Eagles Die Too

Eagles Die Too

▼ ▼ ▼

Meg O'Brien

A PERFECT CRIME BOOK
DOUBLEDAY
NEW YORK   LONDON   TORONTO   SYDNEY   AUCKLAND

A PERFECT CRIME BOOK

PUBLISHED BY DOUBLEDAY
a division of Bantam Doubleday Dell Publishing Group, Inc.
666 Fifth Avenue
New York, NY 10103

DOUBLEDAY is a trademark of Doubleday,
a division of Bantam Doubleday Dell
Publishing Group, Inc.

Grateful acknowledgment is made for permission to reprint the following:

"Coming Home" by Douglas R. Lunsford. Reprinted by permission.

Book design by Tasha Hall

Library of Congress Cataloging-in-Publication Data

O'Brien, Meg.
Eagles die too / by Meg O'Brien.
p.   cm.
"A perfect crime book."
I. Title.
PS3565.B718E18   1992
813'.54—dc20   92-949
CIP

ISBN 0-385-42265-2
Copyright © 1992 by Meg O'Brien
Printed in the United States of America
August 1992

1   3   5   7   9   10   8   6   4   2

First Edition in the United States of America

For Douglas R. Lunsford . . .
Musician, songwriter, teacher, friend.

You give me reason to laugh, and to love.

Grateful acknowledgment is made to Lee Runkle,
for sharing his expertise in firearms,
the desert, and small aircraft. . . .

And to Bud Friedman of Tiffany Executive
Charter Services, Rochester, New York,
for his valuable assistance regarding charter flying,
particularly in New York State and the Thousand Islands.

Eagles
Die Too

Chapter 1

▼ ▼ ▼

"Come in, Outlaw. Over." The low voice issued from a two-way radio attached to my belt. It was accompanied by a crackle of static.

Outlaw. The name, much as I despised it, seemed appropriate enough. My mom had labeled me Jessica when she was still in and out of the ether and Pop was on a drunk. It never even occurred to her that with a last name like James, I'd be known as Jesse by third grade. When I was twelve I hung out with boys, and I wanted to change my handle to Spike, or Bugs, or something equally amusing, but Mom wouldn't allow it. Just as well. In Rochester, New York, in my neighborhood, changing your name was the sort of thing you did when getting married, or (same difference) on the way to jail.

I pulled the radio from my belt and punched the talk button. "This is Outlaw. Come in, over."

"Judas is heading in your direction. He's wearing a black leather windbreaker, work boots, brown cords . . ." I knew the rest of the description well enough: thirty-seven, six feet tall, light hair. A nasty scar running straight down the middle of his cheek. "He's armed with a .308 sniper rifle, and he knows we're here. Don't blow it this time."

I clicked off without saying over. My mouth was too dry. I shifted the weight of my own rifle, an M-16, and raised it to shoulder level—peering through the sight and scanning the quiet street.

It was a small town, colonial in style like so many in New York State. An ordinary village, except that a child killer, a sniper —code-name Judas—stalked its streets.

The temperature, I thought, must be in the seventies. Warm for April. The time was 2:07 P.M. We were too far inland from Lake Ontario to get a breeze, but every now and then a truck rumbled by, raising dust in the air. My black sleeveless tee stuck to my back, and my long brown hair, tucked inside a fatigue cap, bled sweat onto my forehead.

I leaned my back against the brick siding of the Town Hall and tried to relax. *Breathe in. Breathe out. Don't let your nerves take over.*

The crackle again. "Outlaw? He should reach you in less than ten seconds. He should be in your view. Over."

I snaked a look around the building again. I didn't see him anywhere. Nor did I hear any sounds. No birds, no dogs, and even the traffic had quit. I felt like the abandoned marshal in some Wild West movie. Was everybody hiding indoors, like in *High Noon*, that old Gary Cooper flick? And what would I do when Judas appeared? Would I step out, cool and brave as Coop, and shoot him dead? Or would I turn tail and run?

I had blown it yesterday. I couldn't fail again.

My hands shook. The rifle slipped from my grip. I caught it before it hit the ground.

I didn't want to do this. I hate guns. I hate killing. To me, heaven is a place where people leave people alone. But my job was to make sure Judas was killed. "It shouldn't be that difficult," they had said in the briefing. "The man is a monster. He deserves to be killed."

Keep telling yourself that, Jess. He deserves to be killed.

A sound, like that of a twig snapping. A grunt a short distance away. The hairs rose on the back of my neck. *Behind me.* I swung around. *Judas! Killer! Monster!* He stepped out from the shelter of a mom-and-pop grocery store less than forty feet away, his weapon raised to shoot. I jerked back and felt my legs turn to liquid as bullets slammed above my head. From other areas I heard loud reports begin. Someone was covering me; drawing his fire their way. Maybe they'd get him first.

I closed my eyes, willing myself far away in Florida, the Caribbean, Duluth—anywhere but here.

At some point, the gunfire settled down. I took a deep breath and dared a look at the store again. A gun barrel glinted in the sunlight. It was pointed directly at me. I yanked my rifle up. Sweat blurred my eyes, and I had to pull back and hurriedly wipe them. I sighted into the sun again.

That quickly, Judas disappeared. Where the hell *was* he? One moment he was there, and the next—

Shit! Movement only thirty feet away now—across the street by the bank. Judas? I couldn't be sure. Then something metallic clicked, so close it stopped my heart. I whirled sideways and aimed the M-16 as a projectile slammed into the ground at my feet, spraying pieces of asphalt everywhere. I wasn't thinking then about how I hated killing. I pulled the trigger without thought, in a knee-jerk response to fear. The rifle bucked, slamming into my shoulder. The sound blasted my eardrums. I realized I hadn't put the automatic on, and I closed my eyes and squeezed the trigger over and over, not wanting to see the bullets strike their mark.

I heard a baby cry.

My eyes flew open, and with horror I saw that where Judas

should have been, there stood instead a light-haired woman, holding a baby. In my mind, a look of terror crossed her innocent face. (You understand, I tell this now from hindsight. It all happened simultaneously that day. The woman. The baby's cry. My finger squeezing the trigger.)

My bullets struck and the woman fell, clutching her child. They lay motionless in the dust.

I dropped the rifle as pain enveloped my heart. "You always do everything wrong, Jesse . . . never do anything right." Pop used to say that. He'd say it in a drunken stupor most of the time, but that didn't change the fact that I believed every word. Even at thirty-one I was still hearing it—a family recipe, handed down from one drunken Irish generation to the other: *You'll never amount to anything good.*

I stumbled the few feet across the street and stood above the woman and baby. Her chest, her face, the baby's frail body, were riddled with holes. Shaking with rage, I kicked the woman. She flopped a little, but otherwise, she didn't move. I kicked the baby. I stomped on his face. "God damn you both," I yelled.

Then, turning my back on the painted plywood target, I left the Davies School of Defense for Executive Bodyguards. I never wanted to see the goddamned place again.

I stopped in at a bar on the way home. Not Harrigan's, where the bartenders knew me and knew I'd been to a treatment program a while back. A dreary little joint called Jack's, somewhere along the river. Jack's had rotting green window shades and was dense with smoke. Factory workers were drinking their lunch with sides of polish sausages and pickled eggs.

I ordered a Genesee Screw—Genesee beer over sliced oranges, my old favorite from drinking days. I had to tell the bartender how to make it, and when I specified Genesee, he quirked a scraggly gray brow. Genesee is usually only ordered hereabouts by merchant marines, mass murderers, and embittered reporters like me.

When it came, I stared at it awhile. While I stared, I remembered how I'd gotten into this mess.

Marcus Andrelli, head of an elite branch of the mob in Western New York, had offered me a job some time ago as his bodyguard. This is the New Mob, you understand—no drugs, prostitution, or ordinary street crime will ever tarnish its smooth white cuffs. A cabal of Harvard Business grads, Marcus's group is dedicated to the proposition that all men are created to move money and land with the least amount of legalities and the highest level of profit possible.

I make no excuses for the fact that Marcus is my friend and sometime lover. The reasons are unclear, even to me, but have something to do—I suspect—with that old adage about moth to the flame. As for the offer of a job as bodyguard, being a reporter has its frustrations, and I guess Marcus noticed. I love writing (as Peter De Vries, I think, has said); what I can't stand is the paperwork. Marcus, on the other hand, offered $60,000 a year, a company Beamer, and travel to foreign countries.

You probably think that as a woman with very little cash in her pocket, a '68 car with bad karma, and a job I hate, I jumped at the chance.

Are you *crazy*? Me, Jesse James, work for—(wait a minute now, what's that euphemism?)—the *Organization*? Become an outlaw for *real*? My ingrained sense of guilt would never allow it.

Take the woman and baby, for instance. I will carry that moment of stupidity around with me all my life. The problem being: What if they'd been for real? That, of course, was the whole point of the Davies exercise, and why it had played havoc with my nerves: What would you do if the scenario were real?

As the kid of an alcoholic, I'd learned early on that more often than not, I fail.

So I could never work at a job that required I carry a gun. I opted instead for doing a little independent study at the Davies School of Defense—research for a story on women as executive bodyguards. *Newsweek* bought the idea, and that's how I ended up making a goddamn fool of myself in front of a class of twenty-eight men and one beautiful blond broad who never once blew a move in the whole two weeks we were there.

I pushed my cap back on my head and shivered as the air-conditioning finally had its way with my sunburned arms. I fiddled with the frosted glass of the Genesee Screw, but didn't drink. Eventually, with the kind of mental acrobatics I'd honed to a fine edge over the years, I came around to the comforting illusion that I hadn't blown it too badly. After all, I'd stopped shooting almost immediately upon hearing the baby's cry. That was the first clue: an automatic wail issuing from a speaker high above the exercise ground, once you hit the woman and child. A signal, to tell you you'd done it wrong.

So, okay. I hadn't shot up the whole damned town. Which was akin to being the awkward kid in school who only stepped on a crack and broke her mother's back seven times instead of eleven. Mom would still be in traction the rest of her life.

I finally left the beer untouched and went in search of a phone. The wall around it was decorated with graffiti, and among its many offerings—the Salvation Army, Travelers Aid, 1-800-HERPES2—was an AA number. I ignored it, of course. Since drying out at St. Avery's a couple of years ago, I'd been seeing a New Age shrink in Pittsford named Samved. He and I had concluded there was nothing worse than imprinting a belief on one's consciousness like: *I am an alcoholic.* I mean, when you've already got a bad self-image, where do you go from there? I much prefer Samved's approach: *You have a problem with drinking on this plane, today. In reality, however, you are a perfect child of God. Children of God can be healed.*

I eyed my beer, back there on the bar. Wet my lips.

Uh-huh.

I lifted the receiver and used my calling card to reach *Newsweek* down in New York City. When my editor, Nina Barrett, came on the line, I told her I didn't think I'd finish the bodyguard story after all.

"I've got another idea instead! Listen, Nina, God, it's so fucking great, you'll *love* it. No, for crying out loud, of course, I won't have any problem with the deadline. Huh? About? What's it about? Uh, it's about this . . . this dog . . . yeah, that's it, this dog, and he's been trained to sniff out Elvis fans—"

Racket from the other end of the line.

"Well, jeez, you could at least listen. I mean, we've got to get these people, you know? The streets aren't safe—"

Real yelling now. I paced as far as the phone cord would take me. Sweat trickled down my neck. "How about The Great New Chefs of Bangor, Maine? New England cooking is in, it's hot—"

I stared into the dead receiver, then dropped it back on its hook.

A cool voice spoke behind me. "Couldn't take it any longer, huh?"

I turned with irritation to face the owner of the voice. He had come up behind me a few minutes ago, and I'd felt him standing there, but didn't turn around then because I figured he was waiting for the phone. If you acknowledge people like that you have to either talk faster or put up with their sullen glares.

What I saw at eye level was a cracked leather jacket, bomber style. Wide shoulders, and above the jacket, a tanned, weather-lined, cynical face.

Cary Grant?

John Wayne?

No . . . Mac Devlin, flying instructor for the Davies school. He sported a cocky pilot's cap, and pinned to his lapel were silver wings. The face was sharply chiseled and not bad-looking, but world-weary.

Gregory Peck, then. Starring in a remake of *Twelve O'Clock High* at the age of forty. Probing gray eyes, though, not at all like Peck's. Probing, and bitter as the Genesee beer he held in one big, tough, calloused hand.

"I saw you fall apart today," Mac Devlin said. He leaned against the wall with a contemptuous air. "I knew you wouldn't make it; most women don't." He sucked down some beer, then smacked his lips. "Barbie dolls. A bunch of Barbie dolls, trying to be G.I. Joe."

Barbie dolls.

Two weeks of crawling in mud, shooting at targets by flash-light, defensive driving at 130 mph, being "shot at" from every angle, scars from barbed wire, cuts from landing on concrete when some "assassin" jumps out of an alley and aims for the guy you're protecting—

I sighed, stuck my chin out, and jammed my fists on my hips. Poor old Jack. His bar was about to see a reprise of World War II.

Well, it wasn't my fault. All I'd come in for was a Genesee Screw.

Chapter 2

▼ ▼ ▼

"Call me a relic, a thing of the past,

Or any damn thing you please.

Call me a poet rhyming too fast . . .

I only write what I see."

—"RELIC," BY D. R. LUNSFORD

"I've always felt that pilots who wear their wings off-duty are on the prowl." I sneered from across a table at Mac Devlin's silver pins.

"Prowl, huh?"

"For women—the kind who hang out in bars near the airports looking for husbands."

"At least they've got taste."

"Ha. More like they know that pilots make big bucks and aren't around much to get in the way."

"Is that the kind of man you're looking for, James? So you can spend all day getting your hair fixed, like Barbie?"

"Beers," the bartender growled. He slammed them down. "You two gonna be at this all night?"

For ten minutes, Mac Devlin, Flying Ace, had been trying to best me in the thing I do best: arguing. Somehow, we'd worked our way over to this scarred little table in the middle of the room. Now we were sitting, arms folded, glaring nose to nose. A potentially rowdy bunch of barmates had spun their stools our way and cocked their ears, just waiting for the first physical blow to fall. The tension was escalating nicely.

Devlin shoved one of the beers in front of me. I shoved it away—not from any noble decision to maintain my nine-month sobriety (this time), but because I wanted my wits about me.

Pop would've been proud. He'd had a few verbal fisticuffs in bars, too.

But Devlin's words brought to mind that I hadn't touched comb to hair since that morning at Davies. It looked more like a tangled brown fuzzball at the moment than Barbie's demented, Ophelia locks. I knew this because I saw myself in the reflecting mirror of Mac Devlin's scornful gray eyes.

But those eyes had strayed as the bartender broke in, and Devlin was staring at someone who'd just walked through the front door. The man stood there a moment, a tall figure framed in the soft April light. His glance swept over Devlin and held there a couple of seconds before he moved on. He sat at a corner table near the door, his back to the wall, only fifteen feet away.

"Somebody you know?" I said. The newcomer was dusty and worn, like he'd just come in off a stagecoach from the West. Over a khaki shirt he wore a tired suede vest. His hair was dark blond, to the collar, and there was stubble—at least a couple of days' worth—on his cheeks and chin.

For all that, he blended right in with the rest of us sartorial wizards here at Jack's.

Mac turned his attention back to me, and I saw a flicker of emotion before he could close it off. It might have been anger—but it was too quickly gone to tell.

"No," he answered softly. "Nobody I know, or would want to know."

But the battle was over; I'd lost my sparring partner. After a few desultory sips at his now-warm beer, Devlin excused himself. He headed in the direction of the men's room and the phone.

The man by the door followed. They disappeared from my line of sight.

Hmmmm.

Well, it wasn't any of my business. And it didn't look like a story for *Newsweek*. I should be getting home.

But what the hell . . . reporters are supposed to be nosy. It's what they pay us for. So I ambled over to the hallway myself, and found it empty. I picked up the receiver of the phone, and leaned my back on the wormy molding around the men's room door.

"I told you, *no.*" It was Mac's voice, muffled a bit, but loud.

The other man's voice was softer, cajoling at first, and then rising with anger. "You owe me!" he argued. "It's collection time."

"I don't owe you that."

". . . owe *her.*"

Mac's voice grew louder. "Don't ever . . . her name." There were sounds of a scuffle, then silence. Footsteps, coming toward the door.

I moved away a split second before Mac came barreling through. He saw me, stopped dead, and gave me a look that would freeze Lake Ontario. I spoke into the receiver like I really had a call on the line. "See you later, then. Thanks!" Hanging up, I followed Devlin back to the table.

"Trouble?" I asked casually. "I couldn't help overhearing."

He took a deep draught of the warm beer. While he was doing that, the other man came out of the hallway and walked with an angry stride, out the front door. Mac watched his departure with those searching gray eyes.

"What did you hear?" he asked.

"Not much, just raised voices. I wasn't really trying."

He gave me a calculating look, then changed the subject— smiling widely. The smile was crooked, the eyes flirtatious. I heard Gregory Peck say, *Let's bring her in now, men. Easy does it. A little trim there on the right rudder.* Or something like that.

"I've got an idea," Mac Devlin said.

"Oh?" I answered vaguely, still in *Twelve O'Clock High.*

"How about, I give you flying lessons?"

That brought me around. I blinked. *"You* give *me* flying lessons. Why the hell would you want to do that?" Why the hell would *I* want to do it? I was scared to death of flying.

"Well, look at it this way. I've been pretty tough on you, James. Maybe you're not as bad as I thought. I'll give you three lessons, absolutely free—provided, of course, you can hack it that long."

"I can't think of a single reason to do that," I said firmly.

"Well, for one, it'd give you some more input for your story. Sounded like you were in hot water with your editor a while ago."

"So? What do you care?"

"I don't, especially. I'm just trying to be fair."

"Well, thanks a whole bunch, but I don't *need* you to be fair."

"What *do* you need me for?"

"Nothing! What makes you think—"

The grin was outrageous now. "Then why are you hanging around me like this?"

I swept to my feet, tossing out a couple of bills for my untouched beer. "I'm not. I'm going home, in fact. Right now."

He tilted his pilot's cap with a thumb and left it at a jaunty angle, folding his arms across his chest. "Think about it. Offer's always open."

I stormed out the door—just in time to see Mac's "friend" jerk back into the shadowed entry of a poolroom, across the way.

The curbs were crowded with cars and pickup trucks, and my restored, temporary car—the old Dodge Dart—was parked a half block down. Curious, I got into it, kicked on the gas, and moseyed to the corner. There, I U-turned and came up to within a half block of Jack's again. I made the pass slowly—in time to see Mac Devlin come out of the bar. He didn't see me; probably didn't know my car. He walked across the street and stood there talking angrily to the man he "didn't know and wouldn't want to know."

A horn sounded behind me. I moved on, U-turned, and made another pass—but Devlin and his friend were gone.

I wondered who the "she" was that Devlin owed something to. The man's sister? His wife? I wondered if Mac Devlin went around leaving broken hearts from East to West, around the world. Or was it something else?

If only I'd known, as they used to say in the old-timey mystery novels.

But I didn't . . . and maybe that's just as well. Pain, as Samved is lately wont to say, is ofttimes good for the soul.

Chapter 3

▼ ▼ ▼

*T*he reason Samved says dumb things like that—now—is because he's gone from New Age guru to Fundamentalist preacher, in one fell swoop this year. The silly to the ridiculous, if you ask me.

One thing about Samved—my guru/shrink—he never does things by halves. He's got an 800 number these days for donations, wears a stiffly cut black suit, and intones strange opinions like: *Pain is good for the soul.*

Hah. What would Samved know? He's over seventy, makes more money than I'll ever have (he makes it from counseling fools like me), and has all the time he needs to play.

Whereas I haven't had much time lately at all.

Truth is, I haven't *taken* much time. To have fun, that is. I've kind of been in the doldrums since Mom got married last December. I mean, look, it's bad enough having an on-again, off-again love affair with a yuppie mobster who's too busy wheeling-and-dealing world-class real estate to see beyond his nose. It's worse when one's fiftyish mother has a *better* love life and ends up married to someone as dashing—and dangerous— as Charlie Browne.

Now there's a con for you. Charlie Browne looks like Paul Newman. He's caring and attentive, he's younger than Mom, and he's wealthy—or at least, he keeps coming up with bucks. I've never quite figured out how. Charlie is a mystery, in and of himself. We know where he came from, but not where he's (always) been—at least, not in the past twenty-three years.

Mom married him anyway. Which only goes to show that if a man looks like Paul Newman, a woman'll overlook anything.

Most women. Not me. I haven't accepted Charlie yet, and maybe I never will.

Mom says I'm a curmudgeon. "A thirty-one-year-old curmudgeon, Jessica Rosemary James. Good thing Marcus doesn't mind your snarling at him all the time. You'd never be able to hold a man who wasn't that strong."

Mom likes Marcus Andrelli. She sees, in his scamming mobster heart, the son her daughter became.

That's the sort of thing I was thinking about as I cooked garlic dinner—my new diet. You put a whole bulb in the oven, roast it, then spread it on thick soft chunks of sourdough French.

It doesn't take off weight, but it does keep men away.

I stood at the kitchen counter, ruminating over the pros and cons of continuing with this sort of fare. During the long, freezing Rochester winters, people say, "Well, it works for me." (Pasta, wine, garlic, the old Italian warm-up binge.) But then . . . along comes spring.

Hail to Spring! That's what *I* say.

Spring in Rochester, New York, means warm days and balmy nights. It means the boats are out again on Lake Ontario. The trees are in bloom. The dogs are in heat. The lilacs—

The lilacs come to visit for a few weeks, at the most. And

17

when they do, I turn into this whole other person, this blathering idiot who feels shivery little chills up and down her spine at a man's mere touch . . . a mindless, gutless being without initiative or spunk, wearing makeup and skirts and swinging my hips —*giggling*, for God's sake, at the world's worst jokes—

"Spring is here . . ." the minstrels sing. And it is. Right now. A glance at the calendar on my fridge told me that.

The memory of my foolish argument with Mac Devlin confirmed it.

Well, I hadn't agreed to flying lessons, that was one point in my favor, and a big one. I've been known to do truly idiotic things while in hot pursuit of a man.

I picked up the phone and called Marcus at his penthouse apartment in the Rochester Towers. Alfred, his bratty assistant, answered as I was stuffing a huge, thick hunk of garlicky bread down my gullet.

"Andrelli Enterprises."

"It's me, Alfred. Your good friend, Jesse James."

"Mr. Andrelli is out of the country," he said snippily. "I was supposed to tell you yesterday. I guess I forgot."

"I'll bet you forgot, Alfred. Where is he, anyway?"

"Spain, I believe. Perhaps Berlin."

"Right. No forwarding number, I suppose."

"None I can remember."

"Uh-huh. When's he coming home?"

"Who knows?"

"*You* know, you jerk."

Alfred fired off his final salvo. "He's with Christopher, Ms. James. *And* his mother."

Marcus was out of the country with Christopher? His son? *And* his son's *mother*?

Shit.

I said it aloud.

"Same to you, Ms. James." Alfred hung up.

I sat there, stunned. Why would Marcus have taken a trip like that without letting me know?

With me pushing on him to do it, he'd begun seeing his son in the past few months. Christopher was eight now, and Marcus had been keeping a distance since he was born, afraid that his mob connections would cause trouble for the kid. A few months ago I'd finally convinced him that the kid needed a dad, and he should see to it somehow.

So more and more Saturdays and Sundays, lately, had been spent in the presence of Chris—and his mom. Marcus had sworn there was nothing going on anymore between him and her, and Marcus, more than anyone I've known, will tell the truth when confronted with an outright question.

So the thing that worried me wasn't the past, known Saturdays and Sundays—but the unknown ones, stretching out into an uncertain future.

And I'd sure never had anything like this in mind, when I pushed for those father/son get-togethers—not a trip out of the country with Chris and his mom.

Where the hell had they gone? Rome? Madrid? Paris?

Paris was awfully romantic in the spring.

Of course, Marcus did leave a message for me. Alfred was just being his bitchy little self, in "forgetting." He never passes messages along—and Marcus reprimands, but never even threatens to fire. Partly, he says, because it would spoil my fun. The other reason being that Alfred speaks nine languages—or is it nineteen?—and deals most diplomatically with business clients round the globe.

He hates only me.

Fair enough. I can be a rotten bitch too. Truth is, I can find out where Marcus is anytime I want, just by calling Tark. I'd interrupted Alfred out of a sheer stubborn need to harass someone.

I looked at my watch. A little after six. Not a good time to reach Tark. Marcus had moved him up from bodyguard to head of security, and he'd be making supervisory visits to some of the many towering buildings Marcus had taken over in his reign as head of the corporate mob in Western New York State.

I took a glass of iced tea and went out on the roof of Mrs. Binty's porch to think. It's a wide roof, with two double-hung windows opening onto it from my living room. There are big old trees out there for shelter from the street, and now and then a breeze comes by and blows the branches. At night, you can see the lights on in the old Colonials, across the way. Now, at near-dusk, they provided welcome shade from the day's heat.

A plane buzzed overhead. I thought of the irritating Mac Devlin, Flying Ace, and then—moving back in time—of my ig-nominious, lackluster, two-week performance as a reporter/stu-dent at the Davies School for Executive Bodyguards. Someday, I thought, I'll have to figure out how to get through life without screwing things up.

A gentle wind picked at my hair. Leaves rustled softly, and there were scents all around of various dinners cooking. I looked over Genesee Park Boulevard to Mr. Garson's house. His wife had died last year. There were a lot of older people on this street, with no one left to talk to now. A few houses with young fami-lies, but more with people who had grown up here, worked their asses off for forty years to pay their mortgages, and who now sat in their homes alone.

A scent of lilacs drifted up from Mrs. Binty's garden. Lilacs make me crazy. They trigger old sentimental buttons—and I realized suddenly that I didn't want to be alone tonight. Or any night, this spring.

Such was my state of mind when the Red Baron called.

I'd brought the phone over to the windowsill so I wouldn't have to move if it rang. I reached back and grabbed it.

"Marcus?" *Oh, hopeful heart.*

"James? Jesse James?"

"Who is it?" I growled.

"Devlin here."

Devlin here. "What the hell does that mean, 'Devlin here'? It sounds like leftover dialogue from a 1940's British war movie: *Devlin here, old chap. Bring on the kidneys and kippers, eh wot? Ta Ta.* And how did you get my number?"

"Easy. You're in the book."

"Oh . . . yeah. I forgot. Well, what do you want?"

"Boy, you are one tough cookie. It's a beautiful night, clear as a prism, lots of stars. I thought you might like to go up with me."

"Go up? Up where?"

He laughed. "Into the sky. *Fly.* Remember?"

"Oh. Sure." Into the sky. No way did I want to go up into the sky. "I can't."

"Can't? You busy getting your hair done, Barbie?"

My hand went to my hair, still damp from a shower. "No . . . I just can't."

A silence. I tapped a foot.

"Hey, wait a minute," Devlin said softly. "You're not afraid of flying, are you?" He said it in a way that told me that if I said I was, it'd be a surprise, but he wouldn't laugh. I closed my eyes and saw the classic Gregory Peck nose, the hell-bent-for-leather grin, the cocky tilt to the cap.

"No . . . I'm not afraid," I said. I wasn't sure at the moment just what it was that I meant.

"I only ask because you were so quick to turn down free lessons. Being a reporter, I'd've thought you'd have jumped at the offer. Of course, if you're afraid . . . A lot of girls are."

That was about all it took.

Next thing I knew I was several thousand feet up, clutching a queasy stomach, the contents of which, I feared, might soon be in some farmer's field, way down there on the ground.

Chapter 4

▼ ▼ ▼

*M*y knuckles glowed white from the moon. My face must
have glowed white, too, but that was only fear.

Get me out of here, I prayed silently. *Get me the fuck out
alive.*

Below, when I dared to look, were silver rivers, silver lakes
and streams, city lights, and the red blink on transmitters and the
tops of tall buildings. Then, suddenly, there was nothing but
darkness as we headed north over Lake Ontario.

For long minutes, my hands gripped my stomach. My
mouth tasted bile, and my jaws ached from clenching them in
terror. Then, slowly I felt the jaw ease . . . the bile return to its
natural resting place . . . the stomach settle down. After a
while, I could almost believe I was on the ground. The seat was
solid beneath me, with only the throb of the engines, and their
dull roar, to remind me of where I was. The air was cool, almost
cold, the moon and stars brighter than I'd ever seen them before.

I've flown on large commercial jets, plenty of times. And that's not too bad, once you're in the air. I never sit by a window, but stolidly pretend to be home in my living room reading. In the old days, I used to drink myself blotto before, during, and after every flight. Could've been in Harrigan's, downing one with the guys, for all I knew.

So I never saw the moon and stars. Not like this.

The plane was a Cessna 310, Mac had said. A smallish plane. You step on the wing to get in and out of the cabin, and tonight there were four seats—two front, two back. The seats were removable, he said, adding that at night, when charter companies aren't transporting people, they fly cargo.

"The banks are our best customers. They move checks from city to city at night. FedEx, too. Lots of film from Kodak. On any given night there might be five thousand small planes in the skies over New York State. Flying trucks, sort of.

"How about a little pass over the Thousand Islands?"

I turned to see his face intent on the instruments, then on an imaginary horizon. I couldn't see a thing out there—but I could believe Mac did. He was in another world up here, where vision had nothing to do with sight. "Aren't the Islands a long way?"

"Oh, just up the Seaway a bit. Fifty minutes, maybe. You ever been there?"

"No." In my life there hadn't been much money for travel or vacations. I went where my work took me, and it had yet to take me up the St. Lawrence Seaway. Roughly, it begins at the eastern end of Lake Ontario, above Watertown. That's where the Thousand Islands are, both on the Canadian and American side. Then the Seaway meanders north through Canada until it reaches the Atlantic above Nova Scotia. (Geography isn't my strong point, so don't base your next trip itinerary on this.)

"We could stay over in an inn there," Devlin said.

"An inn, huh?" Cozy.

"Sure, why not?"

"I have to get back. I've got work tomorrow."

"You're free-lance, aren't you?"

"That doesn't mean I can just take off." Why is it non-writers always think that writers don't really work?

"Don't you ever relax?"

"Sure."

"When?"

"When the mood strikes."

"Hey, it's a fantastic night." The moon had come from behind a cloud. The sky had been brushed with snowy white streaks. "Look at those stars. You ever see them sparkle like that? What better time for a mood to strike?"

We were back to the subject of the inn. "Look, I'm involved," I said. At least I thought I was. With Marcus galumphing around faraway places with his sweet little "family," who knew?

"Oh." Devlin was silent a moment. "You're seeing someone? Who?"

"A guy."

"Just 'a guy'? No name or anything?"

I folded my arms. "I came up here for the ride, Devlin. I never promised you my life story."

"Sheee-it, you are one ornery cuss, Jesse James."

Mac jumped down first, then turned to help me. A service guy in uniform approached, and Mac arranged to have the tanks refueled. "Hangar it for me, will you?"

He was distracted by something across the field. I stood by Devlin and followed his eyes to a distant spot—to a figure standing by a larger plane. The plane looked old and solid—a workhorse breed. The figure was in semidarkness, just on the edge of a spot of light from the hangar. It didn't take much, however, to see it was the man from Jack's, the one with the soldier-of-fortune look.

Mac put an arm over my shoulders and steered me toward the parking lot, which was halfway between us and his friend. "Do me a favor, Jess . . . go on back to the jeep. I have to take care of a few things."

"Okay. But if I'm ornery, you're secretive," I said. "Who's the guy?"

"Nobody you should know."

"You either, it looks like."

He didn't answer.

His jeep was one of those gray things, with a black canvas top. Not the new Suburban Cowboy type—more a working vehicle. The top was folded back, and I sat and watched Mac approach the man by the plane. Mac stood in the light from the hangar, but the other man was still half in shadows. They talked. A match flared. Mac waved his arms, the set of his shoulders angry.

Finally, he headed back to me and the jeep. He climbed in silently, stuck his key in the ignition, and ground it thoroughly. His hand shook.

"You want me to drive?" I offered.

He seemed to think about it. "Thanks. But I need something to do."

The airport was near my apartment, but Mac drove in the opposite direction. "Mind if we get some air?"

There seemed to be plenty as it was, tearing through the open canvas top. But Devlin, it was clear, needed time to cool off.

"Sure," I said. "Take that road over there. It goes past Miller's farm."

He swung left. "I know. I drive out there all the time."

Within fifteen minutes, we were surrounded by farmland, out in the country where the roads were empty and moon-struck—

Moonstruck. I love that word. Everything in the countryside that night was "struck with moon." The hillsides, the trees, the little streams that meander through farms—all were spilled, liquid moon. As the jeep whizzed by, stirring up air, you could hear the leaves on the trees jingle like shimmery silver coins.

"This is my favorite place." Devlin pulled up to a rise that overlooked a small valley. "You should see it at dawn, from the air. Everything turns pink from the sun."

He turned off the engine and we sat there a moment. Then he slid from his seat and came around to mine, grabbing my hand. "C'mon. Let's sit on the hood."

"You come here a lot?" I said.

"Once a week, maybe, when I want my feet on the ground. A reality check. What about you?"

I drew my knees up to my chest, hooking my arms around them. The warmth from the jeep's engine filtered through the hood to my rear. "Not since my last birthday."

"You came here to celebrate your birthday?"

"To mourn it, actually." I told him how I'd spent the one before that—my thirtieth—sobering up, at St. Avery's Treatment Center. Marcus had sent me balloons by way of a clown, in an effort to teach me to play. He said I took life too seriously, and needed to loosen up.

I didn't mention that part to Mac; it was pretty obvious I'd lost the knack of late.

"So anyway, that year was sort of a rebirth. It wasn't until my thirty-first, last year, that I really got the blues. I brought a six-pack of Genny and sat out here just like this, on the hood of my car." I looked down the road, to the left. "Over there, actually, where we used to park in high school. I never opened the beer that night, though. My 'anniversary fall' didn't come until summer."

"You've got a drinking problem?" Mac said.

I shrugged.

"Sorry, I didn't know. I wouldn't't've tried to push that beer on you earlier."

"It's okay, I'm a big girl. I can say no these days." Sometimes. It still isn't easy, though.

"When is your birthday?"

"Please . . . don't ask."

"Hell, girl, thirty-two is nothing to get worried about. Wait'll you're forty-two, like me. Now, that's old."

I gave him a look. In the moonlight, the world-weary lines were barely visible. He had taken off the ever-present pilot's cap, and his hair was thick and dark, just brushing his neck. The eyes were the thing, though. They wouldn't let me go. "Next week," I answered finally. "My birthday's next week."

"No kiddin'! Well, now, we'll just have to do something about that. Dinner, maybe? We could fly wherever you want. Just name it."

"Can't," I said firmly. "I'm planning to sleep all day."

"Fat chance of that, with me pounding down your door."

"When's *your* birthday?" I asked, more to change the subject than anything.

"November. The twelfth."

Aha. A Scorpio. It all became clear.

Samved had given me a brief course, once, on astrological signs. I'd scoffed at first, but then he started pointing things out to me about people I knew. Showing me how they fit their sign.

Take Marcus, for instance. Like Mac, he has a direct, piercing look. That's one of the hallmarks of a Scorpio, Samved said. He hit it on the nose with Marcus—his birthday's on November 19.

Another thing about Scorpios—whose higher symbol is the eagle—is that they're heroic, loyal, dedicated to family and the people they love. And they never forget a kindness. Or an injury. I wondered what injury the man at the airport had done to Mac.

Not that I believe in all that astrology shit.

Meanwhile, an arm was not-too-casually finding its way around my shoulders, and there were fingers not-too-casually stroking the far side of my neck.

I turned my head and stared at the owner of those fingers. "Mac Devlin—are you romancing me?"

He grinned. "What if I was?"

I thought about it, and shrugged. "I don't know." All else aside, it had been a long time since I'd "dated" anyone new. Like somebody who'd been widowed after years of devoted marriage, I'd almost forgotten the program.

I hadn't forgotten how to be cautious, though. With a macho guy like Mac Devlin, you gotta wonder how long it'll take before he whips it out and waves it around.

"I don't think I'm ready for this," I said. "Besides, I'm not much into making out on the hood of a car, under the moon. It seems so . . . so *teenage.*"

He sighed and dropped his arm. "Somehow, I thought you were an adventuresome gal. C'mon, I'll take you home."

Mac insisted on seeing me to my door. We crossed Mrs. Binty's porch, then climbed up my gray wool-carpeted stairs. At the top, I said, "Well, thanks for the ride. Flight. Whatever." I turned my back and slid my key in the lock.

"Wait a minute." My escort rested a hand on the doorjamb. "Why do you think I brought you home?"

I faced him and shrugged. "To get rid of me, I guess. So you could go to some bar and find somebody more amenable."

"Amenable, huh? *Amenable?* Lordy, you reporters use big words."

He leaned forward and kissed me. A nice soft kiss, non-threatening, so I didn't pull away. But then the kiss became more earthy, more sensual . . . ardent . . . hot. (Hold the presses; I'm struggling for all the right adjectives here.) A hand at the small of my back drew me close, while a tongue did warm, wanton things to mine. Mac's other hand wandered lazily, stroking over my thin cotton shirt, from my ribs to my breast—(I was going for it, God help me, I was going for it!).

I leaned into the kiss and the hand on my breast. My fingers went to Mac's dark hair. My tongue was somewhere in Peoria.

Until my door opened abruptly, and I fell through it.

"Jesse! How the hell are you? Long time no see!"

I looked up, dazed. It was Charlie Browne . . . in my living room.

Charlie—for God's sake—Browne.

Charlie had caught me as I was falling. I struggled out of his arms and onto my feet . . . no longer lusty, but furious.

"Goddammit, Charlie! What are you *doing* here?" I glanced quickly around. "Where's Mom?"

Charlie smiled his too-innocent, blue-eyed smile. "She's taking a nap on your bed. It was a long flight from California, and we got held up in Chicago for nearly five hours. Kate's exhausted—"

"How did you get in?" I didn't even try to keep the suspicion out of my tone. Charlie has all kinds of talents in the area of breaking-and-entering.

"Mrs. Binty let us in."

"Oh, swell. Fine. Great!" I'd have to speak to my landlady about opening my door to just any riffraff that comes along.

I'd almost forgotten Mac, in the meantime. He was giving one of those long, piercing stares to Charlie. I introduced them.

"Mac—Charlie Browne, my—uh, stepfather." The words still stuck in my throat. "Charlie, Mac Devlin."

They eyed each other like two dogs pissing off at a fire hydrant. Finally, they nodded and said all the right words. Shook hands, that sort of thing.

I turned to Charlie. "What exactly are you doing here?"

He ran a distracted hand over his crinkly silver hair, and gave me an aw-shucks grin. "Your mother and I are on our honeymoon, Jesse. Naturally, we assumed you'd like us to stop by."

"You came from California to Rochester, New York, for a *honeymoon?*" I didn't buy it for a minute. If I knew Charlie, there was something else going on. With him, there always is. Whether it's legal is another matter.

A voice came from the bedroom. "Charlie? Is that Jesse? Is she home?"

I met my new stepfather's eyes.

"Kate's really looking forward to seeing you," he said.

I threw up my hands and headed for the bedroom. Leaving Paul Newman and Gregory Peck alone.

My bedroom is large—the back half, actually, of the apartment —and it looks out on trees. I'd left both windows open, and a soft breeze was blowing through sheer white curtains. My bed is queen-sized, with a simple white down comforter. I recently added black accents, and a few red. Simple fare, for a simple brain. Keeping things uncluttered helps my concentration.

With Mom here, though, there were paisley suitcases all over the place. My plain white bureau was littered with perfume bottles, makeup jars, and creams. Froufrou dresses hung from every possible door or window frame, apparently losing wrinkles. In one corner, neatly stacked, were three tan leather suitcases that I knew to be Charlie's. Charlie—despite his many flaws— doesn't litter. He's almost military that way.

Mom sat on my bed, her back against pillows. Her short brown curls were flattened on one side from sleep. There were occasional glimmers of gray through the brown—on the top and sides—but her face was younger than ever. Lines that had been there before Charlie had somehow miraculously disappeared. "Pisces," Samved had told me, "never grows old. Old soul, true

. . . but wisdom brings us back to youth again. A time to explore, to adventure, to play. . . . You'll have your hands full when she's seventy."

Mom was, indeed, a classic case of the reverse-age process in action. Tonight, however, she was wearing her yellow robe—and that, in the past, had always been a sign that she was in need of comforting.

"What's going on?" I asked. "You and Charlie were married in December. What are you still doing on a honeymoon?"

"A honeymoon?" She ran fingers through her curls and looked blank.

"That's what Charlie said."

Mom laughed. "Oh, you know Charlie, he's so romantic that way. Any trip we take is a honeymoon, to him."

"Of course. Good old Charlie, what a prince. I should have known."

"Now, Jesse, don't start with that, please." She patted the bed, inviting me to sit beside her.

I sat. And sighed. "Sorry, Mom. I'll try to be nice."

"That's my girl. Jesse, who else is out there? Who is Charlie talking to?"

Their voices could be heard—deep in earnest conversation, it seemed.

"A friend."

"A man, it sounds like. Is it Marcus?"

"No." I frowned. "Marcus is out of the country. And he didn't exactly invite me along."

"So you're seeing someone else? Oh, Jesse . . . don't tell me there's trouble between you!"

I never could understand Mom's passion for Marcus Andrelli. Not that I haven't had a little passion of my own for Marcus over the past few years; but c'mon, upscale or not, the man's a mobster—not the sort a girl usually brings home to dinner.

"He's good to you," Mom said. "And you told me he's changed a lot in the past few months."

It was true. Marcus was being more careful not to hurt people in his business dealings now—even if those people aren't downtrodden. That was the thing about Marcus, in the past: He always stood tall for the downtrodden. Now he's even kind to the middle class. (Well, hell, it's the middle class, now, who *are* downtrodden.)

"Mom, you wanta tell me what you and Charlie are doing here?"

"We're on our way to the Thousand Islands, dear. We've got reservations at an inn."

(See what I mean? It's probably the same inn I was invited to by Mac, and turned down. My mom's got a better love life than I'll ever have.)

"And it was Charlie's idea to stop off and see you," she went on. "He really does like you, Jesse."

"And I like him, Mom." Or I will—when pigs fly.

"I don't think I like your tone." Mom lifted her chin and put that light in her eye. *The evil eye,* I always called it when I was a kid. The one that made me—*makes* me—quake.

And that's the other thing. You can be thirty-one years old, have your shit together—or at least feel that you do—and then, by golly, your mom shows up. *Whammo.* Instant childhood again.

"How's Aunt Edna?" I said to change the subject.

"My sister is fine. She likes having her little house back to herself now that I'm married, so don't feel sorry for her, if that's what you're thinking."

It was a bone of contention between us, my feelings for Aunt Edna. Mom has always felt I loved her sister more.

"No way would I feel sorry for Aunt Edna. She's the only woman I know who's got balls."

"Jesse!" Mom blushed.

"Well, it's true."

It was also true that Mom had balls . . . as evidenced by the fact that she had up and married Charlie Browne. She'd gone for what she'd wanted—which was love, adventure, and a new life. Before Charlie came along, Mom had been living with Aunt Edna in California. In Marin County, she had six long years to put up with Aunt Edna's chanting, with her gardening at midnight—by the light of the (New Age) moon, of course—and with her treks to the missions to feed the poor.

None of which Mom really minded. It was the smoke that got her in the end. Aunt Edna, a chain smoker, is almost continually surrounded by a dense layer of smog. If she lived farther south, she'd be declared a suburb of L.A.

Anyway, a year and a half ago Charlie came along, with his mysterious past and his mischievous blue eyes. He caught our attention right away—Mom's and mine—but for different reasons. Mom thinks he's a saint. I still think he's a crook.

Which brought me back to the present.

"Anybody special Charlie's seeing on this trip?"

"Only you, dear. Then we're off to the Islands."

Only me. Well . . . I'd better watch my back.

Mom fluffed her hair again with her fingers. "Why don't we go out and join him? And your new friend."

"Mac's not really a friend," I explained. "Not like you mean. And we probably won't see each other again."

"Oh?"

"Well, you know . . . we haven't got much in common."

"Since when did that stop *you,* Jessica Rosemary James?"

Mac and Charlie were still deep in muted conversation. They stood by the front windows, Mac in his jeans, white shirt, and leather jacket, and Charlie in neat chinos, with a white shirt and blue blazer. Not really alike—but there was something about them. They might have been brothers. I heard a few words like "drugs . . . supply . . . agency," before they saw us and shut down.

Mom went into the kitchen for coffee, and I stood with my arms folded. "You boys going into business together?"

Charlie gave me that disarming smile again. "Just talking flying," he said.

"I didn't know you were into flying." But of course I should have. Charlie's into goddamned everything. Since Mom met him she's learned how to windsurf, to backpack, to skydive . . . Of course Charlie would be into flying.

"You have a pilot's license?" I asked.

"Only small craft," he answered modestly.

"Where did you learn?" A leading question, designed to smoke out some of good old Charlie's past. I gather odds and ends like this. Someday, I hope to put them all together and come up with the real Charlie Browne.

"Oh, it was a long time ago," Charlie said vaguely. "Long ago and far away." His grin was quick. "Like the song."

I looked at Mac, who was avoiding my eyes.

Clue two. It doesn't take long to put them together, with Charlie. You just never know exactly what you've got.

Some sort of connection between Mac Devlin and Charlie Browne, though. Well, now, wasn't that a clever coincidence? Mac taking me on a little flight, and Charlie showing up on my doorstep the very same night.

And who was that guy at the airport and Jack's?

"Coffee?" Mom offered, coming in from the kitchen with a pot and several cups, the handles laced through her fingers. She set them on the coffee table.

Mac looked from Mom to Charlie. Something passed between them. "I think I'd better be going," he said, only half to me.

"So soon? But you haven't even been introduced to my mom yet."

"Oh . . . sorry. Mrs. Browne? I didn't mean to be rude."

Mom fussed and fluttered, doing her Betty White *Golden Girls* thing. "Don't be silly. I should have introduced myself. But, dear, call me Kate. Please."

"Kate." Mac stuck out his hand. Mom looked up from her five-foot-three to his relatively towering six feet, and smiled.

"I do like men who fly," Mom said.

Clue three.

"Mom, how did you know that Mac's a pilot?"

He'd been gone fifteen minutes. Mom and I were having coffee on the couch, while Charlie made phone calls from my room. Charlie's always making phone calls—and to God knows who. My bill, after a visit from him, though, is intriguing. Once I traced a number to a vegetable market in NYC; another turned out to be an espresso shop in Belgium. Charlie always leaves money to pay for his calls. No explanations, though.

"Why, I think you must have mentioned it, dear." Mom's tone was complacent.

"That Mac was a pilot? I didn't mention it to you."

"Then I must have overheard them talking," Mom said. "Same as you."

"How did you know I overheard them talking?"

Mom sighed, tapped a foot, and fussed with her hair, looking the other way. "Jesse, will you please not be an investigative reporter with me?"

"I wouldn't have to, if you and Charlie weren't always so damned secretive."

"I am not being secretive! I just don't care for all your prying questions."

"Mom—"

My next prying question was diverted by Charlie, stalking out of my bedroom. His face was rigid, his eyes worried. He came straight over to Mom, bent down, and kissed her on the mouth. A firm but semilingering kiss. He lifted her chin with a finger and gave her a steady look. "I've got to go out, Kate. Will you be okay?"

"Of course." She said it with poise and aplomb, and didn't even ask him why.

I did. "What's going on, Charlie?"

He glanced my way, but shook his head. "Got an errand to run. Look after your mother, will you?"

I left Mom sitting there, and followed Charlie down the stairs and out onto Mrs. Binty's porch. There, I grabbed his arm. "What the hell have you got my mother mixed up in now? What's going on?"

"Jesse . . ." His face was illuminated by a streetlight. It was haggard and drawn. "Please don't push. Not this time."

"Listen, since my mother's known you, she's been involved in a stolen painting, in murder, and God knows what else—"

"I love your mother very much . . . you know that. And she loves me."

"That doesn't mean you're good for her."

He removed my hand from his arm, but held it a moment. "You may be right about that."

He brushed my cheek with his lips, and then he was gone.

Chapter 5

▼ ▼ ▼

*M*om was singing in the kitchen the next morning (the way she always does), when Toni Langella arrived.

Charlie was still out—a fact that didn't seem to disturb his "bride" a bit.

"Kate! Kate, is that you?" Toni breezed through my front door, yelling, and tossed the morning paper my way.

Toni was fourteen now, the kid from next door nearly all grown up. She had breasts and everything—as she herself liked to point out. Probably why the brat thought it was okay to call my mom by her first name.

"Toni!" Mom came out of the kitchen, her face wreathed in smiles. She and Toni hugged. They blabbered on and on, catching up with things since Mom's last visit in the fall.

I'm convinced they like each other better than either of them's ever liked me.

"How're the gymnastics going?" Mom asked.

"Oh . . . I don't know. Okay, I guess."

Toni was more into boys these days than sports. One day, after we'd worked out (something that Toni forces upon me to help me stay sober), she even let me talk her into a Häagen-Dazs double chocolate ice cream bar. That's how far she's gotten from her previously rigid training.

I think it's neat the way hormones can rage through the body and turn even the most disciplined people into chumps.

Toni sat at my dining room table in the bay, and Mom brought her a glass of milk. They sat talking, the morning sun streaming in on both heads—one with long, dark hair, still glossy with youth . . . the other with short, gray-brown curls, no longer as glossy, but with kind of a perky look still. Mom was in her yellow robe. Toni wore blue-striped shorts and a T-shirt. They might have been a couple of kids at a pajama party. Toni now had a white mustache from the milk Mom had brought her.

I had to get my own coffee.

It was while I was pouring it that the phone rang. I grabbed the receiver, hoping it was Marcus.

"Hi," Mac Devlin said.

"Oh . . . hi." I took a sip of coffee, swallowing disappointment along with it. "What's up?"

"Just thought I'd say good morning."

"Oh."

"Did you decide about the lessons?"

"What lessons?"

"*Flying,* remember? Three, if you can last that long."

"Uh . . . no, I guess I forgot."

"It wasn't so bad, though, was it? Last night?"

"No."

I wasn't sure what we were talking about: the flight—or, at my front door later, the fancy.

"So?"

"So, what?"

A loud, exasperated sigh. "Lordy, girl, are you dense in the morning, or what? Do you want the lessons?"

I did *not* want the lessons. While I was willing to admit it had been okay—maybe even fine, once we were there in the sky —the thought of more takeoffs and landings gave me no thrill.

On the other hand, I was intrigued by Mac's dusty friend— or rather the mystery surrounding him. Even more, there was that conversation last night between Mac and Charlie Browne. *Drugs . . . supply . . . agency.* The words had burned along my brain, fueled no doubt by suspicions about Charlie and my desperate need to put together clues about his past.

Which is the *only* reason I agreed to hang out with Mac Devlin some more . . . and dammit, don't anybody think *one word* to the contrary.

"Why don't I meet you at Harrigan's, down on Genesee?" I said. "You can give me some background on flying, for an article. If the piece seems like it'll work, we can talk about lessons."

"Okay. When? Noon or so?"

I looked at my watch. It was nearly ten. "I guess I can make that. I've got some stops to make first."

"Great." A pause. "Oh, by the way, is your stepfather there?"

"Charlie? Not at the moment. Why?"

"Oh, we were just talking last night about somebody we both used to know. I thought I'd ask him a couple of questions."

"Well, he's not here."

"Hmmm. You know when he'll be back?"

"Not a clue."

Another pause. Mom and Toni buzzed in the background. Faint sounds of static came over the phone line. I let the pause ride.

"Well, twelve o'clock, then," Mac said finally.

"Right. Twelve o'clock."

High.

I showered, dressed, and pulled on jeans, a Hawaiian print blouse, and sneakers. Then I interrupted the Junior Golden Girls, still deep in gab. "Mom, I really would like to know where Charlie is. I need to ask him something."

She gave me her vague little smile, the one she always flashes when I ask questions about her new husband. "Oh, you know Charlie, dear. Who knows where he is or what he's up to?"

She said it fondly, as if to say: *Whatever it is, it's for some good reason, I'm sure.* Her faith in Charlie Browne is both unswerving and appalling.

"If you hear from him, will you ask him to call me?"

"Of course, Jesse. But where will you be?"

"Down at Harrigan's, from twelve until maybe one or two. He can reach me there."

"All right. Is there anything you'd like me to do around here?"

I hesitated. "Well . . . there's a huge pile of laundry in my closet."

Mom laughed. "I didn't mean that sort of thing. I meant research or something."

"Research?"

"For articles. I could straighten out your notes, pull them together for you. Help you condense them, you know."

I stared. "You don't want to help me with the housework?" Mom always wanted to do housework when she was here. In the past, she had bustled about—cooking, cleaning, organizing closets . . .

"Oh, Jesse, I'll help, of course, if you insist. But since Charlie and I have been married, I've learned a lot of new skills. I was hoping not to spend my time with something so meaningless as housework."

I was pretty much speechless, I guess.

Once recovered, I gave Mom a pile of notes a foot high, ideas and research for articles I'd drafted out, hoping to sell them over the next year. I placed them in front of her on the dining room table, along with pencils, a yellow legal pad, and file folders labeled with each article's working title. Later, the pieces would be submitted to national magazines, and to various large newspapers around the country. A few might end up in Sunday supplements, but I had a couple of biggies on the fire that *Newsweek* would be almost certain to buy.

Provided they didn't deep-six me for missing the deadline on the Davies story.

When I left the apartment twenty minutes later, Mom and Toni were poring over my scratchy notes and deciding how to organize the folders even further: with a list attached to the outside of each one, describing its contents.

"Let's start by putting the exposés in one pile," Mom was saying briskly, "and the straight political news in another. This piece on Senator John Shales, for instance. It belongs under Defense Department—unnecessary expenditures. A dreadfully overdone topic . . . but then it does seem to have a twist, according to Jesse's notes." She shoved a pencil behind her ear and picked up another pile. "The congressman from New Hampshire, on the other hand, is a fairly straightforward story about a man who worked his way to the top . . ."

A *dreadfully overdone topic?* Indeed! I bristled all the way down my stairs, wondering what other skills Mom—who had never done anything but waitress work in her life—had learned since being married to Charlie Browne.

Chapter 6

▼ ▼ ▼

O ne of the calls I'd made was to Tark. His apartment/office is next to Marcus's penthouse, but with a separate entrance, so I don't have to pass through Alfred the way I do when I need the boss.

Tark had been grousing over all the paperwork his new job entailed. So even though I could have found out anything I wanted to over the phone, I thought I'd just wander on over there and cheer up his day.

It wasn't easy.

We sat on his terrace in the sun, overlooking Rochester and drinking orange juice. "I told Marcus I'd do this for six months," Tark said. "But God knows if I'll last." He set his glass down heavily. "Making rounds of corporate offices? Flying here to there on a company jet? It's not exactly make-work, but there's not much action in it, either."

"What *do* you want to do?" I asked. "Do you know any more now than last year?"

Before he'd moved up as head of security a few months ago,

Tark had been Marcus's bodyguard for over twenty years. Always loyal, Tark had gone through a kind of mid-life crisis last summer, a situation that might have been laughable—mob bodyguard, tough guy, and all that—except that I like Tark. And I knew exactly how he felt.

His new life had included a woman for a while, and he'd gone off to Italy with her. But she wasn't in the picture anymore.

"When I came back from Italy last fall," he said with a far-off look, "I thought I might just retire. Get a place in the country near my parents—somewhere down around Canandaigua." He laughed. "Can you picture that?"

I had to admit I couldn't. Tark is six-four, with shoulders that stretch from here to Canada. He has a decent-looking but worked-over face, short, bristly black hair tinged with gray—and Northern Italian gray eyes. I like the way he looks, personally. I find his size reassuring, and his amusement over my escapades edifying. But he doesn't quite fit the country squire image.

On the other hand, Tark's got the soul of a philosopher. I could picture him in a hut in the Himalayas, clothed in a white robe, keeping silence all the day. With Tark, it would have to be like that, from one extreme to the other. Organized crime—or retreat the whole way.

The problem with staying on here—no matter what the job—was that even though he and Marcus had been friends since childhood, there was still that one big wall between them: Marcus was the one who gave the orders.

"He's leaving me plenty of space now," Tark said, picking up my thoughts. "He's really trying. And that's the hell of it."

"I know. With me too. So if we hang around, it's because we want to, not because we have to. How can we fault him for that?"

On the other hand, too much space wasn't always to be desired. "Tark? I . . . uh . . . wanted to ask you something."

He glanced my way, lifting a dark brow. "I wondered when you'd get around to it."

"Yeah, well, you know . . . I just wondered."

"The only thing I can tell you is that Christopher and his mother are with Marcus in Switzerland. I don't know why. But I thought he left you a message."

"He left it with Alfred. You know how that works."

Tark gave a soft laugh of amusement. "So does Marcus. He probably wanted to give you something to chew on."

"Hmmm. He's still pissed that I turned down his offer to take over your job?" At various times, the offer had been as bodyguard, then as corporate investigator.

"Not really pissed, I don't think. But turning the heat up."

"So what do *you* think they're all in Switzerland for?"

"I know Marcus has a business deal going on over there. A hotel that he's buying, on Lake Geneva."

"So they're probably staying at this hotel?"

"Not probably—they are. You want the number?"

"Oh . . . I don't know." I set my own glass down, and got up and walked to the railing. "It's a game two can play—turning the heat on. Maybe I'll just give *him* some space this time."

"Make sure that space isn't a hole—and that you don't fall into it." A warning tone slipped into Tark's voice.

I turned back to him, leaning against the rail. The sun was warm on my shoulders, and from inside the apartment I could hear the strains of classical music. Something light and airy—perfect music for a perfect spring day. Which reminded me: "Do you know a Mac Devlin . . . gives flying lessons out at the Davies school, and has his own charter company?" It was Tark who had originally referred me to the Davies school for research on my article. He knew several people out there, both administrators and teachers.

"Devlin . . ." He thought a minute, steepling his fingers against his chin. As always at work, he wore a well-cut dark suit.

But he wore it easily. . . . jacket open, tie loose. His long, muscular legs were stretched out, ankles crossed. "Used to own one of those cargo airlines," he said. "In Nam."

"You mean like Air America, the airline that flew drugs for the CIA? The Golden Triangle?"

"That's the dark side of it. Air America was owned by the CIA. But they carried regular cargo, too, like rice and machinery . . . and they flew rescue missions. Picked up refugees, and went into the jungle for downed Air Force fliers. A lot of good men, good pilots."

"Most of whom, now, claim not to know that there was sometimes heroin in those sacks of rice."

"Well, you know, Jess . . . in times of war, people do things they'd just as soon forget in another time, another place. Devlin, now . . . his company wasn't connected with the CIA or Air America, I'm sure. He had one of those smaller, independent cargo lines. A lot of those lines went under because they couldn't get the lucrative contracts that Air America got from the CIA."

"So he came back here and opened up his own charter company. . . ." I mused. "CHARTER 10, it's called. You know anything about how he operates now?"

"I haven't heard anything bad, if that's what you mean. I could check him out."

"Would you?"

"Sure. But what's your interest in this guy?"

Good question. Curiosity? The yen for every reporter's dream—a story that would "knock their socks off"?

Or was it only spring?

"I'm not sure yet. But he's got an old friend hanging around . . . someone who looks like bad news."

"A pilot?"

"Seems so. Soldier-of-fortune type—looks like he was dressed by a wardrobe master at MGM."

"You want me to have Devlin followed?"

"Thanks, but I think that might be an overkill. I'll just poke around a bit myself for a while—see what skeletons I can dig up."

Tark looked worried. "Why does that have an ominous ring?"

H-A-double R-I-G-A-N spells Harrigan.

And D-R-U-N-K spells what I used to be when I came here to Harrigan's all the time. Now I only drop in now and then to meet people . . . say, when I'm doing an interview. Or, to re-new acquaintances with all the friendly cops whose hangout this is.

Not all of them are friendly, of course. Some are mean and uppity—like Grady North.

"You drinking again?" he growled when he saw my approach.

"Not today." I slid into the back booth, opposite Grady and facing the door.

"A fine distinction."

He was gnawing on a Harrigan's corned beef sandwich . . . fat and greasy, half a cow. I picked some pieces from around the edge, and nibbled on them.

"Well, my mom's here visiting," I said. "So who knows about tomorrow?"

"Kate's here?" He brightened. "I'd like to see her. How long is she staying?"

"That's up to her husband, I fear."

"Ah-ha. The infamous Charlie Browne." Grady wiggled his sandy brows like an old-time villain.

I sighed. "There are times when I regret the fact that we cleared him of that murder rap last fall."

He gave me a sharp glance through hazel cop-eyes. "He's being okay to your mom, though?"

"It sure looks that way. She's happy as a clam." I wondered why people say that. How do they know that clams are happy? For that matter, how happy can a clam be?

I asked the last question aloud.

"I think," Grady answered, "that we assume they're happy because they appear to be mindless. Nerveless—so what else can they be, but happy?"

"You think my mom's like that? Not enough sense to be anything else?"

"No . . . no, I don't, actually. I think Kate is pretty smart."

"And getting smarter every day." I had a quick flash of her sitting at my dining room table with Toni. Knowing all about senators and congressmen, about national defense and things. She sure wasn't the Kate O'Donnell James that I used to know.

Obviously. She was now Kate *Browne.*

"Get your fingers out of my food," Grady grouched.

"One lousy potato chip." I grabbed it. "You're getting a belly, you know."

He yanked his plate out of my reach. "I haven't gained an ounce since high school."

He was right; I'd lied. Grady was slender, about five-eleven, with nice taut muscles. He got them working out and teaching self-defense classes to women at the high school, nights.

"I never get to eat a whole meal with you around," he complained. "What are you doing here today, anyway? Looking for trouble?"

My eyes had been on the door. It was after twelve, according to my watch. Mac Devlin had yet to appear.

"Could be. I'm meeting someone. And speaking of trouble, I haven't seen you around for a while." Grady and I used to watch old movies together at my place, have dinner, hang out. At one time, I thought there was going to be something between us.

It turned out there was: Marcus Andrelli.

"Well . . . I'm seeing someone," Grady said, kind of shy-like. He passed a hand over his sandy curls.

"Yeah?" Why did I feel a pang? "Who? Somebody I know?"

"I don't think so. Her name's Sissy. I met her at this year's charity hop."

"Sissy?" I laughed. "You're seeing some girl called *Sissy?*"

Grady glared. "She's not a girl, Jess, she's a woman."

"What kind of woman has a name like *Sissy?*"

"What kind is named for an outlaw?"

He had me there.

Grady is such a nice guy. He's all the things a girl dreams about when she's growing up: decent, honorable, nice-looking, hardworking, and with a code of ethics that would fill a book. Any woman in her right mind would go after Grady Ryan North, rope and tie him, and never let him out of her sight.

Me, I've never been in my right mind; I always look for trouble in a man. Usually, I get it.

And there it was . . . right now . . . walking in through Harrigan's door.

Trouble.

"Mac Devlin," I said, introducing them. "Grady North."

Grady looked him up and down, warily. Mac did the same.

It's a funny thing. Men don't want you themselves, they aren't prepared to make any kind of serious move on you—or, heaven forfend—a *commitment.* Yet, let another man show up, and that look enters their eyes—that age-old primitive instinct to defend the territory . . . as meaningless as that territory may be to them.

So there were Grady and Mac facing off with each other, the same way Mac and Charlie had the night before.

And my name's not even Sissy.

Grady did ask Mac to join us. But Mac took my arm and very deftly led me away, to another booth, by ourselves. "Nice meeting you," he said over his shoulder to Grady. "Another time, maybe."

I do like a man who's masterful that way.

Mac, thankfully, hadn't worn his pilot's cap—or his wings—today. I'd have heard about that from Grady. As it was, Grady simply moved on out a short while later, with a stiff nod in Mac's direction. I got ignored.

I turned my attention to my lunch partner. He was dressed in leather jacket, blue shirt, jeans, and boots. One unruly lock of brown hair fell over his forehead, giving him that dashing World War II flier look.

"How're things going?" I asked. We had corralled our own cattle, and had heaping plates of corned beef before us.

Mac swallowed a mouthful of sandwich and wiped his chin with a napkin. "Fine." He gave me a long look, the face a mask of nonexpression.

"About last night," I said uneasily.

He grinned. "Last night was . . . nice."

Whew. I'd thought he was going to pretend it never happened. Men do that: the Morning-After Syndrome. Of course, a kiss *is* just a *kiss* . . .

But to ignore it would have made it more important than it was. Better to face it, laugh about it, wipe it off the memory banks that way.

"A great moon," Mac said.

"A great ride. Flight. Whatever."

"Only thing is . . . something's come up since we talked. I'm afraid I have to back out on the flying lessons for now."

"Oh, that's too bad."

Whew II.

"There are some things I have to take care of—old business. But I should be free again by next week."

I could be in Utah by then.

"Is this about that guy who's been hanging around?" I ventured.

He shrugged again.

"And the woman he says you owe?"

I was treated to an empty stare. A Scorpio, Samved had told me, may seem open and friendly, but he needs a lot of privacy. Masking emotions with a blank look is one way to get it.

"Like I said, I couldn't help overhearing, yesterday, when I was on the phone. Anything I can do?" *Any bits of information I can pry loose?*

He took another bite of his sandwich. "I told you before, it's nothing serious. An old score to settle, that's all."

"And Charlie?"

He blinked. "Charlie?"

"Browne. My stepfather. Surely you haven't forgot."

"I don't know what you mean." But his jaw went rigid, and the gray eyes closed in spirit if not in fact. He set the sandwich down.

"You and Charlie seemed to have something in common," I pushed. "And he disappeared off our scanners right after talking to you. When Charlie does that, there's always trouble brewing."

"I . . . wouldn't know."

"Of course not. Silly me."

He grinned again, suddenly, changing the whole drift of things. "Are you gonna give me more trouble today, lady? Next time I get you a thousand feet over the lake, I just might dump you in."

"So . . . you going out of town? This week, I mean. With a charter?"

"Maybe. Something like that."

"With your friend . . . the one who's been hanging around?"

"No. And he's not a friend. Not since Nam, anyway."

"Yeah? He fly for the same line as you there?"

"Awhile. We were partners, sort of, for a while."

"I see. And just how is Charlie involved?"

Mac rolled his eyes. "Lordy, lady, don't you ever give up?"

I called across to Harve, the bartender, and asked for another bottle of mineral water. "You want another beer?" I asked Mac.

"You buying?"

"Sure." I always bought, when it was for a story. This—I had decided—might just be a story.

The only problem was—with Charlie Browne involved, would it ever get told?

Chapter 7

▼ ▼ ▼

"*I* grew up in Kansas," Mac said, an arm draped easily over the back of the booth. "But I've always liked it better here, what with the lake. I like water."

Start with basics, I always say. Get 'em talking about themselves, their childhoods, and one thing leads to another. But Mac wasn't that easy. We'd been sitting here a half hour, and all I'd heard was the "I like water" stuff. Even a couple of beers hadn't loosened him up, and if this went on any longer, I might be tempted to have one myself. Or seven or eight.

At least Mac hadn't asked me any more about my "problem." Most people do. Now that every recovered souse in the world is letting it all hang out in books and on talk shows, people think it's okay to pry. To ask the Big Question: "I see you're not drinking. Are you an alcoholic?"

I mean, what do you say to a dumb question like that? Yes, but I'm lapsed—like a Catholic?

"Look," I said, irritated suddenly. "Why don't we cut to

the chase? You know and I know that what I *want* to know is
how you met Charlie Browne."

"Well, there's nothing mysterious about it," Mac said
calmly. "We met a few years ago in Mexico. *El Terremoto.*"

"The Mexico City earthquake? What was Charlie doing
there?"

"Browne was one of the American businessmen who set up
a relief agency to help the survivors."

I laughed. "C'mon."

He spread his hands palm up. "I flew supplies for him.
Food, medicine, equipment. Hate to disappoint you, but that's
all there was to it."

I let that sink in. It was easy enough to see Charlie in Mexico at the time of the earthquake—he'd always traveled a lot,
according to what I'd dug up about him. But that he might have
been involved in a philanthropic cause there, rather than something illegal? It was a new picture of the too-charming, too-
mysterious man my mother had married. One I wasn't sure I
believed.

"If that's all there was to it, why didn't you come right out
and say so? Why pretend you didn't know Charlie?"

Devlin took another draught of beer and leaned back in the
booth, folding his arms. He gave me an easy smile. "Did I do
that? I didn't mean to."

I was beginning to feel I'd met my match. When it came to
answering questions with questions, Mac Devlin had it all over
me.

"This thing you've got to do this week—is it something for
Charlie?" That would explain the sudden, way-after-the-fact
"honeymoon." And it was too much of a coincidence that Charlie had shown up at my apartment the same day I'd gone out
with Mac—or that they knew each other.

What I couldn't figure out was how I fit into all this—if
at all. Maybe it wasn't me—maybe it was my apartment. A

convenient place to meet, without any outsider knowing about it?

"This man who's been hanging around," I said. "What's his name?"

Mac sighed. "Why do I feel I'm being grilled by a cop?"

"I'm a reporter. It's my job to ask questions."

"Is this an interview, then? Should I watch what I say?"

"No, it's off the record. I'm just curious. Of course, if you've got something to hide . . ." I smiled.

Mac hesitated, then gave in. "Nothing to hide. His name's Garner. Sam Garner. I suppose you could have found that out almost anywhere—being such a hotshot investigative reporter."

"I suppose. So, he used to be your partner? In Vietnam?"

"Yes."

"But the company folded."

The gray eyes flicked up to mine, their look sharp. "How did you know that?"

I shrugged. "I was at Davies awhile. Word gets around."

He seemed to weigh, without accepting, the explanation. "I don't—"

We were interrupted by Harve, the bartender. His flaming red hair was silhouetted by sun, which flooded through stained-glass windows above the bar. Harve looked like a saint—rail-thin and pale—being burned at the stake. "Jesse? Phone for you."

I crossed to the bar and picked up the black receiver. Here, the sun glinted off colored bottles and crystal-clean glasses. I didn't like being this close to these bottles at Harrigan's anymore. It brought back too many memories, memories of all the tensions sliding away with no fuss at all. I turned my back to the shiny oak bar, and gazed at Mac across the room.

"Hello, Charlie?"

But it wasn't Charlie. It was Mom. "Jesse? Oh, thank God you're there! You've got to come home!"

"Mom? What's wrong?"

"It's Charlie, dear. I went down to that corner grocery on Thurston, to buy some lemons? And when I got back, there was a message on your machine. I thought it might be from you, wanting to tell me something, so I played it . . . and it was Charlie. He's gone somewhere!"

My hard gaze fixed on Mac and stayed there. "Slow down, Mom. What do you mean Charlie's gone somewhere?"

"He said he'd be out of town and out of touch, for possibly a week. He didn't say why, or where, and that's not like him. If that man has gotten himself into trouble again—"

Oh, hell. "Mom, what's going on?"

But Kate O'Donnell Browne had clammed up suddenly. She wouldn't tell me another thing.

I slammed the receiver down, and virtually flew across the room to Mac Devlin, taking the booth by storm. Leaning my palms on the table, I breathed anger and corned beef fumes into his face.

"My mom is upset."

If I thought he was going to admit to knowing why, I was wrong. Mac looked startled, confused.

"She's upset because her husband has disappeared. For a week, Charlie says. Out of town. No explanation. But we both know you can give me that explanation, and I want it right now."

"I told you, I don't—"

I grabbed the beer bottle out of his hand and slammed it down. "Listen, you may think this is a game. Maybe you've spent your whole life thinking it's all a game. But if you don't tell me where Charlie is, and what he's up to, I'm taking you out of play. Understand?" I grabbed his blue shirt and yanked on it, pulling him out of the relaxed position he'd been in. I had the advantage of surprise, but not for long. His eyes turned angry, and one large, strong hand wrapped itself around my forearm. A

55

nerve screamed, and I had to let go. I didn't back off, though. Somewhere in the back of my head I knew that Harve, and other customers, had stopped everything to watch and listen. But it was all a red, angry haze. "Listen, nobody hurts my mom and gets away with it. Whatever you and Charlie and that ex-partner of yours are involved in, you'd better make sure that it *doesn't hurt her.*"

Mac's gray eyes took on the look of a boxer when he realizes he's misjudged his opponent. But he didn't give in, or tell me anything. Somehow, I knew he wouldn't. Finally I left him sitting there, and stormed out to a phone booth on the corner, for privacy. Tossing in a quarter with a shaky hand, I punched out Tark's number.

"Hi, it's me. Listen, I've changed my mind. I want Mac Devlin followed, and I want a background check. He's at Harrigan's Bar, right now. How soon can you get somebody over here? Ten minutes?" I checked my watch. I could hang around, myself, until the tail came. "Okay." I gave him a description, even though he'd seen Mac out at the school once or twice. Height, weight, and what he was wearing. I didn't know what he was driving, for certain, but mentioned the jeep. "I'd also like you to run a computer check on a Sam Garner, used to own that cargo company with Devlin in Vietnam. I don't know anything else about him. And listen—I know I told you to lay off Charlie for now, but I've changed my mind. It seems he's gone—leaving my mom behind. Personally, I wouldn't care if he never came back. Unfortunately, I'm sure he will. In the meantime, I want to know what the hell he's up to."

"I'll let you know Devlin's every move," Tark said. "And I'll get right on this Sam Garner."

"Great. He's been hanging around Devlin. Can you get a tail on him, too, if he shows up again?"

"No problem. What do you want us to do when we find Charlie?"

"Don't do anything for now, just let me know. Call me at home when you've got something, but don't leave any specifics on my machine, okay? Mom might hear it. I'll call you at regular intervals if I go out."

"Got it. Oh—by the way. Marcus phoned."

"And?"

"And he said to tell you he'd be back next week. I think he wants you to know there's nothing to worry about."

"Did he say that?"

"No . . ." A pause. "I did."

"Thanks. I won't worry, then. About you."

Tark laughed softly.

Meanwhile, I had enough on my plate, with Charlie Browne.

Chapter 8

▼ ▼ ▼

W hat else can I tell you about Charlie Browne?

Not a whole hell of a lot. Mom showed up with him last fall, announced they had both stolen a valuable painting of a rabbit, and within a week Charlie was in jail for murder. I cleared him of that, but it's a long story . . . having to do more with Mom, and her trust in him, than my own.

The thing is, so far as I can see, he really cares about her. And I never could get anything on him—nothing illegal I could prove, just suspicions. And as Mom could tell you—I'm suspicious about everyone. Samved (my guru/minister/shrink) says it's myself I don't trust, and he's a sharp old bird, so I have to believe he's at least half right. That leaves me with the other half. The other half tells me I'm right about Charlie Browne.

Oh, sure, he's handsome, he's truly charming when he wants to be, and he is, for all I can tell, good to my mom. They travel together, stay in the best hotels, and he always seems to have enough money for this. Mom, in turn, is nuts about him. They laugh together, play together, sing together . . . (a ludicrous picture, the inscrutable Charlie Browne singing, but it's true. The oldies, you know, like "Smoke Gets in Your Eyes.")

I've always wondered if Mom had smoke in her eyes when she first met Charlie Browne. They met through a dating service —the old-fashioned, matchmaker kind, in California, that hooks up people of wealth and means. Mom had gotten tired of waiting for her prince to come, and had claimed to have money so she could get into this thing. Charlie soon found out the truth, but that didn't deter him. I honestly think he loves my mom.

Which doesn't explain the goddamn shoes.

That's my main reason, actually, for not trusting Charlie. The *shoes*. See, when Mom and Charlie were here last fall, there was a package delivered to my apartment by UPS. In it were several pairs of men's shoes—all brand-new, but not in store boxes. Wrapped singly, in newspaper. And they were weird—in various styles, none of them Charlie's sort at all. (More often than not, he wears L.A. Gears.) Mom explained it away like this: "Oh, those are Charlie's, dear. He always gets them sent to him this way."

She didn't even see anything odd in it.

Charlie, when I finally pinned him down, laughed off my suspicions. "There are codes in the lining," he had teased— those brilliant, blue, Paul Newman eyes sparkling.

Like I wasn't to believe a word of it . . . a joke.

Uh-huh.

When I got back to my apartment, I headed straight for those linings. But the shoes were gone.

Oh, I know what you're saying. You're saying Samved is right—and Mom is right—and Charlie, too. Hell, everybody's right about me, you're saying—I am a suspicious broad.

Well, just you wait.

I sat in the rotten old Dodge Dart and ruminated along those lines until the tail arrived. I was a few doors down from Harrigan's, and if Mac had come out before Tark's people got here, I'd have followed him myself. But he didn't. I wondered what was keeping him.

Within the promised ten minutes, a car pulled to the curb, behind mine. I recognized it as one of the Andrelli Enterprises fleet, a steel-gray Volvo. "What could be more nondescript than a Volvo?" Marcus had said, in explaining his choice of this kind of car for his foot soldiers. *Yuppie* foot soldiers. Ordinarily assigned to tail bank presidents, real estate moguls, and CEOs, they could go anywhere—even valet-park at all the "in" restaurants—with a Volvo.

Organized crime is dull these days—some of it, anyway. I have to laugh at the people who get all hot and bothered about "glamorizing the mob." I mean, *somebody's* got to. The further up they get in Corporate America—the further they get from the streets—the less real grit we reporters have to write about. Grit like curbside killings, and burials at sea with cement blocks. Good, solid, headline news.

And Marcus's men are good at their jobs—so they seldom get caught or go to jail. Most are Ivy League-educated, smarter than some of their counterparts in the FBI.

Something about that appeals; I'm not sure why.

It was still early afternoon, the sun high, the traffic a little heavy. I pulled out into it, anxious to get home. Mom must be hysterical by now, I thought. Weeping, pacing, a bundle of nerves . . . If I didn't find Charlie, I'd be up holding her hand all night.

Wouldn't I?

Right.

"You take a cup of flour, half a cup of sugar, and a handful of crushed pecans," Mom was saying. "Add the lemon custard later."

"But that's so simple!" Mrs. Binty piped in.

"Simple and quick, but delicious. Here. Have another."

The two of them—Mom, and my tiny little landlady—were on the couch, pigging out. Toni sat cross-legged on the floor. On the coffee table was a plateful of lemon bars—one of the treats Mom used to ply me with, back in the bad old days. Whenever Pop went on a drunk, she'd start baking. She never cried.

I should have remembered that.

I went into the kitchen, still redolent with baking flour and lemon, and poured myself a cup of coffee. Coming back, I sat next to Toni on the floor and said carefully, "I thought there was some kind of emergency going on, Mom."

She gave me a bland, innocent look. "I'm sorry, Jesse. I think I overreacted, dear." She flushed. "You know, it makes a world of difference to have friends to talk to." Her tone implied that I should try it sometime.

Mrs. Binty looked from her to me and wiggled back in her seat a little. She was so tiny, her feet didn't even touch the floor. "Oh, Jesse has lots of friends. And they're all such fun! Gangsters, cops, robbers, the homeless—" She broke off at Mom's disconcerted expression, and tugged at a white curl with a crumb-laden hand.

Toni laughed. "Your mom got a call from Charlie. Everything's okay."

"You got a call, Mom?"

"Yes, and everything's fine. He had some business to take care of in New York City, that's all. Nothing mysterious. You know businessmen, dear, and as Dora was saying, her husband used to do the same thing, go off just like that—" She snapped her fingers.

"Dora?" Who the hell was Dora? I must have looked blank.

"Jesse—your *landlady!*" Mom said. She put an arm around Mrs. Binty's minuscule shoulders and gave her a squeeze.

Shit. I'd never known her name was Dora. *Why* hadn't I ever known Mrs. Binty's first name? Was I that thoughtless about other people these days?

No. It was just that I always wrote my checks out to Mrs. William Binty. And I'd always called her "Mrs." Out of respect, I suppose. She must be near eighty by now.

So how was it my mom could come into my life and take it over this way? In ten minutes flat she knew things about my neighbors, my landlady, my friends . . . hell, she even knew more about Marcus, probably, than I.

Maybe she could tell me why he was in Switzerland with that bimbo and her son.

"So, Mom, you're just baking because you got hungry for lemon bars, is that it?"

"Something like that, dear."

"And it has nothing to do with Charlie being gone?"

"Nothing at all," she said airily.

"In fact, you're not worried about him a bit."

"Not one whit." She smoothed a hand over her jeans—my jeans, actually. I recognized the holes in both knees. Mom's green eyes had a faraway look.

And I was getting more nervous by the minute. This was the way she used to act when Pop went on a drunk. Like nothing had happened, when in fact, the whole world was crashing down around.

"I have to make some phone calls," I said. Mom's eyes bored into mine. "My editor," I lied.

In the bedroom, I punched in Tark's number with a feeling of foreboding. Almost knowing what I'd hear. He picked up immediately.

"It's me," I said. "Anything yet?"

"They're at the airport as we speak," he answered. "You no sooner pulled away from Harrigan's than Devlin came out. Lang and Damato followed. . . . Devlin went straight to the airport, and into that charter company he's got. Lang's going in as a potential customer, if Devlin doesn't come out soon. See what he can see."

"What about Charlie?"

"Nothing yet . . . wait a minute, hold on. Damato's calling in."

I waited, listening to Mom's bright chatter in the other room. Too much chatter—and it was far too bright. Not only that, but Mom was wearing a yellow blouse. She'd been wearing yellow since she got here—and yellow's the color she always puts on when she needs comforting. Something was very wrong.

I lay on the bed, phone at my ear, and stared at fine cracks in the plaster ceiling. Many's the night I'd stared at this ceiling, watching it float or rock, and then, toward the end of my drunken madness, seeing squiggly little black things on it that weren't even there. Many's the night—

"Jess? Two men just went into Devlin's office. One fits the description of this Sam Garner. The other's about fifty, crinkly silver hair. He's nearly six-foot, and he's wearing jeans and running shoes. Sound like somebody we all know?"

Shit.

But that answered one question. Charlie wasn't making a business trip to New York City. Unless, of course, he was chartering Mac to fly him there.

Charlie, Mac, and Sam Garner. Hmm. Still, the pieces didn't exactly fall into place. I could see Charlie and/or Sam Garner being involved in something illegal or below board. But how did Mac fit in? How did any of it fit, for that matter?

"I think I'll just mosey on out to the airport and see what's going on," I said.

"Check with Lang and Damato when you get there. They may have something more by then."

He told me where they were parked, which was more or less where Mac had parked his jeep the night before. From that vantage point, they could see the office, the hangar, and parts of the airstrip.

"Anything on the computer about this Sam Garner?"

"A home address in Arizona. And he owns his own cargo plane, an old Beech 18."

"I've seen it, I think."

"Garner's pretty much a loner, a soldier of fortune. My guess would be that he's transporting drugs and ammo around Central America, for private parties. The money would be good for someone with his background in Nam."

"Any sign of Mac Devlin working with him now?"

"Devlin's clean, I think . . . only one small thing."

"What?"

"He did make a trip to Colombia seven years ago—at a time when I've pinpointed Garner there."

"You think he might have been doing something for Garner then? A drug run, or something?"

"Hard to tell. It's been a while, and we don't really have anyone in place down there to ask around."

"Can you ask some other Family? One that deals down there in drugs?"

"A couple of years ago, maybe. But lately . . ."

"What?"

"Well, Marcus has cut all ties with those people. You know he's never dealt in drugs, but in the past few months he's been removing himself from even a hint of drug connections. He's had some meets with Lucetta, too, trying to convince him to let this end of the business go strictly legit. According to Marcus, Andrelli Enterprises is solid enough now to run half the damned country without benefit of mob backing."

"Not that it would *ever* be strictly legit any more than any major corporate enterprise in this country."

"Well, there are levels, of course . . . but I think he's hoping the Organized Crime Bureau will let up on him if they see what he's doing, stop trying to nail him on something. Ever since . . ." He let it hang.

"Since Christopher," I finished for him. "Since he decided to start seeing the kid."

Silence at the other end. Tark and I both knew that if Marcus was going to such lengths, gradually easing out of organized crime, it could only be because of Chris—and, of course, his mom.

It took me less than fifteen minutes to reach the airport. I pulled into a lot that couldn't be seen from Mac's office, and walked along a concrete path to the executive terminal. The air pounded with the sound of jets from major airliners at the other end of the field. Here, in an area behind a chain-link fence, were smaller hangars with privately owned craft—from corporate jets to charter planes. On the outer fringes, to the left, were single- and twin-engine personally owned planes. I'd done a piece for the *Rochester Herald* last year, when a Piper Cub was stolen. It had amazed me that more didn't disappear; they were simply parked out there on the field, like so many cars in a lot. A hijacker's paradise—with security here, since the latest recession, not being quite up to par.

It wasn't an easy feat, but I managed to take Damato by surprise, coming up behind the Volvo on little cat feet—without even the benefit of fog.

I slid into the seat beside him, and he jumped a mile. "Hey, Joey. How's tricks?"

It was a loaded question. Joey Damato was a pimp for the old mob, before he came to work for Marcus. He was one of the few exceptions to Marcus's rule about hiring only business grads. Marcus took Joey on as a favor to his old boss, Lucetta, and the first thing he did was retire Joey from pimping and send him off to night school. It didn't take. Oh, Joey was brilliant at math—he could add whole columns of numbers in his head. (All that hanging out with bookies in the early days, he said.) Joey didn't apply himself, though. And he drove his teachers nuts. He still wears his dark hair in a fifties-style ducktail, and he still chews gum all the time. Or most of the time. On alternate days, you might find him picking that same gum out of his dentures with a cliché gold toothpick.

I don't like Joey much, but he does provide comic relief.

"Lang inside?"

"The Golden Boy? Yeah." He cracked his gum. A scent of Dentyne drifted through the car. His narrowed eyes scanned the tarmac, the hangar, and Mac's office. Whatever one might say about Joey Damato, he is a good tail. He had parked the car facing the chain-link fence, but behind an airy shrub. We could see through it, but anyone looking from the field to the car wouldn't see who was in it.

Mac's CHARTER 10 sign, white with red letters, was highly visible in daylight, as were surrounding buildings that I'd only gotten a glimpse of the night before. His company was at the hangar end of a row of offices with smaller signs on their windows. Squinting earned me a few words: FREIGHT . . . COPIES . . . MAIL.

"How long's he been in there?" I said.

Joey didn't look at his watch. "Thirteen minutes, seven seconds."

I didn't doubt him for a minute. Joey was good at that, too.

"Seems a little long, just to ask some customer-type questions."

"Lang can handle it. He's smart."

"Even so . . ." I was feeling edgy, itching to go in there myself. To confront Mac, Charlie, and Garner—take them by surprise, and maybe pry a few truths loose.

"Give him a few more minutes," Damato said. "You'll find out more if you give them some rope. You don't wanta go barreling in."

He was right. I always make that mistake—thinking the element of surprise will make people fess up. Hell, I used to fess up, as a kid. I'd have my alibi all prepared, and there would be Mom, with just one particle of what had really gone down, and I'd blab out the rest.

I hate that about mothers. They con you into thinking they know it all, and within five seconds flat, they do.

It's just too bad the technique doesn't work on adults, most of whom had mothers just like mine and are wise to the scam by now. So I sat by Joey and tapped my nails on the ledge of the car window . . . in rhythm to Joey's snapping gum.

Fortunately, Lang appeared before we drove each other nuts.

Lang is tall and smooth, with neat blond hair and always—always—a three-piece suit. He never checks to see if his tie is neat. Lang knows. He's Joey's opposite number, physically—but their brains complement each other. Joey is quick—blunt and decisive—while Lang is slow-moving, thoughtful. Once the two of them decide to move, it's all a magnificent blur.

I watched Lang amble across to the parking lot, hands in his pockets. Now and then he'd stop and gaze around the field, the way any curious customer might. Eventually, he reached the Volvo. He didn't even react when he saw me in the front seat, just slid into the back.

"There are two men in a back room," he said. "Your stepfather and this Sam Garner guy, according to the descriptions you gave Tark. The man who owns the charter service, Devlin, talked with me. I told him I had a meeting scheduled in Toronto next week, and was bringing several of my staff along. He referred me to an executive charter service down the line, one with jets, which is what I'd expected him to do. His planes are too small to handle that many people."

He stopped for a breath, and I jumped in. "I thought he moved cargo as well as people."

"He does. But these smaller charter companies use the same

planes—Aztecs, usually, or Cessnas—at night. They pull the seats out and hump freight all over the state. My impression is that this is not an expensive operation. I asked him for brochures, rates, and so on, and he had to go in the back room for them. That's when I saw the other two men. They seemed to be arguing, but broke off when Devlin opened the door."

"You didn't hear anything they said?"

"Didn't get a chance. The mood in the office was definitely secretive. Devlin couldn't wait to hustle me out of there."

Dammit all. What were they up to?

"I say we tail all three of them," Damato put in with a crack of gum. "Get Tark on the horn. Tell him I'll take Garner, you take Browne, and Jesse here can keep tabs on Devlin." He looked at me. "You got any problem with that?"

I hesitated. I'm not very good at these games. When things start to happen, I don't always react well. Look at how I'd screwed up at Davies. And I had a handicap here, in that both Mac and Charlie knew I was on to them—on to *something*, at least. I'd have to convince them I'd dropped my suspicions.

Well, I could play on the entrée I already had to Mac. After all, *he* had pursued *me*. Maybe I could take it into my sweet girlish head to start hanging around, sort of groupie-like. He might not like it, but what could he do about it? I could even insist on taking—God help me—those flying lessons. I could become a nuisance. A pain in the butt.

That shouldn't, I figured, be hard.

Chapter 9

▼ ▼ ▼

I went back to my car, leaving Lang and Damato on their
phone. They were ordering up another car, which Lang
would use to follow Charlie. I didn't want to go into the hangar
so soon after Lang. I went back to the old Dodge Dart to plan
my own course of action.

Go home, change into something more alluring for my flying lessons, something Jacqueline Cochran might have worn to a
Powder-Puff Derby? And call Mac from there, insisting the lessons be now or never? Plead a deadline emergency?

Or wait here until Charlie and Sam left—and go in then?

What if it took hours for Charlie and Sam to leave?

That finally decided me. I was turning the key in the ignition, thinking I'd go home first, when something loomed at my
passenger door, blocking out the light. I jerked around in my
seat and sucked in my breath. The door was wrenched open, and
a figure slipped in. It wore faded jeans and L.A. Gears, with a
soft blue V-neck sweater that matched its eyes. It sat sideways,

facing me. The teeth were even and white, and they flashed into a knowing grin.

"Jesse, Jesse, Jesse . . . you do show up in the strangest places, at the oddest times."

I scowled. "They only seem strange or odd because you're there, Charlie."

"Nothing odd about it this time," he said easily. "I'm making travel arrangements to the Thousand Islands. For my honeymoon with your mother . . . remember?"

"Of course. And I'm here to learn how to fly."

He laughed. "You? Fly? Now, that I've got to see."

"I think I can manage it without an eyewitness."

"I'm thinking in particular," he went on, a chuckle still in his husky voice, "of the morning after Kate's and my wedding. The hot-air balloon, in Napa. You remember that? We did invite you to come along."

"Right. My dream date—you, me, Mom, and Aunt Edna in a wicker basket, hundreds of feet above the ground." I folded my arms. "You know, it defies any sense of logic. Why would *anyone* think it's smart to go hundreds of feet into the air in a goddamned nylon *sack*, for Christ's sake, and then light a *fire* under it? It makes no sense, no sense at all."

"And you turned down the para-gliding, day after that. What a day that was! There is absolutely nothing like para-gliding! You ever have dreams where you fly, Jess?"

"You mean the ones where I flap my arms like wings, desperate to get away from some mad killer who looks like you, and I can't even lift off the ground?"

"A sign of inner conflict," Charlie mused. "Doesn't surprise me. Well, para-gliding is like those dreams, except that you don't have to flap your wings. You just sit there and sail. You're like a bird, soaring over treetops and villages, lakes and streams. Nothing but silence, and the wind on your face."

"All in all, I'd rather be in Minnesota."

He laughed. "Kate loves that sort of thing, you know."

"She never did, until you came along."

His blue eyes met my frown. "But I did come along." He said it softly, touching the side of my cheek briefly with a finger-tip. "Accept it, Jess. I love your mother. And I've made her happy, maybe for the first time in her life."

I pulled away from his finger. "Yeah? Well, why is it I always feel that's temporary? That she's happy today, but God only knows about tomorrow?"

"Is that what you're waiting for from Marcus Andrelli? Guarantees?"

I didn't answer. But I've got to admit, that's one thing about Charlie . . . he knows all my buttons. He fingers the problem and lays it right out there, not letting me squirm away. It's this sort of thing that made Mom fall in love with him, I'm sure.

I'm sure because it makes even my cold heart flutter now and then.

The difference between Mom and me is that I see this and know it for the trap it is, and I'm smart enough not to fall into it. It's all part of the con, the technique.

"There are no guarantees in relationships," Charlie was say-ing. "And no one can be there for us all the time. Someone said . . . was it Merle Shain? . . . that sometimes the people we love can make it through—and sometimes they can't get to us, no matter how much they try."

"Merle Shain?" I was more or less dumbstruck.

"Canadian author. A journalist, too—like you."

"I know that." I'd been carrying around a beat-up copy of *When Lovers Are Friends* for years. Every few years or so I take it off the shelf and read it again, finding new things to underscore. Most recently, I'd been taken by something about people being friends in spots. That there are parts of people you want to be-friend, and parts you don't want anything to do with at all. That you have to learn to be grateful for what's there for you, rather than annoyed by what can never be.

I always wonder when I mark a new paragraph if it means I've grown—since I now see its message as a truth, one I accept as my own. And I often think that if I could just put that book—that one, slim, hundred-and-six-page volume—to work in my life, many of my trials would be over.

I remembered then that one of a con's tricks is to deliberately find out what books a woman likes, and casually mention them, to create a bond. "Why would somebody like you be reading Merle Shain?" I scoffed.

"Maybe I'm not who you think I am," Charlie said. "Or *what* you think I am. Maybe you just see me as you want me to be."

I gave a short laugh. "I *want* you to be a crook?"

"It would give you one more thing to gripe about . . . one more person not to believe in."

"Christ Almighty, now you sound like Samved!" And Samved was an old fraud.

I stared out over the tarmac and decided not to give Charlie Browne, the master puppeteer, any more strings to pull between him and me. "So, have you made those honeymoon arrangements already?"

"Just a few minutes ago, in fact—with your friend, Mac Devlin."

"Mom said you had to go to New York City on business."

"Right. But only for a couple of days. And that'll give Kate some time to visit with you first."

I recalled my plan to act as if I'd dropped all my suspicions. "Well, that'll be nice. I left her at home baking lemon bars with Toni. They're becoming friends again."

"Does that still bother you?"

"That Mom and Toni are joined at the hip, when Mom and I have always had problems being close? Not at all."

"And that's why, while they're home in the kitchen cooking, you're out here walking into danger without a backward glance, the way you always do?"

I threw a suspicious glance his way. "Danger?"

Charlie smiled. "The flying lessons," he said smoothly. "For you, that must be scary. But is it easier than hanging around the house and getting close to your mother?"

"Hardly. It's just that Mac offered the lessons free, to help with research on a piece I'm doing for *Newsweek.*"

"And you think it's important to do that, right now?"

"Absolutely. My editor's not happy with me. I guess I kind of messed up my hands-on research yesterday."

"Don't be too hard on yourself about that. It's a tough course they give at Davies."

I almost stopped breathing, but didn't. In fact, I didn't move, not a muscle. I hoped that my cheek didn't twitch, or my eyes widen.

What did Charlie know about Davies? How did he know that I'd been out there, and that I'd screwed up yesterday on the field? I'd never told him about it, nor Mom.

Would Mac have talked about it? And if so, why? I somehow couldn't see Mac and Charlie nattering on . . . gossiping . . . having light conversation.

"Well," I said, smiling, "sitting in a tiny box with two wings, high above Lake Ontario, can't be much worse than Davies."

The Paul Newman eyes were steady on mine. "As long as you don't run into any buzzards up there."

"Buzzards?"

"Birds of prey. I'd hate to see you get carried away."

I watched Charlie walk to a jazzy car with rental plates, a red Porsche, and unlock it. With a kind of loose, lazy grace, he eased into its low seat. While I watched, he maneuvered the car smoothly out of its slot and down the lot. The requisite Volvo glided past, following. Only Lang was in it; I hoped he knew he'd have to use all his skills to keep Charlie Browne from knowing he was being tailed.

Charlie Browne. Shit Almighty.

What, I thought, if this guy is for real? What if he's some kind of government agent (as I've often speculated), and he's legal—although secretive—and on the up and up?

Not that I believed it for a minute.

It always astonishes me, though, that Mom—who is late-fifties-Betty White—landed this forty-nine-year-old hunk. He isn't my type, and I wouldn't take him on a silver platter, as they say. So I'm not jealous. It's just that I can't quite see it—Charlie and Mom, together. Charlie could've had his pick of pretty young things. Instead, he chose my mother, a woman who'd spent most of her life waitressing to hold her family together— and who had the lumps and lines to prove it. Not that Mom isn't pretty—she just isn't Patty Penthouse. And for years, I've been thinking that that's what men want.

Maybe I've been wrong. Maybe men—*real* men, secure in themselves—don't need a nubile teenager on their arm who makes them look good. Maybe some of them want real *women*— even if they're lumpy here and there.

(Yeah, right, I hear you—not likely. But it's a fantasy I have now and then.)

I slid out of the Dodge and started back around to Mac's office, remembering something about impossible relationships that Samved had told me:

Say you walk through a jungle and don't see the pit, so you fall into it. Eventually, you get out, and it's okay because you didn't see the pit, and it wasn't your fault. But if you walk through the same jungle and fall into the same pit again, you've got to question your mentality.

One level up is when you walk through the jungle, but have sense enough to circle round the pit.

The final level, according to Samved, is when you walk through a whole 'nother jungle.

God bless Samved. He tells me everything in pictures, which is about all my gray cells, so long numbed and eroded by alcohol, can deal with.

Chapter 10

▼ ▼ ▼

*I*t was getting late. Not much point, I had decided, in going home now. By the time I got there in late-afternoon traffic, Mac might have closed up here. And I didn't know where he lived.

Funny, isn't it, how you can be kissing a guy one night—his hands can be all over your *body,* for God's sake—and twenty-four hours later, you realize you don't even know how to *find* him? He's got your address, your phone number, hell, he may even know the size of your bra—

And you don't know diddly-squat.

They do that on purpose.

Men.

The office was open, but there wasn't anyone there. It was a small room, about twenty-by-twenty, with a desk and a row of black metal filing cabinets along one wall. Opposite that were three chairs, presumably for customers. Nothing fancy, but clean lines, and cheerful, with chrome frames and red leather seats and backs. The overall feeling was of a working office, but not one where a lot of activity took place. Competent. Nice enough to reassure the average customer.

A door on the wall opposite the entrance was closed. Presumably, it led into the back room where Lang had seen Mac with Charlie and Sam Garner. Garner might still be in there. I stood quietly, listening, but didn't hear voices.

"Mac?" I called out, thinking he might be in the back room. No answer. I knocked. Still nothing. I rattled the knob, but the door was locked. Maybe they'd gone out to the hangar. I decided to wait, and take a look around the office while I had the chance.

The desk was piled high with papers. Receipts for parts and equipment. Invoices from Mac to various companies, for cargo he'd carried. FedEx . . . Kodak . . . Marine Midland and other banks.

On the wall above Mac's desk was a 1940's-vintage poster, a pinup of a Betty Grable type. She wore red tap shorts, and a blue halter with white stars. On her head was a sailor cap. She saluted smartly. But the wink of one eye and her saucy, curving mouth held a hint of sensual promise: *When Johnny comes marching home again, hurrah, hurrah . . . We'll give him a hearty welcome, then, hurrah, hurrah . . .*

A black telephone had three lines; each button was blinking slowly, the way they do when they've been put on hold. People calling in would get a busy signal, and not think the office was closed for the day. That, and the unlocked front door, told me I didn't have long before Mac would get back.

I pulled out the top desk drawer. Pencils, rubber bands, paper clips, fingernail clippers . . . the usual office crud. A stapler, and scissors. In the next drawer was blue and white stationery: CHARTER 10 AIR. A careful search through the rest of the drawers revealed only more of the same. Carbons, envelopes. There was no computer, but a spiffy red Royal typewriter.

I tried the file drawers. Each was locked. Maybe—

I stiffened, hearing a noise. From the back room, I thought. After a moment, I went over there and knocked again. "Mac?" A rustle. Or maybe not. It could be a cat; a lot of offices have cats, to keep the mice away.

"Mac? Are you there? It's me, Jesse."

Nothing.

I ran my fingers along the edge of the door and tapped in several places, sure that it had a steel inner core. I wondered what was in this room, what made the steel core necessary.

Probably just a safe. And business papers. Like I said, out here at this end of the airport, the security isn't all that great. There are burglaries reported in the papers all the time.

I did have an itch to see into that room. And since Mac hadn't returned—

I could pick the lock. If Mac came in and caught me, I could pretend the door had been open. Lying about these things —and breaking-and-entering—is something I'm good at, having built up considerable skills along those lines as a youth. Running on the streets, as a kid, with all the Bad, Bad Boys of the neighborhood, I'd learned a lot of neat stuff—like how to heist cars, how to break into people's houses just for kicks, how to wind up in jail . . .

It was excellent preparation for becoming a reporter. Or a thief.

I went back to the desk and took out a paper clip. Opened it out to its full length. Returned to the lock. Kneeling, I started to work on it. After a couple of long minutes, I began to sweat. Damn, what was wrong? The tumbler wouldn't budge. Maybe the clip was too thick. I went back and looked for something else. There is always—*always*—something around to pick a lock with. That was something I'd learned from the Genesee Three. If a lock has a new look to it, however—which this did—you could forget the credit card route. You might end up with nothing more to show for a day's work than a broken card.

Still, there's always something . . .

Fingernail clippers.

I picked them up and opened out the skinny little file at the end. Went back to work again.

Ahhhh. . . . A satisfying snick. Music to my lawless ears.

I was in.

But so was Mac.

In the back room.

Flat on his face, trussed up, on the floor.

"I never thought I'd be happy to see somebody break in here," he said after I'd pulled the packing tape from his mouth. It must have hurt like hell, but he didn't do more than grunt. His expression was grim.

"What the hell happened?" I was wrestling with thick, tightly wound tape around his wrists and ankles. It was strapping tape, with fibers throughout that were too strong to break. It wouldn't unwind. I went out and got the scissors from the desk.

"Burglar. Tied me up to give himself time to get away."

"Burglar?" Possible. But I couldn't help thinking there hadn't been much time for that.

Charlie, then?

I worked the scissors beneath the tape—not an easy task. Whoever had done this knew his business.

Charlie knew his business. He was adept at every god-damned thing he did.

"This, uh, burglar—" I managed to slit an inch of tape. "What did he take?"

"Uh . . . money. From that safe." He gestured with his head to a heavy gray monster by the back door. "Ow! I'm not sure what else."

"Hmmm. What did he look like?"

"A kid. Just a kid, looking for drug money, probably. Watch it!"

"Sorry. Hold still." Little by little, I was getting through the blasted tape. Oh, I could see Charlie Browne doing this, all right.

I didn't realize how pissed I was, until Mac said irritably, "What are you trying to do, finish me off?"

"Look, I'm trying to get you out of this thing. There." I ended with the wrists, and started on the ankles.

"Give me that!" he yelped, grabbing the scissors.

I stood, arms folded, watching him. "Boy, you sure don't know how to be grateful."

"On the contrary. I'm *very* grateful. So much so, in fact, I won't even ask why you were picking the lock on my door."

"I was picking it because I thought you might be in trouble in here! I heard a noise."

"Sure."

I threw up my hands. "So all right, don't believe me. Crimin*ee,* I loathe men. You are all so goddamned difficult. You don't communicate, you don't give any woman a decent break, and even a dog responds better to kindness than a man."

The ankle tape gave, and Mac stood, flexing the stiffness out of his long arms and legs. "Yeah?" He grinned. "You loathe men? Didn't seem that way last night, on your stairs."

I flushed. "A momentary madness. Spring fever. It will not be repeated . . . ever."

He lifted my chin with a finger and kissed me square on the lips before I could move. "Okay," he said, straightening. "Fine with me. I just thought I'd thank you for coming to my rescue."

My ears felt like they were on fire. "With a kiss—like a pat on the head? You jerk—"

He grinned. "What *do* you want?"

"Nothing, not a damned thing." I remembered about my plan, for being a pain in the butt. "No, wait a minute. I want flying lessons. I just decided."

"Okay, great. I told you that. Next week—"

"No, I want them now. I mean, I *need* them now. I've got a deadline—I have to get this piece in to *Newsweek.*"

"Out of the question." I followed his back into the front office. "I've got a couple of charter jobs this week. I'm all booked up."

"Oh, and that's how you show your gratitude? You just leave me dangling here? I thought friends were supposed to be people who were there when you needed them."

He leaned against the desk, rubbing his wrists. Smiling widely, he cocked his head to the side. "Is that what we are now —friends?"

I frowned. "Something like that, I suppose."

"Then I guess I can ask you not to say anything to anybody about this little incident here today."

"This *burglary,* you mean?"

"Yes, this *burglary.* Insurance, you know. My rates could skyrocket if they heard about it."

"Hey, okay. Sure. Fine. It's none of my business. I just really need those flying lessons now."

He appeared to think about it, then nodded. "All right. But I'll need you to be available whenever I can fit you in."

"Whatever you say. I'll stick like glue."

It was, after all, what I'd wanted to do.

Chapter 11

▼ ▼ ▼

We made plans to meet at the airport the next morning at 6:30. Until then, it was my job to follow Mac—but I'd been worried about Mom since seeing Charlie out here. It was a tough call, but I decided to check on her first. Mac did say he was going home and would be there all night—and he even gave me his home phone number in case I needed to call for anything. He wouldn't have done that, I thought, unless that was where he'd be.

Of course, if he had games to play with Sam Garner and/or Charlie Browne, he could always just leave an answer machine on and tell me later that he'd been asleep.

(And yeah, sure, I know what you're thinking now. You're thinking I don't give men a chance. That I'm suspicious and unfair—one of those women who just doesn't like men, no matter how good, kind, and innocent they are.

Uh-huh. Well, like I said . . . just you wait.)

I found Mom at my dining area table once more, working

alone on my files. The late sun, slanting in through the side bay window, was square on her attractive face. Only a few lines were revealed; mostly, around her green eyes, which were intent on a sheaf of papers in her hand.

I leaned over and kissed her, feeling protective and loving. "How're things going?"

"Just fine, dear," Mom said absently. She was still focused on the papers.

"Great. I'm glad to hear it. Is Charlie around?"

"Hmmm? Oh, I told you, Jesse . . . he left for New York City, around noon."

"Right. I guess I forgot. What are you doing?"

"Doing?" She was still distracted. "He's supposed to call tonight. . . ." She frowned, and picked up a red pencil. Made a few marks on the top paper.

"Jesse"—she peered up at me critically—"you do use parens a lot, you know."

"Parens?" I sat in the chair next to her and smiled uncertainly.

"Parentheses. When you write."

"I know what parens are, Mom." I frowned. "But what do you mean, I use them a lot?"

"Like this, here . . ." She held a page up to my nose. It was one of my drafts. On it were red lines . . . marks . . . *editing* notes—on *my work. My article.*

Mom had edited my work!

I shut my mouth, which had dropped open, but it fell slack again. I stared at one of the paragraphs savaged in red.

Randolph Batters spoke to reporters outside his hotel ~~(the American Arms, on West 87th Street)~~. "We definitely do not plan to close the Westside Heights Apartments," he insisted. ~~(Interviews with tenants, however, clearly indicate otherwise.)~~

The parentheses were crossed out. "I . . . I can't believe you did that!" I choked.

Mom's green eyes were vaguely innocent. "Did what, dear?"

"Don't give me that, you know what I mean! Why did you edit my work?"

"I don't understand, Jesse. . . . You said I could help."

"Help *file*, Mom. *Organize!*" I ran a hand over my face.

"But I can be of so much more value to you this way. See this? You write in italics, too. A lot. Well, you always did talk that way, and I've noticed you write the way you talk. Which isn't necessarily a bad thing," she added quickly. "It's a very immediate style."

My mouth worked. No words came out. I couldn't believe this. Sure, Mom had gotten a degree in English Lit before she married Pop. But that was thirty years ago—and she'd worked all her life as a waitress!

I cleared my throat and moved my mouth again. "Mom, I'd have gotten to this myself. I always edit my work before it goes out. I'd have removed the parens—"

"Well, I'm not so sure, dear. That last article of yours in *Newsweek* had several. I think perhaps you don't see them anymore. That happens sometimes, I hear, when writers are too close to their work."

"Mom, for Christ's sake! The last thing I need in my life now is another editor!"

She smiled complacently, laid down the papers, and folded her hands. "You really should limit your use of exclamations, too," my mother said.

"I don't know what to do with her." I was lying on my bed, with the phone at my ear, and I was whining. I knew I was whining, but I couldn't help it. "Every time she comes here, she just takes over. First it's my friends, then Marcus, and now she's meddling in my work! Why can't she just mop the floors or something?"

"Where is my sister now?" Aunt Edna said from Mill Valley, California.

"Out. Remember Emma Hughes? She owned the Knit Knook, next to the restaurant where Mom worked just before Pop died? They went to dinner. But Aunt Edna, she even took it upon herself to tell me, before she left, that I should condition my hair! It's getting too long, and too dry, she said!" My fingers twisted absently in one long brown snarl on my shoulder.

"Well, your mother didn't have much control in her early life. Maybe she's overcompensating."

"You mean, for being an abused wife all those years? But things are different now. She's got Charlie." Or maybe they weren't so different after all. Women who were abused by the men they loved felt abandoned. And women who were abandoned for nefarious reasons—by a husband like Charlie, going off alone the way he was doing now—must feel at least a little abused.

"Things are different for you, too," Aunt Edna pointed out. "You don't drink now. But Jesse, you are still one hell of a difficult child."

"I . . ." Well, shit. *"You* should talk," I grumped.

I could hear her puffing on the ever-present cigarette between sentences. Although Aunt Edna firmly believes in New Age precepts—health foods, chanting, meditation, Save the Environment, and all that shit—she's never been able to break herself of smoking. "Are *you* completely grown?" I said.

"Of course not," she answered with satisfaction. "No one is. That's why it's important."

"What?" I plumped my pillows behind my back and bit into the turkey sandwich I'd brought in with me. "What's important?"

"To just take people the way they are. There are five-year-olds in all of us, and the only difference is that we're five years old in different ways. One person stomps the floor, another goes silent. Somebody else might wheedle her best friend out of her school lunch. Jesse, there is absolutely no one in this world who doesn't have some vice. Your mother's, right now, may be a need to control."

"You don't think it's Charlie? That he's made her like this?"

Aunt Edna sighed. I could almost see the smoke billowing out of her throat, making puffy clouds around her frizzy red hair. A sense memory returned the scent of cigarette to me, a scent I'd always liked even though it made my eyes smart. It brought back moments that Aunt Edna and I had shared—tooling around in one of her ratty old convertibles, the wind in our hair. Pigging out on hot fudge sundaes after an outing in the country.

"Will you let up on that poor man?" Aunt Edna said now.

"Let up on Charlie? What do you mean?"

"You know damn well. You might as well accept him, for God's sake. Your mother is gaga in love."

"Yeah, well maybe it's that five-year-old that's in love. And maybe it's got the grown-up Kate James bamboozled."

"It's Kate Browne, now," Aunt Edna reminded me. "Kate James *Browne.*"

"Yeah." I sighed. "I know. That's what I'm worried about."

Aunt Edna's tone went sharp. "Is there something wrong in the marriage?"

"Not that I can see. But you know how they are together, like a couple of kids with a secret. They never tell me a damned thing."

Aunt Edna laughed. It was more a cackle. "You never could stand not being in on everything."

"I'm telling you, it's more than that. This so-called honeymoon? Charlie's using it as a cover for something illegal, I'm sure. And Mom just blithely looks the other way. I'm really worried this time."

"Well . . ." There was a short pause. "I have to admit, I've had my doubts about good old Charlie Browne. If we could only find out what it is exactly that he does, it'd help. Not to mention where he's been all these past twenty-three years. For a man to have no past since leaving West Germany and the Army in '69— nothing that can be tracked on a computer—isn't natural these days." Aunt Edna puffed. "But what can you do about it? You can't convince your mother of anything, you've tried that before."

"I know." I was silent, thinking.

"So how's *your* love life?" my aunt said bluntly.

"Huh?"

"You sound lonely."

"Well . . . Marcus is out of the country right now."

"Hmpfh. It's spring. What you need is somebody new, an other energy."

"Another energy?"

"Not like that. Three words: An Other Energy. In caps. Someone to defuse all the feelings you always get in spring, the ones that run rampant in those obstinate female veins like at no other time of the year. Serve Marcus Andrelli right, going off and leaving you like that when the lilacs are in bloom."

"There is someone . . ." I said tentatively.

"Oh?"

I laughed, feeling silly. "No one, really. Anyway, it's beginning to look like he's mixed up with Charlie."

I could hear her satisfied grin, in the way she jumped on it. "Ah-*ha!* Well, if he is, you like him *because* of it. You're just like your mother, Jesse! You always *did* like mysterious men!"

I scowled into the phone. "Aunt Edna? Did you ever notice that you talk a lot in italics? And exclamation points, too?"

Chapter 12

▼ ▼ ▼

"Feeling the changes in all the many ways . . .
I feel them just like you."

—*"*FEELING THE CHANGES,*"*
BY D. R. LUNSFORD

"*I* don't have a car phone, unlike some people I know with unlimited budgets. Otherwise, I *would* have called in sooner."

I wasn't really pissed at Tark, but at myself, because I'd spent all that self-indulgent time on the phone with Aunt Edna, instead of calling him first. Because of that, I'd missed hearing the not-too-astonishing news right away: that Charlie—slimy creature of the deep—had slipped through Lang's net.

"Lang's chewing nails," Tark told me. "In ten years with Marcus, he's never had this happen before."

"He's never tailed anyone like Charlie Browne before. Damn!"

"Not to worry. Sam Garner wasn't so careful. He led Damato right to a meeting with Devlin and Browne—"

"Devlin's there, too?" So he wasn't home sleeping.

"You got it," Tark said. "And Lang's there with Damato now. Jess—"

He sounded like he had something he didn't want to tell me. Finally, he spit it out. "Do you . . . uh . . . know where your mother is tonight?"

I laughed. "You mean, like, 'do I know where my child is tonight'?"

"Something like that."

"Well, sure. Mom's having dinner with Emma Hughes, an old friend from the Knit Knook—" The last traces of turkey sandwich stuck in my suddenly dry throat. "Or maybe not."

"There's a woman with our tricky trio," Tark said. "She's short, attractive, fiftyish, and has gray-brown, curly hair. She arrived at this meet with Charlie Browne."

I jumped up and dragged the phone with its long cord into the kitchen. Poured some water and choked the turkey down.

"Jess? You still there?"

"Where are they?"

"At a farmhouse, way out in the country. It's about a half hour from here."

I scrambled in a drawer for pencil and paper. "Address?"

"It's hard to find. Tell you what—I've got a few things to wrap up. Can you come right over? I'll drive you out there."

"That's okay. Give me the address, I can find it."

"Not as easily as I can."

"Oh?"

"I already know where this place is," Tark said.

"You do?"

"I do. And so does Marcus."

Another pause while he obviously decided whether to tell me the rest. Or maybe he was going for effect.

"Marcus owns it," Tark said.

I took a clean fork from a drawer and picked at leftover risotto on Tark's plate. He was hurriedly running water into a pot, putting it in the sink to soak. Garlic and wine aromas hung in the air. A bottle of imported Italian red was still open. I picked up the cork to sniff it, and sighed. You can have your Obsession, your Ciara, your Chanels Number Whatever. I'll take garlic and the scent of an Italian red cork anytime.

"I just don't understand what game she thinks she's playing," I said. "Charlie, sure. He's always up to no good. But Mom . . ."

"You want a plate of that? There's more in the fridge."

I shoved another forkful of creamy, spicy rice into my mouth. "No . . . I'm not really hungry."

In a basket was garlic bread—with tons of garlic and butter, a thin layer of cream cheese, and grated Parmesan. Tark makes the best garlic bread I've ever tasted in my life. I picked up a piece and munched on it. Cold, but no less gratifying.

I eyed the wine. Tark caught me, lifted a brow, dried his hands, and capped the bottle—putting it away on a glass-and-chrome shelf that held other wines and liqueurs.

Brandy . . . Grand Marnier . . . amaretto. I've always loved amaretto. It's warming and sexy—

I love men who cook, too. That, I think, is warming and sexy.

I do fantasize about Tark now and then. He's big, and broad—a major consideration for someone as small and insignificant-feeling as me—and he's not bad-looking, if a bit battered from years of bodyguard work. He's also smart, and tough, and, well . . . kind of lovable.

(If Tark knew I thought he was *lovable*, he'd bust my nose.)

"You've only been here three minutes," he said with an amused look, "and you've already grazed your way through most of my leftovers. We could pack them up, take them with us, if you're in that much need of nurturing."

"Hey, yeah, a picnic," I said morosely. "Just the ticket for a spring evening in the country."

"You haven't even heard the worst of it yet."

"I don't think I want to." I scooped up some more risotto. Tark grabbed the plate away and scraped it into the garbage disposal. Giving it a quick rinse, he stuck it in the dishwasher. Then he wrapped the garlic bread and shoved it in the fridge. "Let's move. I'll tell you on the way."

He herded me out of the kitchen, flicking off lights behind us.

"Could we stop for dinner at some nice little inn along the way?" I tried.

It took him a moment to see I was only kidding—playing for time.

The black Fiero zoomed along the dark country highway. Classical music played softly on a tape. Bach. Beyond the glistening black hood, halogen headlights picked out blossoming trees. The tires sang as they ate up miles.

"How much longer?"

"Ten minutes. You ready to hear it now?"

I scrunched down into the buttery leather seat. "I suppose."

"Sam Garner is serious bad news. He and Devlin grew up together in Kansas, and joined the Air Force together during Vietnam. They trained as copter pilots in Texas. After their tour, while the war was still going on, they operated a small cargo company out of Saigon. They flew the usual—rice, guns, supplies —between Vietnam, Thailand, and Laos. There was a lot of competition between those companies, and the ones that weren't affiliated with the CIA, like Air America, didn't get the most lucrative contracts. They had problems getting parts, too, and keeping their planes and choppers in repair.

"Devlin and Garner's company, Indo-Kansas Air, was legit to all appearances. But just as the war was winding down in '73,

Garner got into some kind of deep shit with a Thailand drug lord. Word is he was in the business, up to his neck. He may have double-crossed this drug lord. There was a price on his head, and Garner disappeared—leaving Devlin holding the bag. The company folded. Devlin came back to the States and dusted crops for a while in Kansas. A classic case of burnout, according to my source."

"And Garner? What's he been doing the past fifteen or so years?"

"His name surfaced once in Central America during the Ollie North/Nicaragua blowout. Whether he was flying for the CIA or simply cashing in on the arms issue, I don't know."

"Was Mac moving drugs in Vietnam?"

"Hard to tell. But you've got to assume he at least knew about Garner's involvement."

"Yeah."

"Like I said, Garner and Devlin were boyhood friends in Kansas. Devlin was the high school football hero, class president . . . a small-town boy with an edge. Father owned the local newspaper—still does. Devlin had a steady girlfriend through all four years of high school. Mariana Samorano. Her family was from Colombia, the only foreign family in town, in those days. Probably why people remembered."

"And Sam Garner?"

"He was a hell-raiser, the town's bad boy. Never anything serious, no arrests . . . but my source says he came close more than once. Devlin was his only real friend. They learned to fly together at a local field. Got into trouble barnstorming—scared hell out of the local farmers, put the chickens off their feed and the cows off their milk."

"How did you find all this out in just a few hours?"

"Personnel office at Davies pulled Devlin's resume and faxed it to me. After that, it was easy enough. I called a few people in Kansas City—they put me onto somebody whose football team played Devlin's every year. Everybody in the county knew everybody else."

"So now Mac is here in Rochester, with a company of his own . . . and he's teaching at the Davies school. Have he and Sam Garner seen each other over the years?"

"That I don't know. I'm still checking a few things."

"Mac didn't seem too pleased when he showed up." I thought back to the argument they'd had in the men's room at Jack's Bar. The "she" that Sam had said Mac owed something to.

"There are several possibilities. According to my source, a lot of the soldier-of-fortune types who flew cargo in Nam live more or less regular lives now. They may be insurance agents, or own hardware stores—but their names are on a list. And when the CIA needs somebody to fly a mission, they get called. They do it for bucks, of course, but they also get bored with civilian life, and this is one way of making it through. It's my guess this Sam Garner is either doing this, or he's full-time, and working on his own. He may be in some kind of trouble . . . and Devlin may be in it with him."

"Dammit, Tark! These are the people my mom's mixed up with? And what the hell is she doing out here in the country in the middle of the night, anyway? Why did she lie to me about going to dinner with an old friend? And more important"—I finally had to ask it—"why are they all at a house that Marcus owns? How the hell is he involved?"

Tark pulled into a narrow lane, thick with trees, and slid the Fiero to a stop. "I've got a call in to Marcus, but he hasn't gotten back to me. You remember last year, though, when Charlie Browne was arrested here for murder? I heard later that Marcus went to see him at the jail, while you were in California. Shortly after that, Charlie was out."

"No shit! I remember it wasn't long before Charlie showed up in California. He was out on bail—and you know, it never occurred to me until later, but how can somebody on bail leave the state like that?"

Tark didn't answer, but we both knew. It took the right connections.

"Marcus never told me he'd talked with Charlie," I said.

"Did you ask him?"

"No. There wasn't any reason."

"Maybe you should talk to him about it now. I've never known him to lie to you." He laughed shortly. "Of course, there are all those things he just never mentions. . . ."

The dash lights were still on, and in their glow I met Tark's eyes. "We're really on our own where he's concerned, aren't we? He doesn't much coddle."

"You always wanted it that way, Jess. You changing your mind?"

"No. It's just . . ."

He sighed. "Spring."

I laughed. "Yeah. Spring."

"Don't feel bad. It turns even the best of us to mush."

Leave it to Tark—more Diogenes than Dillinger these days —to understand that.

"We'll walk the rest of the way," he said.

"Where are Lang and Damato?"

"Around, somewhere. They'll find us."

Wear jeans and a dark sweater, he'd told me earlier on the phone. He should have mentioned shoes. His jeans, black sweater, and black boots made sense—and so did my own dark jeans and sweater. But my white Nikes, even though they weren't new, stuck out like a pair of headlights in the dark.

Tark led the way, since he'd been here before. "I had to check out the grounds for a security system," he told me. "Marcus never did say what he planned to do with the place. You know how close-mouthed he sometimes is." At one point, the path branched off in two directions. "They meet at either side of the house," he said. "You take one, I'll take the other. That way, if anybody's leaving, we won't miss them."

It was okay by me—or at least, it was until I got several yards alone into the brush. I don't much like being out in the country at night. There's all that weird hoo-hooing and whoo-whooing, and furry little things that just might scurry up your sleeve. To take my mind off it, I thought about another furry little thing—Bastard the Dastardly Dog. The Genesee Three had taken him to NYC for a couple of weeks, and I sort of hoped they'd lose him, maybe drop him down a grate.

I hate anything with fur that moves. Where I grew up in Rochester, the only furry moving things were rats—and cats. Cats are okay, but predictable. Sort of like men. You ignore them, they come rubbing up against you. Cats—and men—always want what they can't have. But you go letting them think *you* want *them*—just once—and they're here to hell and gone.

The boyfriend who left Bastard with me is gone now too. It happens that that story has a sad ending rather than a bitter one. But generally speaking, one has to protect oneself from hurt in today's world, so I try to develop a tough attitude about dogs, and men.

I brushed past something with sticky branches—bayberry, it felt like. My arm smarted where the sleeve of my sweater was pushed up. I rubbed at it and felt a thin line of blood. The nearly full moon had gone behind a cloud. Ahead, a glimmer of light appeared through the trees. I was so relieved that I'd finally be out of the woods and into a clearing, I guess I got careless. I should have been watching for somebody leaving the house. I should have been more quiet.

Shoulda, shoulda, shoulda . . . I never will be good at this shit.

A hand reached from behind and smothered my mouth. Another gripped my waist and lifted me off the ground. Panic washed through me. I couldn't breathe, and without my feet on the ground, I had no purchase. I reached back frantically, found hair, and yanked. A grunt—but the grip didn't loosen. I doubled my efforts, squirming and kicking, but hitting nothing. The moon came out and I saw it in a blur. There was an odor. A crack. I sniffed.

And went limp.

It's what they teach you to do at the Davies School of Defense, when attacked by a total idiot.

I may not be good at sneaking up on people, but there's nothing wrong with my sense of smell.

I gave the owner of the hand another moment to see who I was and to relax the hand over my mouth. When he did, I said, "Would you mind putting me down, asshole?"

My feet hit the ground, and I rubbed at my lips, facing Joey Damato. In reflected light from the sky he looked disappointed, and more than a little hurt. "How'd you know it was me?"

"The gum, dummy. The Dentyne."

He frowned. "Never thought of that." The gum cracked again.

Heaven protect me from the Old World mobster—the kind without a brain.

"Where's Lang?"

"Someplace behind the house. Where's Tark?"

"Right here," Tark answered quietly, coming in from the right.

"You're losing your bodyguard skills," I complained. "Didn't you hear me getting grabbed?"

He smiled. "More and more, I'm learning how well you take care of yourself." He squinted at Damato. "Seems pretty quiet in there. Are all four of them still here?"

"Nobody's left this way."

Tark nodded thoughtfully, gazing off at the house. "Jess? This is your show. What do you want to do?"

I peered at the house, too, visible now beneath a bright moon. It was a couple hundred yards from where we stood, set in a large clearing. Sprawling and white, the Victorian-style farmhouse was sheltered on either side by huge, spreading trees. Tall windows had dark shutters, but they were open. Soft light poured from a downstairs room, flooding the lawn. The rest of the house was dark.

"I'm tempted to just walk right in there," I said. "See what they've got to say."

"Up to you."

"On the other hand, I've never yet gotten a straight story out of Charlie Browne. Or my mom, for that matter—at least, not lately. Let's see if we can hear anything first, from a window."

Tark nodded. "Joey, you stay here and keep watch. If Lang comes back, tell him to wait too."

The Dentyne Kid faded back into the bushes. Tark and I crept forward, crossing the vast lawn on our haunches, more or less. The reason why escapes me, since the lawn was so open and the moon so bright, a field mouse would've been spotted instantly. Maybe it's *de rigueur* in these things to hunch—like in war movies, where the G.I.'s are always running in a crouched position, as if the enemy doesn't have sense enough to shoot anything that short.

We paused beside the thick trunk of one of the trees next to the house. The lighted room was at a corner, so there was a window at both side and front. Neither window would be easy to reach, though. The house was high off the ground, with a two-foot basement foundation before the wood siding began. The bottom of each window was a couple of feet above that. Completely surrounding the house on this side were lilac bushes that must have been fifty years old. They were easily five feet wide and seven tall. You could reach out one of those windows, I thought, and pluck one. Anytime.

My jealous imagination created an instant vision of the

woman who might live in this house. She would be pale and delicate, with long, silky hair. She would wear gauzy white gowns and picture hats, and on gentle evenings she would play Chopin on a spinet . . . or a harpsichord. A summer breeze would play through billowy white curtains, and behind her would stand a man who was good and kind, loving and steadfast. . . .

I remembered that Marcus owned this house, and my envious fantasy grew.

Did a woman like that live here, even now? It was possible. I sometimes conjure up visions that turn out to be remarkably true. Samved says it's a metaphysical toss-up as to whether I'm psychic, and see things that exist—or whether I create them, actually make them happen, out of my mind.

I murmured to Tark, "I'll take this window, you take the other. Okay?"

He nodded, pressed a huge hand on my shoulder, and moved off.

I pushed quietly into a lilac bush, trying to get into a position to raise myself by the window's outer ledge. Large purple blooms brushed my face, their sweet, wonderful scent like a newly sharpened knife. I hardened my heart—not ordinarily that difficult a chore—and spread the branches farther, lodging my foot into their approximate center. The branches bent a little, but they were old and thick. They held. I leaned forward, grasping the window ledge, and was in a perfect position to see . . .

Nothing.

An empty room with a ceiling light, no more. No spinet, no harpsichord, no woman in flowing white female vesture . . .

No Mom. No Charlie. No Garner or Devlin.

I held that way for a moment, thinking. When there was movement behind me, I dropped down, rubbing my hands. "Where do you think they are?"

Tark shrugged. He stepped back, looking at the upstairs

windows. "Let's go around back. Maybe there are lights that we can't see from here."

"I wonder where Lang is. Funny he hasn't spotted us yet and shown himself."

"I've been thinking the same thing. Listen, maybe you should go back to Damato, let me do this from here on out—"

"No chance. C'mon."

We were more cautious now, though. I could see tension in the set of Tark's mouth, the tight lines around his eyes. I felt it in my back, which was rigid. My knees weren't quite as flexible as they had been. My crouch, perversely, grew taller as I tried to shrink, and I took long, deep breaths, knowing that when I'm tense I make mistakes. I stumbled a couple of times. Tark moved ahead of me. I followed his black sweater and jeans, wondering at every inch of crawl if we were being observed from some dark window.

And if so, why? What the hell was going on here? Why were Mom and Charlie meeting with Devlin and a disreputable character like Sam Garner?

I wished my mom had settled down with some nice old grandpa type who fixed broken toasters in his garage while she rocked in the kitchen and knitted booties for their grandchildren.

On the other hand, Mom would probably never have grandchildren—at least, any that were normal—since I'm an only child.

"Jess!"

It took me a few seconds to look up from my crouching position and see Tark, looming above me. "What the hell are you doing?" he said.

"Oh . . . uh, thinking, I guess." I stood and wiped loose grass off my palms. The lawn had recently been cut. Someone was tending to this place.

"This is not the time to think," Tark warned.

"I know." But hell, I couldn't turn it off. My mind goes down all these steep bends and curves, it wanders into dark countries . . .

We were behind the house, looking up to a screened-in porch. "There's a light back here," I observed.

"Kitchen. You finally noticed." His tone was more reproving than amused.

"What do you think?"

"I think I'm more worried now that we haven't seen Lang. I wonder what's going on in there." His big body moved silently up the two or three stairs to the porch. "You stay here."

"Right."

He stopped to look back, and found me bumping into his spine. *"Please* stay there," he said.

"No."

Tark sighed.

When his first step hit the porch, there was a loud creak. We both froze. When no one appeared, either at the kitchen door or the window, we moved on. At the door, Tark held me back with a hand. He bent to look through the upper half, which was glass. Then he made an angry grunting sound, grabbed the knob with one huge hand, and shoved. The door flew open.

And I saw the source of Tark's anger.

The kitchen was cozy and warm. Early American furnishings, with blue and white delft tile. Copper pans and molds hanging on a wall. A clearly new stove in an old-fashioned style, white with a copper hood. The double sink was a shiny, upscale, dark blue enamel. There were pots of red geraniums scattered about. I felt like I'd walked into a photography set for a layout in *America's Award-Winning Homes.*

Except for one thing: There was a Harvard-type mobster sitting at the round maple table, arms folded. Waiting patiently for our arrival.

"Lang?" I spoke first. Tark was simply looking at him, eyes narrowed.

"Where is everybody?" I said.

"Gone."

"Gone where? And when? Did you at least hear what they were up to first?"

"Not a thing," Lang said. He shrugged. "They were gone when I got here."

"Damn! Tark—"

But Tark's light gray eyes were still fixed on Lang. They were as cold as an out-of-season frost on a Northern Italian vineyard.

"Gone when you got here?"

Lang nodded.

"Funny Damato didn't see them leave."

"I suppose they must have left the back way. There's a road that leads to the state highway."

"I know that. Why weren't you covering it?"

"Hell, Tark, I can't be everywhere at once."

Tark lifted a heavy brow, but said no more. I felt Lang's explanation being tucked away into some dark recess, to be exposed to a brighter light at a more opportune time.

"Let's look through the rest of the place," I said.

We left Lang, and I followed Tark into the living room we'd seen from the front window. The light was still on, the room just as empty as before. No picturesque furnishings here. There were floor-to-ceiling French doors along one wall. It wasn't a vast room, but larger than those found in the average farmhouse. Most likely, walls had been knocked out of two or more rooms to make this spacious one.

A flight of stairs led up to the second floor. The banister was polished and smooth, the kind a kid might slide down without getting splinters in his rear. It brought back a memory—but I couldn't quite get a fix on it. Something about my youth. . . .

Upstairs, we flicked lights on as we went. There were three bedrooms and two baths. The bedrooms were large and empty, the baths as complete as the kitchen, obviously newly redone.

One had dark blue tile and touches of lemon yellow, the other was aqua and white. Hi-tech, but welcoming: Big, wide tubs that you stepped up into had wide ledges around them. Tall windows came down to the ledges, so that when you bathed you could look out on what I knew must be trees and hills.

The farmhouse was in a state of repair. The plumbing and kitchen contractors had come in first, it seemed, carrying their heavy loads of unmixed plaster and uncut tile . . . they'd been working here, most likely, for months.

The house was being readied for someone. It was becoming a home. And I was sure, now, that I knew for whom. Marcus had taken care of his son, Christopher, financially, from the day he was born. For the kid's sake, he'd stayed out of his life until just recently. But Marcus was one of the most responsible men I'd ever known. Christopher would always be provided for—and so would his mother.

And Christopher loved the country. We'd had a long talk about it once, one day when I visited him . . . before Marcus had begun to see him all the time. "I want horses someday," the kid had said. "And I want to grow vegetables and things. You know, be self-sufficient."

I'd looked into his eight-year-old eyes, dark and observant like Marcus's, and connected. "It's always been a dream of mine, too."

Until that moment, it was a truth I hadn't fully realized. But Christopher had a way of bringing out truths. You could tell him anything, and not be afraid of being made fun of. There aren't many grown-ups like that.

So . . . Christopher was getting his home in the country. The only question left was: Would Marcus live here, too?

For a long while now, I'd known it was only a matter of time. And in the back of my brain, I'd been planning for it. Moving away, little by little, from the possibility of anything long-term with Marcus.

Smart move, Cookie.

I came back to the present as Tark laid a hand on my shoulder. "No one's here," he said gently. "Shall we go?"

"Sure." I cleared my throat. There was a giant lump in it. "Let's get the hell out of here."

Chapter 13

▼ ▼ ▼

T here was a message on my machine when I got back to my apartment.

"Jessica, it's your mother."

She only calls me Jessica when she's playing the role of firm, unyielding parent.

"Charlie and I are going on to the Thousand Islands tonight, dear. I'm sorry we didn't get to see you before we left. Bye."

Bye.

I sat and thought about it, drumming my fingers on the desk. What was wrong with that message? Something.

Well, for one thing, Mom had told me that Charlie would be in NYC for a few days—and now she wasn't even commenting on his sudden reappearance. For another—nitpicky as it may seem—she hadn't said "take care," or any of those mother things Mom usually ends a conversation with when she's not going to see me for a while.

Oh, sure, Jess, and when she does you always say to yourself: "Puh-lease, Mother, I'm a full-grown woman now. You don't have to zip up my parka or straighten my hair."

Maybe she had learned to let go at last. And maybe I'm never satisfied.

I checked the bedroom. Their suitcases were gone. Her yellow robe was no longer hanging on the door.

I wandered back into the living room, pacing from window to window. Finally, I picked up the phone and called Toni Langella, next door. "Did you see my mom or Charlie tonight?"

"Sure." I could hear her munching on a celery stick, the way she usually does on the phone. *Sodium and potassium,* she told me once. *When you do gymnastics, you have to pile them in.* "They left about an hour ago."

"Did you talk to them?"

"Just for a minute. I was coming back from practice, and they were getting into a cab."

"And?"

"And what?"

"What did they say?"

"I don't know . . . just good-bye, I guess."

Just good-bye. "Nothing else?"

Munch. "Like what?"

I sighed. *Teenagers. Where did you go? Nowhere. What did you do? Nothing.*

Founts of information.

"Something wrong?" Toni asked.

"Oh . . . I guess I just worry about Mom."

"I'm sure she's fine, Jesse. She's been with Charlie a long time, a couple years almost. And she's still happy and healthy. What more could you ask?"

"I don't know. I keep waiting for the other shoe to fall, I suppose."

"Yeah, well, Jesse . . . I hate to say this, but maybe you need to get a life."

I stared at the receiver, then dropped it by one stung finger onto the floor.

Chapter 14

▼ ▼ ▼

I checked the round gray and white clock on my kitchen wall: 10:42. Nibbling on a leftover lemon bar, I called Mac at home. His machine was on. Not that I'd really expected to find him there. If Mom and Charlie were on the way to the Thousand Islands, he was probably their pilot.

If any of that were even true. I didn't know, anymore, what to believe of Mom's tales.

It was a restless night, with those funny waking dreams popping in and out of the sheets.

At least I had new sheets—having retired the Puff the Magic Dragon ones at the first sign of spring. In a rush of hope and verdant energy, I'd run out to McCurdy's one day and bought these flowery things, all burgundy roses and green leaves. The way a woman does when there's a new guy in her life . . . and she's planning to bring him home.

I couldn't have had Marcus in mind; he never spends the night here. He's old-fashioned that way. Given how well the neighbors know me, and how "interested" they are in my life,

Marcus is afraid tongues will wag and strike a final blow to my already somewhat tarnished reputation. So I've stayed over at his place now and then, but I hadn't had a man in my own bed in all the two and a half years I'd known Marcus.

So why did I buy new sheets this month? Ask any woman. It's something we do in spring—like going on a diet and getting an early tan.

The thing that's *really* sad is how many of us still have virgin, unchristened sheets when that first bite of frost hits, come fall. The percale gets stuffed into a closet along with all the hopes, then out comes the flannel . . . in my case, Puff the Magic Dragon (don't ask) . . . and the cold settles in. Until December, anyway, when we start to dream of diamond rings and proposals on Christmas Eve.

I don't know why we do that Christmas/engagement thing, either—even the most jaded among us. It comes from the mass consciousness, or something. Like bees, we drone romantically on and on. So there I was in the percale bower, with Toni-the-Gymnast's parting tumble somersaulting in my head: *Get a life.*

I couldn't stand it any longer. I got up and wandered into the kitchen.

Mom had made a fresh pot of coffee before she left. The pot was nearly full, and I'd forgotten to turn the warming plate off. I poured a cup into a blue mug with sea gulls on it. Sitting cross-legged in the window bay of my living room, looking out into Mr. Garson's yard across the street, I realized how empty my apartment seemed now. There had been that brief flurry, with Mom and Charlie, Mac, Toni, Mrs. Binty . . . and now everyone was gone. Oh, I could go and roust Mrs. Binty and Toni out of their beds . . . I could "entertain" the way Mom always does. Shit, I could even bake lemon bars.

But that wouldn't give me a life. It wouldn't make me the kind of person who sits and chats, who always has friends around. It wouldn't make me "normal."

Well, I'd made some progress along those lines. I was sober now. Had been for nearly a year, again, this time. But how can you know how long a thing like that might last?

It's "in" now, of course, to get the body clean—drug-and-alcohol-free. But the story wouldn't be told right if it weren't told in its entirety.

The truth is, when one has been on alcohol or drugs, one remembers moments that are like gold glittering in a coal mine. Moments when you'd take a pill, or a drink, and see leaves out your window that formed special, precious shapes . . . moments when the body was released from all its woes, when the mind soared, and you knew without a doubt that this was the way Life was meant to be—except that something awful had happened between the creation of Earth and today, and now you had to take drugs or alcohol to see it this way.

So we go through life now, we sober ones, remembering those feelings . . . and sometimes, God help us, wanting them back . . . yet knowing that the way we got them also included things that led to our destruction: the end of relationships that couldn't hold up under our crazy-seeming difference; the end of jobs for which we never showed.

The great question—for those of us who haven't yet made the final, tough commitment, the absolute decision to be sober the rest of our lives—is: Have we sold out? Or won?

Ah, well. It's not a question to be answered easily—at least not by someone as unevolved as I.

Go to sleep, Jess.

Chapter 15

▼ ▼ ▼

I slept until after eight in the morning, then came awake like a shot. I was late for my flying lesson. Messing up, all the way around.

I lifted the phone by my bed and called Mac's office at the airport. A woman who identified herself as a temp told me that Mac was out on business and would be back later today. "He said to tell you, if you called, that he couldn't wait."

Damn.

"Has he gone to the Thousand Islands, by any chance?"

"I'm sure I don't know." Her nasal, New York City-born twang was perfect for a receptionist in some entertainment industry office; irritating in Rochester. "Ya want me ta take a message?"

"Uh . . . just that Jesse called. Ask him to call me, will you?"

"Will do. So long. Good talkin' to ya."

So long. Good talkin' to ya. Wasn't that an old song? No

. . . it was "So long . . . it's been good to know ya." Mom used to sing it all the time.

And why was everybody these days saying "good-bye" that way? Like some intimate moment had been shared?

I left a message on Mac's machine this time, and went in search of the one heavy gun in my arsenal against crime, injustice, and injury to the common man: Grady North.

"Lieutenant North is off today," I was told by Gus down at Homicide. So I knew where Grady would be—at home, washing his car. If nothing else, Grady is a constant. You can pretty much know where to find him and what he'll be up to on the morning of his one day off. Provided it doesn't rain.

Grady's new apartment is along the Genesee River, one of those upscale places with courtyards and trees. One courtyard is for walking and sitting. Another, behind the building, was built for the parking and washing of yuppie kiddie cars.

It boggles my mind, what's happened to Grady North in the past couple of years. He used to be *Happy Days*-simple, the kind of guy who wanted a house in the burbs, one cat, two dogs, three kids, and a wife who baked apple pies in an apron, her hair tied back in a ponytail. Now all of a sudden he's evolved into this swinging-bachelor type—

Well, not exactly swinging. Not Grady North.

But he dresses up for work, and he's somehow even gotten better-looking. Women flock around him now, making eyes and flirting . . . the way they were doing as I pulled the Dreadful Dodge up alongside his red Pontiac Trans Am.

Grady was dressed in cutoff jeans, his chest bare and beginning to tan beneath the unusually warm spring sun. The women —one a gorgeous blond, the other with disorganized brown hair that looked a little like mine—were hanging around, yakking. They wore skimpy little shorts, skimpy little halters, and a casual, let's-be-friends air. Only their body language gave them away— the kind of posturing women do with their hips and legs, even their chins, when they want a man to see them as graceful and thin.

I clambered out of the Dodge, sweaty and tired from the night's fitful sleep. My white cotton pants were shapeless, my peach-colored T-shirt clean, but stained. I'd pulled it hastily out of a drawer, not bothering to check before I put it on. Next to Grady's girl-pals, I looked like his frumpy little cousin, arriving from the Arkansas farm for an uninvited, unwelcome visit.

'Twas ever thus.

I ran a quick hand through the tangles from my shower, gave it up as a loss, and joined the trio. Grady's hazel eyes flicked to mine, assessing, then slid away to the blond. His mouth twitched, but he didn't stop rubbing the wax on his car.

"Morning, Jess. What brings you by?" He peered at a dime-sized spot and intensified his labor.

"Just wanted to ask you some questions." I smiled at the two women, who were in their twenties, I guessed, and said "Hi." They gave me a once-over and apparently decided I wasn't a threat.

"Hi," said the blond gorgeous one. "How're you?"

"Hi," repeated my tangle-haired twin.

Grady looked at me again, then smiled at them. "Uh . . . see you later, okay? My place, seven o'clock?"

They smiled at us both, swallowed whatever disappointment they might have had at being displaced, and nodded—sauntering away, trailing words and hopes behind them like a bridal train. "Sure . . . later . . . can't wait."

"You didn't introduce me," I observed.

"I know," Grady said. "I couldn't remember their names."

"Typical." I sat on the trunk of the Dodge.

"Of me? How would you know?"

"Not of you, necessarily. Of all men who do the bachelor scene. You don't really care about the women you play with. Not even enough to know their names."

"Jess, I was *talking* to those women, not playing with them."

"Right. And tonight you're having a six-handed knitting circle? What ever happened to *Sissy?*"

He threw back his cute sandy head and laughed. "We're having a condo maintenance meeting tonight. And you are as suspicious as ever."

I relaxed. (And don't ask what all that was about, except maybe that even when you don't want a man yourself, you like to know he's there if you decide you do want him someday. And there may not be anything fair about that, but for cryin' out loud, who said life's fair?) "Speaking of suspicious . . . You know I told you Mom and Charlie were in town? Well, they're gone again."

"Oh?" The red lacquer of his hood got a final swipe before he wiped his brow, tossed down the rag, and perched on the Dodge trunk beside me. Around us, other cars—BMWs, Hondas, convertible Toyotas—were in various stages of wash. Some were worked on by couples, laughing together and splashing each other with hoses. Bright, nearly-noon sunlight sparkled through the spray. At one gray Mustang with a black top, a woman worked seriously, off in a world of thought. The nineties version of tilling the soil, I supposed.

"I thought we were supposed to be in a recession," I said.

"All these bright new cars, you mean?"

"And careless faces. Nobody looks very worried."

"Well, what you see before you are the teenagers of the eighties. Takes a while for things like recessions to become a mind fix."

"A while and a few lost jobs," I said. "And what about you? You're closer to my age. I thought we teenagers of the seventies weren't going to buy into all this shit."

"Do you think I've bought into it?"

"What else would you call it?"

"Enjoying life, maybe—for a change. You should try it, Jess. It'd do wonders for your attitude."

"I don't have an attitude."

"You've always had an attitude. You were born with one. Listen, what did you really come here for today? Other than to bait me, I mean."

"I need you to help me find Mom and Charlie. Quietly. They're supposedly on a honeymoon in the Thousand Islands, and if that's true, I'd just as soon they didn't find out I was asking."

"What makes you think it's not true?"

"Because they've been hanging around with a couple of questionable characters."

I told him about Sam Garner, and the stuff Tark had found out.

"Where'd they meet this guy?"

I told him about Mac Devlin.

"The guy I met at Harrigan's? I know Devlin—by reputation, anyway. Nothing bad—he runs that business out of the airport, keeps his nose clean. Never been in any trouble, not here anyway."

Grady kept *his* nose—and his eye—on so many things roundabout Rochester, he should've been the reporter instead of me.

"Maybe Mac just hasn't been caught," I said. "Maybe he's been lucky."

"Any special reason you're suspicious of him—aside from the fact that you're always suspicious of men?"

"Not always."

"Oh, right, I forgot the one person in the world you've chosen to trust with your life—the King of Crime. An upstanding citizen if there ever was one. Pure as the driven snow."

"Hardly. But I already *know* everything about Marcus. There's a security in that." Well, I knew *some* things about Marcus. When it came to his personal life, I obviously knew nothing, lately, at all.

"Why don't you ask Andrelli to look for Kate and Charlie?"

"Tark's already helping. But Marcus is out of the country."

"Not anymore."

"Yes, he is, he's—" I frowned. "What do you know about it?"

"His private jet flew in at 4:01 this A.M. Funny he didn't call and let you know he was back."

My chin went up. "Not funny at all. It's early still. Anyway, why are you keeping tabs on his arrivals and departures?"

"I've always kept tabs on Andrelli, Jess. You know that."

"Yeah, I know. But anything specific, right now?"

"With Andrelli, it's always specific. Why don't you ask me in a couple of weeks or so."

"Jesus, Grady, you are the most aggravating—"

"Would you like to come up for a cup of coffee?"

"In singles heaven? I don't think so."

He laughed. "You don't know what you're missing."

"Let's say we keep it that way."

Chapter 16

▼ ▼ ▼

"So tell me, where did we go all wrong,

And what were we to do?

I tried to give you my everything,

Open up my heart to you."

—"COMING HOME,"
BY D. R. LUNSFORD

I found Marcus out at his cabin, on Irondequoit Bay. It's
where he anchors his yacht, the *SeaStar*, now, and where
we'd been working at rebuilding the Tancook Whaler. We've
spent a lot of weekends out here, Marcus and me, weekends that
were so perfect, they made this day more poignant than I would
have liked it to be.

He was down at the nearest dock, the legs of faded jeans
rolled up to the calf. Beside him sat a small boy—eight years old,
with black hair like his father's, angular cheekbones, and nearly
black eyes, also like his father's. He had a smile that would one
day knock women off their feet.

Fishing rods dangled. Maybe they hadn't heard that the fish
were off their bite this year. Maybe they didn't care, and were
just doing the male-bonding thing.

Marcus looked up, saw me, and smiled. Christopher followed suit. "Hi, Ms. James." He started to get to his feet,
and even though I said "Don't get up," he was standing and

rubbing a hand on his jeans before sticking it out for me to shake.

The impeccable manners were due in large part to a socially prominent grandmother who had helped to raise him. At her house, Chris primarily wore eastern-boarding-school dress: suit and white shirt with tie. With Marcus, the tie came off and the jeans came on. Today, he wore a T-shirt with holes in it and purple stains. They had probably been berry-hunting, or wood-gathering. With Marcus, one never knows. He's a master at spontaneous activity, at thinking up things that are different and fun to do.

At least, he is when he can drag himself out here to the cabin. At his penthouse in the city, it's another world—that of hi-tech gadgets, noisy faxes, and phones. Business first, last, and always.

"I thought I told you to call me Jesse," I said to Chris.

His eyes flicked uncertainly to his father. "Dad said . . ."

"I said that I want him to show respect for you," Marcus finished. "It's important that he do that."

"Oh." I raised a brow, but didn't know what to say. It wasn't often people were taught to "show respect" toward me. Was I starting to look really old, or what?

"Join us," Marcus added, getting to his feet. "I can find you a rod . . ."

"Thanks anyway. You know I can't bear to see a fish with a hook in its poor, soft mouth."

"Too bad some of that warmth doesn't rub off on your dog." He stood before me, put both hands lightly on my shoulders, and kissed me on the cheek. The virgin kind of kiss he gives me these days when Christopher's around. I wondered if that had to do with "respect," too, or if he just didn't want Christopher going home and reporting what he'd seen to his mom.

"Bastard is on a perfectly nice trip to the Big Apple with the

Three," I said. "With any luck, he'll be eaten by hordes of hungry homeless, and I'll never see him again."

Christopher laughed, unimpressed. He's seen me with Bastard, and insists that I really do love that dog.

"Yeah, right," I always say. Rolling my eyes. He laughs at that, too. The kid is unbelievably easy to amuse.

We sat on the dock, with Christopher between us. Sunlight glittered on blue water, making me wish I'd brought sunglasses. The *SeaStar,* at another dock about two hundred yards away, bobbed gently. It's not an overly large or luxurious yacht, but her lines are sleek, her engine powerful. Marcus uses the yacht for meetings with visiting business associates. At those times, she's anchored at the marina, downcoast; never here. In the past several months, since Christopher arrived on the scene, this place has been Marcus's retreat from that other, often illegal world. The security is intense now, here. I'd had to go through four different levels of it on the way up the winding, forested road this morning. Marcus, of course, had been informed I was on my way from the minute I hit the grounds.

Before Christopher, it wasn't this way. Security, yes . . . but not like this. Marcus's fear was that his enemies from the Old Mob, the tommy-gun faction, would attempt to kidnap his son, or worse. There were a lot of bad feelings about the way he had thrown a monkey wrench into their scams around here, how he had weeded out the drug dealers, and the porn rings that used and abused children. Not that Rochester is clean now. But the old-type mobsters who are left are bottom feeders; they only get what trickles down, what's left over after upscale wheeler-dealers like Marcus skim the top. They're the ones you see in the *Herald,* the ones the OCB pulls in. You'll see their pictures, too, the guys in CAT caps, with cigars sticking out of their mouths. They're the bookies, the low-level enforcers, and the ones still laundering money through steakhouses. It's kind of sad, when you come to think of it—a bunch of old men, put out to pasture, their skills no longer needed by the Harvard grads, who've learned how to make money in "legitimate" business. As legitimate as any business gets, that is.

And yes, as my new editor—Mom—might say, I'm mixing my metaphors. From fish to horseflesh in one fell swoop.

Christ, that's the other thing about editors. All they have to do is mention something to you *once,* and you never forget it as long as you live. I swear to God, I'll never use parens again.

"We had a great time in Switzerland," Christopher was saying blithely.

I met Marcus's eyes over his son's head. Looking for signs of guilt. Or apology.

Nothing. A mask. I glanced away.

"I guess it's a good time to go there," I said, clearing my throat. "Is there still snow on the ground?"

"Nah, not in the cities. Up in the mountains, though. We saw this one place—"

He rattled on and on, while I half listened. I watched the *SeaStar* ride the gentle waves, and remembered nights on its deck, summer nights with stars and full moons, with warm breezes . . . and with the closest thing I'd ever had to love.

"Chris, how about if you give Jess and me time to talk," Marcus said. I could feel his eyes on me. My skin tingled, and my chin trembled a little. I wasn't sure anymore that I wanted to talk.

"No problem," Chris said with a grin. "We're not catching anything, and I s'pose we've bonded enough for one morning." He gave me a private smile as he reeled in his line. "Dad overworks this bonding business sometimes. My therapist says it's guilt, for all the years he wasn't around."

Marcus groaned. "Eight, going on forty-three," he muttered.

I ruffled Christopher's hair, a girl-thing that irritates him no end. Or so he says. He blushes and grins when he says it, which leads me to believe that he kind of gets off on it somehow. At any rate, he never holds my girl-stuff against me. I use it so seldom—with hardly anyone but Chris, in fact—that I'm glad he doesn't. It keeps me in practice.

"By the way," Chris said as he stood, "you look real nice today."

I flushed up into his very dark, very young eyes. "Thanks," I mumbled. I'd conditioned my hair, and it was soft and shiny as polished maple silk, in loose curls to my shoulders. I'd worn new, faded jeans that hugged my legs and pulled in my waist— with a green, sleeveless tee that brought out the green in my eyes and made me look like I had a bust.

"Doesn't she, Dad? Look nice?"

Marcus nodded, gave me a long, hard stare, then glanced away. "She does indeed. Now stop flirting, young man, and get out of here."

When Chris had left, he sighed. "I think we're going to have to have one of those talks about the birds and the bees. And soon. The kid has a crush on you."

"I always was good with kids," I lied.

He laughed. "And dogs."

We took a walk, through the trees to the barn.

"Chris is seeing a therapist? Is there something wrong?"

"Not really with Chris, not yet. He's solid as a rock. But there are a lot of new things to deal with since I came into his life. The increased security . . . having bodyguards around when we go anywhere together . . . not being able to be too public. All the things I was afraid of, those years when I kept my distance from him."

"Are you sorry now that you told him you're his father? I know I pushed for it. . . ."

"No. You were right, Jess, and I'm not sorry. Chris and I

need each other. But I can't help but think that at some time, he'll feel some anger about it all. When he does, he'll need someone outside the situation to talk to. That's what the therapist is for. I'm going too. With Chris's mother."

Family therapy. The relationship was that serious. My heart felt like it had been squeezed between a couple of fifty-ton trucks.

"And the trip to Switzerland?" It came out before I had time to consider whether I wanted to hear about it or not.

"Plans for the future," Marcus said simply, pushing at a low-hanging branch in our path. "But let's not talk about that now."

I heard myself mumble, "Okay."

"Is there any special reason you came by?"

"Do I need one?" I snapped. I'd had a little therapy of my own. And anger, I'd learned, is the best way to survive rejection.

"Of course not. But Tark told me you were worried about your mother and Charlie. I thought maybe you wanted to talk."

"Is Tark up at the cabin? I saw his car when I drove in."

"He's there with Lang. He has some information for you. We can go up there now—"

"No, let's walk a little farther. How's the Whaler coming?"

"I haven't gotten much done since you were out here a couple of weeks ago. There've been so many other things . . ."

The Tancook Whaler had been *our* project. One of the things that glued us together, our way of bonding. It was being supplanted now by more important matters. Like Switzerland . . . and "plans for the future."

Well, I'd known it couldn't last. Nothing ever does. When you're the child of an alcoholic, you learn that. And if you ever once forget it, or even try to forget it, life comes along with some major blow to slap you down.

In the meantime, Marcus and I had had two years—good years, for the most part—of friendship and loyalty . . . something neither of us had had much of before. Tark had been part of that picture. A steadier, more loyal friend, one couldn't ask for.

At least, I wouldn't lose Tark.

I clung to that thought. "Tark said that you own the place where Charlie and Mom had some sort of secret meet last night."

"Did he?"

"Yes. You're the owner of record, he said. A remodeled farmhouse, out in the country?"

"Well, of course, I own a lot of property. Often, I only see it on paper."

"And you don't know this particular place? You don't have a clue as to why Mom and Charlie would meet with people out there?"

"Why did you think I would?"

"Because Tark also said that you and Charlie met last fall, shortly after he was released from jail here. While Mom and I were in California."

"That's true. That was when I was running down those names of art dealers on the computer for you. Charlie asked me for information."

"You never mentioned it to me."

"I'm sorry. Should I have? It didn't seem important at the time."

"That's okay. So anyway, I thought maybe you knew how Charlie was involved with these people now. What they're up to."

"Tark filled me in, of course. On this Sam Garner . . . and Mac Devlin." He frowned. "You know Devlin personally?"

"Sort of. I met him at Davies."

"Jess . . . this is one you might want to stay out of."

"With Mom involved? No way. So, what do you know about it?"

"Nothing that would hurt your mother . . . at least, not—" He broke off.

"Go on."

"Well, I'm just thinking that Kate's a lot like you. She sort of barrels into things, and I doubt there'd be any stopping her if she wanted to be with Charlie. Whatever he was doing."

"Well, then, what about Charlie? What do you think of him now?"

"I think he's certainly unconventional in his approach to things."

"Like you?"

"And he's not always legal."

"Like you."

"But I believe his heart is in the right place."

I didn't give him that. It wasn't a day for accolades.

We came to the barn, and I faced the bronze plaque I'd given Marcus last fall: *Work Is Love Made Visible*. We had tacked it onto the door, for the time being. Until the Whaler was complete. It would then be installed over its cabin.

So many memories. Marcus opened the door, and I glimpsed the wooden boat, its smooth, graceful lines, its bow like folded hands in prayer—a goddess in a cathedral. We stood there silently, and then Marcus said, "Building this . . . spending weekends here . . . sailing, making love . . ." He cleared his throat. "What you and I have been doing is playtime, Jess. And it's been wonderful. It came at a time in our lives when we both needed it." I think it was the first time I'd heard Marcus sound nervous. "But it's time for a new era. For commitment, and responsibility. I want to give Chris that, show him about stability—"

I couldn't take hearing it. Not now. I said, "Look, I've got to go. I've got to see Tark." I needed Tark, all of a sudden, more than ever before. I needed someone who wasn't a lover but a friend, someone who wouldn't leave my life the way everyone else had.

"I know it's hard, Jess. But you have to hear this, sooner or later. Our relationship is stagnant, it hasn't been growing. We have to talk—"

"Not today, we don't."

I turned and ran, leaving the door flying. It hit the side of the barn with a loud thud. As I ran I kicked at leaves, pushed at branches, and as I did, I was kicking and pushing at foolish little-girl dreams, the kind that about-to-be-thirty-two-year-old girls should learn not to have.

Shoving their hapless remnants out of my path.

Chapter 17

▼ ▼ ▼

*T*he main dwelling was more a lodge than a cabin, sprawling in an L shape. It had surrounding decks that looked out over the forest, the hills, and Irondequoit Bay. Inside, Tark and Lang were clearly not in deep conversation. Tark stood with hands in pockets, his old bodyguard posture showing. He had his back against the fireplace, his eyes on the door. He saw me before Lang did. Lang sat nonchalantly in a chair, one leg thrown over its arm. Tark was in jeans and a gray sweatshirt, Lang in his usual three-piece suit. The two-story living room was thick with tension.

"I've got an address in the Thousand Islands for Kate and Charlie," Tark said abruptly as I entered. Lang made a small movement of protest, which Tark ignored. "Greenspire Inn. It's on a private island. I didn't know you were coming out here, so I left a message on your machine."

"Thanks. They are there, then?"

"According to the desk clerk, they were at six o'clock this morning." He gave a meaningful look to Lang. "Hopefully, they still are now."

"What's going on?"

Tark shook his head, his eyes still on Lang. "I don't think I'm really sure. But when someone who's normally sharp gets this careless—"

Lang shrugged and unfolded his legs from the chair. "I think I'll just go get a glass of water."

"You need help with that, too?"

Lang gave a disdainful look, and headed to the kitchen. It formed the L with the living room, but Marcus had recently put up a wall and double doors, for more privacy between the two rooms. Another door from the large kitchen led onto one of the decks. After a minute, we saw Lang out there, standing and looking over the bay, drinking from a glass.

"He deliberately let them get away last night, didn't he?" I said.

"That's my assumption. I could be wrong—but I don't think I am."

We had talked about it in the car, on the way home from the farmhouse. We didn't think Damato was in on it, but we weren't sure. Why Lang might be was another question.

"He plays it real close," Tark said. "But Marcus wouldn't have anyone on staff who couldn't be trusted."

"That was my thought. You think Marcus gave him orders to let them get away before we got there?"

"I've asked Marcus that. He won't say. Only that we should keep out of it."

"He's hooked up with Charlie somehow. Charlie wouldn't tell me, either, but I know. Are you going along with Marcus's order to keep out?"

"You know . . ." He looked thoughtful. "It wasn't an actual order. A suggestion, I'd say."

"Wow. Letting you make your own decision? Don't go and get all crazy, now, all that personal power."

He smiled. "You sound bitter."

"Oh . . ." I sat on the couch and twisted my newly shiny hair with a finger. "I'm just wondering if I've turned too much of my own power over to Marcus in the past couple of years."

"I thought we had all that out a year ago."

"We did. Don't mind me." I stared at a spot on the floor. "He's getting married, you know."

Tark was clearly stunned. *"Married?* To whom?"

"Christopher's mom, who else? He wants to give Chris a stable life."

Tark was shaking his head. "I don't believe it! He hasn't said a word."

"He was saving that particular word for me. He tried to break it to me, just now. I didn't want to hear it."

He simply stood there, silent.

"You know that farmhouse?" I said.

"Yeah?"

"It's the honeymoon cottage. I'm certain of it now."

Tark began to pace. "Marcus loves *you.* I'm certain of that."

"Love!" I gave a short laugh. "Marcus is more Old World —at least personally—than you think. A mistress is one thing; we're talking the kind of woman you *marry,* here."

"Don't do that," he said angrily.

"Do what?"

"Put yourself down like that. Marcus doesn't see you that way."

"He doesn't see me as marriage material, either."

Tark frowned. "I wouldn't know about that. But he has been strange lately, more introspective than usual."

"Yeah . . . well . . . look, can we get off the subject? What about Mom and Charlie? Are they okay?"

"You sure you want to drop this? You don't want to talk about it?"

"What is there to say? When the game is over you pick up your marbles and go away. Anyway, I need to worry about something else. What about Mom?"

He was silent, not buying my tough act for a moment. Finally, he shrugged. "Far as I know, they're okay. It's a nice inn, a good name. Maybe the honeymoon story is true."

"What about Garner and Devlin? Are they there?"

"I'm not sure. Since it's on a private island, I don't have anybody there to nose around. I could take some time off, now that Marcus is back, go up and see who's there."

"How about if I call you later and let you know? Meantime, Lang is supposed to be following Charlie. What happened?"

"I pulled him off—when I decided he might be more of a flaw in the plan than a help."

"And Damato?"

"He's still supposed to be on Garner, but he hasn't caught up with him since the farmhouse last night. They may all be in the Islands."

"Mac's assistant said he'd be in later today. He may have flown them. If he is back, I'll stick with him. That may be the best way to find Garner again."

"Okay. But be careful. And stay in touch. Jess—there's something really off about this thing. You know how sometimes it feels like a shadow is crossing your grave?"

Tark was more astute at these things than most people. I should have remembered that.

He always knew when something bad was coming down.

Chapter 18

▼ ▼ ▼

*T*elephonitis: *The only thing to do sometimes, when depression hits.*

Mac still wasn't back. The day was on hold, and so was my life. My stereo played in the background. George Michael sang that he didn't want to hold me or touch me or think he was mine, which certainly made him part of the in crowd.

I was in bed with a box of Kleenex, sniffling into the phone. My eyes were nearly swollen shut. "He's getting married, Aunt Edna. Marcus is getting married."

"Balderdash!"

"Balderdash? What kind of a word is that, balderdash?"

"I read it last night in an old English novel. It seems to fit the occasion." I heard the *puff, puff* as she smoked.

"What does it mean?"

"Look it up."

"Wait a minute." I reached for my pocket dictionary by the bed, and flipped through, sipping coffee. "B . . . b . . . baldachin . . . bald eagle . . . here it is, balderdash. It means nonsense—or twaddle."

"Twaddle? What the hell does twaddle mean?"

I thumbed the pages. "Silly . . . or boring. That positively does not fit this occasion."

"Still, if one is reaching for words beyond the profane— which, by the way, I am striving hard to do these days—it's not bad."

"Not bad at all. But it doesn't fit. There's nothing silly or boring about the fact that Marcus is getting married."

"Who says he is?"

"He does. In everything but words."

"I only met the man once, when you were both here in California, but my fix is that he'd tell you if he was."

"He tried. I wouldn't listen."

"Now that, my dear, is twaddle."

"More like avoidance."

"Cold, unmitigated fear?"

I nodded into my cup, and drew my legs into a fetal position. "Terror."

"Well, what are you going to do?"

"What can I do? When Marcus makes up his mind—"

"You could fight for him."

"It's not in me to fight. If that's what he wants—"

"Bosh. *Really*, Jesse, *bosh*. And don't bother to look it up. Why don't you just tell him for once how you feel?"

"Aunt Edna, I don't know how I feel. Except that I'm getting old. It's my thirty-second birthday next week! I'm over the hill . . . not fit for any man. No wonder he wants her— she's thirty-five and looks eighteen. She's beautiful . . . accomplished . . . successful. She has their son!" I swallowed a sniffle and wondered if I was getting PMS, aside from everything else. I don't usually cry over men.

"Jesse, don't you have anything more important to do?

Aren't you an investigative reporter? Shouldn't you be out solving some crime or other?"

"I am. I'm doing that tonight. But Aunt Edna . . . you wouldn't believe how beautiful it is here right now. The lilacs are blooming like mad, the sun is shining, the birds are singing—"

"And you're running up a phone bill, calling California on day rates."

"I don't care. It's my *birthday* month! Do you know how often the lilacs bloom in my birthday month? Once in seven years—maybe less!"

"So what you've got is spring fever. You don't want Marcus Andrelli, you want the idea of his wanting you."

"Maybe."

"And it's not like you really *love* him, after all."

"Of course not. Marcus is a mobster. I can't get serious about a mobster."

"So you've just been hanging around him two years for the trickle-down effect of all that illegal excitement."

"That's it exactly." I felt better already.

"Balderdash," my Aunt Edna said.

I tried to call Samved. One conversation with him and I'd feel so stupid for having a New Age guru turned Fundamentalist preacher for a shrink, I'd come back to earth real fast.

But Samved wasn't there. His machine was. It said: "Praise God!" In the background, a hymn played. I was raised Catholic, so I don't know many hymns—but there was the peal of an organ, and the word *"Lord"* was repeated several times. "I'm in the studios, setting up our first Praise the Day! telethon," Samved enthused. His seventy-year-old voice was no longer wispy, but firm. "If you would like to give your time to this worthy cause, please call 1-800-428-5555. And God bless you, each and every one of you!"

Click.

That's the irritating thing about churches: They're always looking for volunteers. In the Catholic church, the women mend altar cloths. The Christians are always building houses for the poor. New Agers don't have churches—and that was what I'd originally liked about Samved. I'd never had to volunteer a damned thing.

I wished I had the old Samved back. He, at least, was good for a laugh or two.

"When are you guys coming home?" I whined next on the phone.

"You in a hurry to see us—or this dumb dog here?" Abe Denton asked. I heard a muffled bark.

"You can lose Bastard in the Bronx for all I care. I miss you guys."

The Genesee Three—Abe Denton, Percy Green, and Rack "Jack"—had been in New York City far too long. Two weeks, by last count on my bedroom calendar. They had taken Bastard with them, saying he'd be safer in Harlem than with me.

"We be just about finished here, Mama," Abe said. He talks, sometimes, like some seventies-hip television black—even though his grammar and pronunciation are ordinarily without flaw. It's an affectation that had grown markedly, I'd noticed, since the Three had been in NYC.

"I know you're not really visiting your aunts and uncles like you said," I accused. "You're only there to learn new schemes and scams that you will then bring back to Rochester to perpetrate upon the unsuspecting. That's why you're talking so weird."

"Perpetrate! Now there's a big word for you. And, unsuspecting? My, oh my—"

"Oh, can it! When are you coming home?"

Abe sobered. "Trouble?"

"Oh . . . I don't know. I guess so."

"Listen, Jess, you need us, we're there. Next flight out."

I felt my spine relax. "Thanks." I sighed. "I guess I just wanted to hear it."

"I mean it. You say the word."

"Okay . . . but not right now. I have to look into things some more myself."

"You don't sound happy, lady."

"Don't I? I can't imagine why."

"I can. Andrelli giving you a hard time?"

"No more than usual."

I could hear Abe's frown over the phone. "You and Andrelli . . . you need to sit down and talk it out one of these days. Ever notice how you don't do that?"

"He tries," I said. "I run."

Abe chuckled softly. "Best little legs I've ever seen on a lady. They just keep takin' you the wrong way."

"I haven't been out on a charter," Mac said, at the other end of the line. "Who told you that?"

"Your temp."

"She said I was out on a flight?"

"Actually, that you were working. I just assumed—"

"I had a late night, but I was right here at home by midnight. You should've left a message."

"You didn't fly my mom and Charlie somewhere? Like the Thousand Islands, for instance?"

Mac smiled that cocky smile. I couldn't see it through the phone, but I could sure hear it. "You can check it out, if you don't believe me. I'd have had to file a flight plan. Can't say I'm sorry to see them leave, though. Now we can get back to what we were doing before they arrived."

I picked at a thread on my sweats. "Not very likely."

"I was talking about the flying lessons," he said dryly. "What did *you* mean?"

"The lessons, of course. I'm just not sure I want to do that anymore."

"What about your story?"

"It's taking a different twist."

"Still, it couldn't hurt to go up one more time."

"Isn't that what the Great Waldo Pepper said, just before he crashed and burned?"

"Goddamn, you are ornery, woman! Did it ever occur to you I just wanted a way to see you . . . to be near you?"

It hadn't.

"That's the difference between just bein' companions, and bein' friends," Mac said. "Companions are people you only do certain things with. Friends are people you want to be with, so you come up with things to do."

"I guess I never thought of that."

"Me neither. I got it off an ACA lecture tape last night."

That got my attention. "Adult Children of Alcoholics?"

"Yeah. About relationships. I thought it might tell me why you're so damn thorny."

I was nearly speechless. A nervous cough slipped out through jaws that felt wired. The guy was closing in! "I, uh . . . I guess I was hoping you could fly me to the Islands," I managed.

"Oh? When?"

"This, uh, afternoon . . . evening . . . soon as possible."

"Well, sure, I can do that. But not until after five. What's up?"

"I just want to drop in and say hi to my mom."

"On her *honeymoon?*"

My eyes narrowed, and my head cleared. "How'd you know she was on a honeymoon?"

A pause. "Charlie mentioned it the other night, in your living room. Remember?"

"Oh, yeah . . . I forgot. Well . . . can we go, then?"

"I don't see why not. I can teach you a few things along the way."

That's what I was afraid of.

"About *flying*," Mac said.

Chapter 19

▼ ▼ ▼

*I*t was nearly four-thirty, and Mac had told me to meet him at the airport at five. I threw some things into an overnight bag, then made sure that the coffeepot was off and the windows locked. Setting the answer machine, I took one more look around.

Alongside the couch, where Mom had been sitting earlier, was something I hadn't seen before. A man's shoe.

I set the overnight bag down and walked over, picking it up. The shoe was obviously new . . . not worn. Alligator, with ties.

It could only be Charlie's. Yet, Charlie didn't wear alligator shoes. He had an aversion to wearing animal hide of any kind; for him, it was always either canvas running shoes or loafers. Even with the loafers, Charlie took great pride in revealing that they weren't leather, but man-made material.

I felt a prickle of excitement—of knowing something, without knowing.

I held the shoe and went back several months in memory, to that time when Charlie and Mom were here last fall. The men's shoes that were delivered by UPS. Like I said, they were all new, but bundled up in newspaper. I never saw Charlie wear any of them, and when I questioned him later, he had laughed. "There are codes in the linings, Jess." Just good old Charlie, poking fun at me.

I never did get to check the shoes out, because when I got back home from California, they were gone.

I wondered what this one was doing here now. Because— despite Charlie's teasing about "codes"—there was something about these shoes. They had some meaning or purpose beyond the obvious. And Charlie wasn't careless enough to have left one behind.

Mom, then? A message of some sort?

I suddenly didn't feel so foolish about tracking her down on her "honeymoon." The meeting at the farmhouse last night was only a glimmer of what was going on here. I was certain of it now.

I opened my overnight and stuck the shoe in. Then, before heading to the airport, I stopped by to see Tark.

It was dark before Mac and I got off the ground. "Last-minute mechanical difficulties," he had said. He never did get them sorted out. "But no problem. I've got an exchange agreement with Northcoast Air, next door. They aren't using their seaplane tonight. Actually, it's better this way. We can land closer to the inn."

"You know where it is?"

"I looked it up. Greenspire's a quiet, out-of-the-way place —one of the old summer estates, rebuilt into an inn. There are docks with boats . . . plenty of easy access for a seaplane."

"Handy."

"Yes."

We had been off the ground ten minutes when I finally opened my glued-shut eyes to see that we were somewhere above Lake Ontario. No lights below, only a few early stars above. I began to have that feeling again of being unconnected, of floating—and liking it. I wondered if there was some Freudian meaning to the fact that I was scared shitless when we were leaving the ground, when I could still see terra firma—and then promptly relaxed when it disappeared.

Whatever, the flight was now bearable. My fists unclenched, and my stomach eased down. After a while I no longer thought about the fact that there was nothing solid below me; that at any moment I might crash and burn. It's like entering another reality. In a way, you almost don't care.

Almost.

Mac's leather jacket creaked as he adjusted his position in the seat next to mine. The throb of the seaplane was different somehow from that of the Cessna. Heavier. We were quiet for long moments, then all of a sudden Mac would fiddle with knobs, humming a tune under his breath. It took me a while to know he was humming *"Coming in on a Wing and a Prayer."* It didn't fill me with confidence.

"Is flying a seaplane different?" I asked. "From other planes, I mean."

"Not much. Worried? Don't be. I've flown everything you could name with wings or rotors."

"You learned to fly in the Air Force?" I knew better, from Tark's report. Still, I can never resist the impulse to see what someone will say, given the opportunity to lie.

"No—as a kid, in Kansas. I had my license for fixed wings by the time I was sixteen. When I went in the Air Force, they needed chopper pilots in Nam. They trained me for that, and afterward, I stayed there awhile and flew cargo privately."

Exactly what Tark had told me. Mac didn't seem to have much to hide.

"What about Sam Garner?"

He flicked a glance my way. "I didn't think I'd told you his name."

"Yeah, you did," I lied. "You mentioned it back in the beginning."

"Funny. I don't remember." He peered at the gauges. "Well, Sam Garner was my friend. We grew up in Kansas together, and learned to fly together."

"He *was* your friend? He's not now?"

"Sam was always a little reckless, but he really got messed up in Nam. He's into things now that I try to stay out of."

"What kinds of things?"

He hesitated, then grinned. "You are a nosy kid."

"I'm a reporter." But I kind of liked being called a kid—now that I was almost thirty-two.

"Are you interviewing me for a story?" Mac said.

"Of course not. Just curious."

"Well . . . Sam Garner is nothing worth talking about."

I wondered what he'd say if I told him I knew he and Sam Garner had had some sort of secret rendezvous with Mom and Charlie last night. Hell, he might already know that I knew. If not . . . maybe I still had the advantage of surprise. I might just hold on to it a while longer, figure out what to do with it.

"Ever been married?" I asked.

"No," he said, short with me suddenly.

"Someone serious?"

"Look—what's this all about?" A quick glance showed a frown of irritation.

"I guess I was wondering about the woman I heard Garner talking to you about—that day at Jack's Bar. He said you owed her."

A pause. "I didn't realize you'd heard all that."

"Well, it's hardly incriminating. What's the big secret?"

"No secret. It was a long time ago. Her name was Mariana, and she was an old friend from back home. She died seven years ago, in Central America. End of story."

"I'm sorry."

"It's okay. I guess I should talk about it more—but I get so damned angry—"

I waited, and when he didn't say any more, I asked, "You want to tell me what happened?"

He sighed. "Why not? Mariana got caught in a private war between drug runners. Sam Garner was the asshole behind it, and I've always been sure he was scamming on both sides."

"Stealing from one to sell to the other?"

"Something like that. Mariana was trying to get medicine for a kid in her village. Sam took advantage of the situation . . . the way he always does . . . and Mariana ended up dead. Sam got away without a scratch."

Mac's voice was controlled, but thick.

"You must have loved her a lot."

"Well . . . it never would have worked, I guess. Mariana . . . she had a mission, sort of. She could have stayed in Kansas, lived in luxury. Her family had money. But Mariana took every cent she could wrangle from them and brought it to Central America. She worked day and night with the poor, dispensing food and medical supplies. With her help, they had warm clothes and at least a minimum of shelter. She ran a relief center down there, and saw to it that when aid came from other countries, it didn't get channeled into the politicians' hands. She didn't deserve what she got from Sam." Mac's face was a study in anger.

"Were Sam and Mariana lovers?" I don't know what made me say it; it just popped out. "Odd, if she chose him over you."

His laugh was bitter. "Thanks. But Sam was always the dashing one. The one with that dangerous edge that women look for in a man."

"But that's what I saw in *you* that day at Jack's Bar—that edge."

"Me?" He looked genuinely surprised. "I'm a pretty ordinary guy. Not a dangerous bone in my body."

I wondered. In every movement of that body, every twist of

the wrist as he flew this plane and the one the other night, there was a controlled anger. A desire to overcome, to win. It was even in his driving. It occurred to me that Mac Devlin didn't see himself clearly at all.

But then few of us do. Sometimes I think we're all just muddling through. It's then that I feel a strange new glimmer of compassion for men . . . replacing the anger I grew up with.

Just a glimmer. But it does give me hope.

"What does Garner want you to do for him?" I asked.

"He wants me to help him make a delivery to Colombia. Medical supplies."

"Illegal?"

"Not according to Sam. He wants me to take the first leg of an airlift. I wouldn't have to go any farther than Arizona."

Tark had said that Garner lived in Arizona now. "Why don't you want to do it?"

"Because with Sam, nothing is ever that simple."

I decided the time was right. "So . . . what's Charlie got to do with all this?"

"Charlie? You mean, Browne?"

"Don't play dumb. Yes, Charlie Browne. And my mother. The four of you met last night in a farmhouse out in the country. What was all that about?"

I could feel him staring at me. "Damn. What are you, woman, a goddamned bloodhound?"

"I just worry about my mom, that's all. I like to keep an eye on things."

He gave a snort. "What else do you know that you haven't told me?"

"Not enough. If you'll tell me about Charlie, it'll save me time."

He was silent. Then he ran distracted fingers through his hair. "Hell, why not? We're almost there. I might as well have you on my side."

"Swell. Are we expecting trouble?"

"Not expecting . . . but cautious. It pays to be cautious with Sam around."

"Is he around? At the island?"

"I don't honestly know."

He expanded, then, on what he had told me about Charlie at Harrigan's. How he was part of an organization of business-people who donated time, money, and supplies to countries where natural disasters had taken place. Some loaned their company planes to the cause, and their company's organizational skills. Charlie had used his contacts around the world to help coordinate all this, for one of the major relief agencies in the world. He and Mac had met just the way Mac had told me—during *El Terremoto*, the Mexico City earthquake.

When Charlie showed up at my door the other night, Mac was glad to see him. He figured that if anyone could help find out what was really going on with Sam, it would be Charlie Browne, with his connections.

Well, it all made for grand sense and excellent timing, I thought. Except that if Mac was telling the truth, he didn't know Charlie very well. Because Charlie and Mom showing up at my door—at just that moment—now made even grander sense. It was all planned by Charlie, I was sure. A way to connect with Mac. The question was: Why? Was Charlie working with Sam Garner on some illegal scheme? What was his agenda in all this? And how did Charlie know Mac would be with me?

I was more anxious than ever to get to the inn. This time, my mother's mysterious husband would have to talk to me. He'd have to tell me what he was up to. I didn't want Mom in the middle of one of Sam Garner's scams; I didn't want her getting hurt, or worse—like Mariana.

I was angry for both of them—Mac's old love, and Mom. Why do men use innocent women like that? How can they put them in the way of danger, if they really care?

By the time we reached the island, I was ready to do hand-to-hand battle, if necessary, with Charlie Browne.

Chapter 20

▼ ▼ ▼

*T*he seaplane circled the hotel like an eagle over its prey, scoping out just the right spot to pounce. The moon was high, now, revealing the sprawling roofline of the main inn, and several surrounding cottages. The inn sat nearly in the center of the small, wooded island. Lighted walks led to various docks around the island, in a kind of hub/spoke effect. At each spot-lighted dock were boats—from rowboats, to kayaks, to good-sized motored affairs. From the sky, one large yacht, anchored farther out, looked like a bathtub toy. It was strung with multicolored lights, lending a festive air to the night.

The inn had a full communications center, Mac had said. He was on the seaplane's radio, confirming arrival and clearing his landing near the yacht. A launch would pick us up and take us to shore.

"Pretty fancy stuff," I said, trying to get my mind off the landing.

"It's one of the best inns up here," Mac said. "Five-star."

"Well, Charlie usually does get the best."

"You don't like him much, do you?"

"Like Charlie? Is it even an option?" The plane dipped and the engines roared as Mac throttled back. At least, I think that's what he said he was doing, in a halfhearted effort to "teach me things." I'd actually paid attention now and then, but this landing on water was making me nervous. What if we sank to the bottom? What if we got eaten by sharks—or, by the looks of things down there, some scary underwater monster? I don't much like swimming in dark waters. Aunt Edna took me to see this movie a long time ago—*Creature from the Black Lagoon*. It scared the shit out of me, and ever since, I haven't been able to swim at night.

The movie was worth it, though. *Creature from the Black Lagoon* was one of those unforgettable thrills of my early life. Sitting there in that darkened theater with Aunt Edna, popcorn flying every time we screamed and clutched at each other's arms and knees, smearing butter all over our clothes. . . .

I was clutching the sides of my seat now. "Actually," I went on, still going for distraction, "I don't dislike Charlie. I dis*trust* him—which is not the same thing."

"How can you distrust someone and still like him?"

"It's one of the great dichotomies of my life."

We were silent, then, as Mac gave his full attention to the landing. Within minutes, the plane's pontoons were smacking down—but gently. I didn't know what constituted a good pilot, but Mac's easiness at the controls, and his lack of theatrics, was reassuring. By the time he'd cut the engines, I was almost sorry the flight was over.

That, of course, might have had something to do with the fact that I was about to see Mom. I could just hear her: "Jessica Rosemary James, I can't believe you are actually barging in on my honeymoon! Don't you have anything better to do?" If she wasn't in trouble, if she didn't need me, I was going to look like a damned fool.

Well, hell—it wouldn't be the first time.

Within minutes of our landing, a small motor launch bore down from the direction of shore. There were two crew members—one at the wheel, and one to take our luggage and help us into the boat. Both wore dark green pants and white shirts, with the logo GREENSPIRE INN across the back and above each right pocket. They moved smartly, spoke courteously, and welcomed us warmly. We might have been visiting dignitary—or paying guests from the nearby yacht, which, I could see now, was in the million-dollar class. No longer a bathtub toy, it stood a couple of stories high. Strings of lights—yellow, blue, red, green, and white—swayed in the warm breeze. Dance music drifted across the water, and laughter came with it, along with the clink of glassware.

It was like we'd been airlifted into another world.

So this is how the rich play, I thought, never having known many rich people—at least, not well enough to join them at play. As an investigative reporter I more often see the seamier side of things—and as for Marcus, he had never, in my two years of knowing him, played this way. Oh, he had all the accoutrements, but Marcus was a workaholic. The yacht and the private jet were for business. And while Marcus was generous with money and gifts—more than I ever wanted him to be—he didn't believe in personal displays of wealth. "There are too many people without it," he would say. "If we flaunt our wealth, we make enemies of people who have only their inner strength to get them through. And those are the people I want on my side."

I agreed with that, in principle.

On the other hand, there's nothing like a party on a well-lit, gently bobbing yacht to stir a girl's heart, come spring.

Ah, well. The motor launch was heading away from the glitter, and toward the Greenspire Inn. As we approached, I saw perhaps an acre of lush lawn before the main house. Surrounding the house in front and on the sides was a veranda, softly illuminated with yellow lights. Along the walk leading up from the dock were flickering torches.

Fantasyland. The perfect place for a honeymoon.

I was feeling really silly about this mission now. "Maybe . . ." I started to say. But then I remembered Sam Garner. His reputation for trouble. And the fact that he'd been in the same room, in an isolated farmhouse the night before, with my mom.

We went up the path, and then the stairs, to the veranda. In the Greenspire Inn lobby, I crossed to the desk clerk, asking the number to Mom and Charlie's room.

His pale face should have been a warning. But hell, I thought he was just overworked. Then he spoke, and it took Mac to get the story down right and explain it to me. I was busy getting crazy.

"Your mom is missing," Mac said gently while my limbs turned to ice. "The police have been called."

"The police?" I repeated numbly.

"There was blood in her room . . . on the edge of the door, and several spots of it leading into the hall . . ."

"Mom . . ."

That's about all I remember saying, until later—when I came out of my fog to find myself talking to cops.

Chapter 21

▼ ▼ ▼

We were in Mom and Charlie's suite, which consisted of a large living room, an equally large bedroom, a bath, and balcony. I sat on a white-and-green striped couch, staring numbly at the floor. The innkeeper had been alerted when a guest reported blood on the beige carpeting in the hall, just outside the door. In here, on thick green carpeting splattered with roses, the spots might have been coffee stains. But the smears on the door were undeniably blood. They had dried to a dark brown, and looked like the mark of fingers gripping the door as someone was forcefully pulled through it—or was fleeing for help.

The closets held Charlie's and Mom's clothes, and their suitcases. I had gone through them, and didn't find anything recognizably missing. Mom's yellow robe wasn't there—but that was hardly portentous. She had probably sent it down to house-keeping to be laundered.

Employees had been questioned, and no one remembered

seeing either Charlie or Mom leave through the front lobby. A quiet check was being made, by Security, of all rooms.

The innkeeper was distressed. On the one hand, there was no real evidence of foul play. The blood might have been from some accidental injury, and Charlie and Mom might have gone off to seek a doctor on another island. There was not yet sufficient reason to disturb the other guests.

On the other hand, everyone's safety had to be considered. Police had been called, a report made. The matter was turned over to a sheriff from the mainland, who was sitting here opposite me now. Captain Ludden—painfully skinny and all sharp angles—had been asking questions as to name, place of residence, why Mac and I were here, and our relation to Mom and Charlie.

"You know anyone who might have wanted to hurt either of them?" Ludden asked me. He rubbed at his right knee and winced, like an arthritic.

I glanced at Mac, who stood behind Ludden, and who up to now had kept out of the conversation except to introduce himself as my pilot. He made a tiny negative motion with his head. I hesitated, then answered, "No. No one."

"And they were here on their honeymoon. That right?"

"Yes. A belated honeymoon. They've been married since last Christmas."

"They know anybody here in this area? Somebody they might have been meeting?"

"Not that I know of."

The captain's pale brown eyes seemed to pierce me through. *Things like this don't just happen,* they said. *What are you holding back?*

Sam Garner, was my silent answer. Mac had said that Sam Garner might be here. But he didn't want me to tell Ludden that. Maybe I would have anyway—except that my first instinct, always, is to not cooperate with the law. Things get too complicated, all tied up in rules and regulations, and what with all the paperwork, things don't get done.

Aside from that—if Sam Garner had hurt Mom, I wanted him for myself.

"I need to make a call," I said abruptly. "If you have any more questions . . ."

Ludden laid that look on me one more time, then shook his head and closed his notebook. "Guess that's all. I'll send over a lab man to dust for prints, but don't expect much, Miss James. Probably find the housekeeper's, the innkeeper's, your mother's and stepfather's . . . and yours."

"What about lab tests to type the blood? Find out whose it is?"

His weathered face looked pensive. "Guess we could do that, young lady. But the way it is . . . until we know something's really happened . . ." He pursed his lips and made a noise like a sucking fish. "Seems a tad of an overkill."

"By the time we know something *really* happened," I said, my voice rising, "it will be too late. The blood will be gone."

He sucked on that one, and finally nodded. "Point, there. You be stayin' here, meantime? On the island?"

"I don't know yet." I glanced at Mac, who seemed perversely blank. "If I hear from my mother, and everything's okay, I suppose we'll go back home."

"Well, let me know if you do. Either way." Ludden stood, flexing his stiff, spindly legs, and groaning. He grabbed at his back, pushing until the spine arched. Bones cracked. "Too much dampness out here. Time to retire. Leave this business to those damned young hot dogs who think they'll never get old." For the first time, he grinned. His teeth were yellow with either age or coffee stains, and a couple were silver-capped. "Young people. You're all immortal, not t'mention wrinkle-free. Like a shiny new polyester suit."

"You talking about me?" I wasn't seeing myself as either immortal or wrinkle-free these days.

Ludden cracked his elbow bones. "You, and that young fella over there."

Mac, too, looked surprised. He lifted a cynical eyebrow, and ran a hand over his thick brown hair.

"Watch you don't both lose your one chance at gettin' old," was the sheriff's parting shot.

As Captain Ludden departed, a uniformed officer entered to inform us that these rooms were off-bounds now until the lab tests had been done. He ushered us out, and we made our way silently to the elevators. It was a silent ride down, too. I was thinking hard. Mac studied the ornate ceiling of what must have been the old mansion's original lift.

Once in the lobby, we moved by unspoken agreement to the doors . . . then to the wide porch . . . and finally, to the path that led to the water. A short way down the path, I grabbed Mac's arm and pulled him into a thick cluster of trees.

"Not one more lie!" I breathed. "Not *one more*. I want to know what that meeting last night was all about. What the hell is going on? And why didn't you want me to tell that cop that Sam Garner might be here?"

"It would only have led to more questions, Jesse. Questions you might not want asked . . . or answered."

"Like what?"

"Like how come Charlie Browne is willing to help Sam with this delivery he's got."

"What are you talking about?"

"All I know is, when I told Charlie about it . . . and when I told him I didn't want any part of it . . . he asked me to hook him up with Sam."

"Does he know Sam Garner? Did he know him before?"

"I'm not sure. But he was anxious to meet with him, and he asked me not to tell Sam ahead of time that he was coming last night. Charlie set up the time—and the place."

"But you were there. You know what they talked about."

"No. I waited outside."

"Where outside?"

"For Christ's sake—on the porch. Why? What does it matter? They were in the kitchen talking, and I didn't hear anything that was said. They wanted it that way."

"What about my mother? What was she doing all this time?"

"She was in there with them. I heard her arguing with Charlie beforehand about it, at the car. He wanted her to stay there, out of the way, and she refused. That is one little spitfire, your mom. Reminds me of somebody I know."

"Right. So you took them to this meet in the country with Garner? How'd you happen to choose that particular house?"

"I told you, I didn't choose it," Mac said. "Charlie did."

"Charlie? He picked Marcus's house as a meeting place?"

"Yes."

"How did he know about it?"

"You'll have to ask him, Jess. Or Marcus."

"Wait a minute. Is it just my imagination, or are you talking about Marcus Andrelli as if you know him too?"

"I'll tell you this much . . . I've never known anyone as cantankerous *or* suspicious as you."

"And another thing—did the meeting last night just end naturally, and then all four of you left together? Or what?"

I saw the lie coming. It was in the shifting of eyes, the negligent shrug. "They finished talking, and they came out onto the porch, and we all left. Charlie and your mother went somewhere together in Charlie's rental car, and I drove Sam to the airport, to his plane. I didn't know where he was going, or why, or what your mother and Charlie were going to do."

Mac was talking too much. It's something you learn as an interviewer: People nearly always say too much when they lie. They think they have to elaborate, to support the lie.

"What about Lang?" I said.

This time, the shrug didn't come. Instead, the eyes blinked. Mac wasn't really a good liar. Certainly not in Charlie's league, for instance.

Or Lang's.

"What do you mean?" he said.

"Stop it! Just tell me. I know he was there before you left."

"Uh . . . I don't . . ."

"Lang. Three-piece suit—Harvard type. I think it was navy blue last night. He found you there, on the porch."

"How—" He shook his head. "Damn, you're good!"

"Never mind the compliments. What did Lang say to you? Did he tell you to get the others, and get out of there? That I was on the way?"

"I . . . I don't know what he said, actually. He went inside the kitchen. I heard him talking to the others. They came out, and we left—that's all."

"So why were you keeping it a secret?"

"Because this guy Lang said—and Charlie said—not to tell anyone we'd seen him there."

"Including me? Did Charlie say, specifically, me?"

He hesitated. "Well . . . yeah, he did."

"But you don't know why?"

"No."

Goddamn Charlie! God damn the man. I *knew* it. I *knew* it. Why hadn't I done something about it? While there was time?

"What is it?" Mac said. "Jesse . . . hey, are you crying?"

"No!" I turned my back on him. "I'm just angry."

"You are . . . you're crying. You're really worried about your mom, aren't you?"

"Jesus Christ! There's blood all over their goddamned room! Of course I'm worried!"

"I know . . . I'm sorry, Jess. I never thought, when I got into this—"

"Never mind! Leave me alone!"

They were all in on it—whatever "it" was. Not only Charlie, but Lang—and Marcus. It was Marcus's house where they met, the house he'd bought for his bimbo girlfriend wife-to-be and their son. What the hell was going on?

Whatever else, I'd always thought I could trust Marcus not to let anything happen to my mom. For that matter—way deep down, I'd believed that Charlie wouldn't let her be hurt, either. He loved her—regardless of anything else, he loved Mom. I had been sure of it. He wouldn't put her in danger.

But apparently, he had.

It was one of several surprises in my life of late. Things were changing all too fast—as in an earthquake, where you're sitting there, doing mundane things like chewing on a carrot stick or filing your nails, and all of a sudden the ground shifts and nothing's ever the same again.

It was that kind of fear. So when Mac turned me around and gathered me in, I reached for something to hang on to—if only for a while—and found it.

"There are leaves in your hair," Mac said. "And moon."

His weight covered me, and so did his lips. They covered my face, moving slowly from brow to chin. His fingers were tangled in my hair. I began to be aroused again, and thought, with wonder, how different men are. How someone like Mac can be so good in the aftermath that sex becomes an ongoing adventure, not a meal to be polished off and cleaned up after.

The moon took a stroll down a path of stars, and when next I looked, it had paused for a visit on Mac Devlin's face . . . highlighting the fine angles, the eyes that didn't tease, now, or even try to look cocky. They were serious, like his tone. Serious about every languorous motion, every promise—

You don't believe in promises, a small voice said.

Shut up, I answered. *Give me this, for now. It's all I'll ever ask.*

"I haven't felt like this since I was sixteen," Mac said.

I've never felt like this, I thought.

"I don't believe we did that." I looked around the Greenspire room we were standing in, an hour or so later.

Mac pulled twigs from my hair, then planted his hands on my waist.

"And coming through the lobby afterward," I muttered, embarrassed, "people looking at us, like they knew . . ."

"I'm sure some of them have made love in the woods," Mac said. He kissed my nose. "Shower?"

"I . . . no." I straightened my spine. "I have to do something about Mom."

"Jess, you heard the desk clerk. They've questioned everyone on the island—all the boat people, even everyone on the yacht—and no one's seen them. I think the best we can do is get a good night's sleep. They'll show before morning—their clothes are still here, after all."

"But the blood—"

"Maybe the innkeeper was right. It could have been a simple accident . . . they could have taken a boat to the main island for medical care."

"No one remembers seeing them. And there aren't any boats unaccounted for."

"I know." He sighed. "Well, what would you like to do?"

I wasn't sure. But I felt guilty for having let myself be distracted—for not doing *something.*

"I need to think." I ran a hand through my hair, and glanced uneasily at the fancy queen-sized bed. "I . . . uh . . . maybe we should get separate rooms."

Mac looked around with amusement, while his hands

roamed up and down my back. "This one seems big enough for two."

"I just mean . . . it doesn't look right."

He held me off a bit. *"Look* right?"

I could feel my face heat up. "You know."

He laughed. "Lady, we have just been buff naked in the woods together, where anyone could walk along and see us at any moment . . . and you're embarrassed, now, to sleep in the same bed?"

"No, I'm not embarrassed, I just—"

"You are. You're blushing." He laughed again—a deep, throaty, Gregory Peck chuckle. His lips found my neck, then my ear.

"Don't start."

"We never stopped—"

"Even so . . ."

When the phone rang moments later, we were in some kind of impossible position on the floor, limbs atangle. I jerked upright, hoping it was Mom. But the phone was on a table that was closer to Mac. He grabbed it. " 'Lo?" He listened, then handed the receiver to me.

"Jess?"

It was Tark. I'd forgotten to call him earlier. "How'd you know I was here?"

His tone was patient. "You told me you were flying over there—remember?"

"Oh . . . yeah."

"I take it that was Devlin who answered."

"Yeah." I glanced at my watch. "You've checked out the shoe?"

I'd taken that mysterious shoe of Charlie's to Tark before heading out to the airport earlier. He had sent it to a local lab that had recently come under the Andrelli Enterprises umbrella, by way of a merger with a giant pharmaceutical company. The parent laboratory was medical—but its tentaclelike branches ac-

tually led to a small technical lab that the Rochester police sometimes use for investigational purposes. The Rochester P.D.
didn't yet know its true ownership.

Marcus's cunning sometimes approaches the Machiavellian.

"You'll love this," Tark said. "Browne didn't lie to you
about the codes."

"You're kidding."

"No. He was telling the truth. At least, it looks that way.
The x-ray turned up four numbers in the lining. 4-0-2-2."

"4-0-2-2." I committed it to memory, and wondered what
it meant. "I can't believe Charlie. . . . It's so cliché," I complained. "Like something from an old spy novel."

"Well . . . sometimes the obvious is overlooked. Maybe
he was counting on that."

"But he actually *told* me. Last year, in California . . ."
He'd flaunted it in my face. Damn Charlie Browne's eyeballs.

"Anything else strange about that shoe?"

"Nothing they could find right off. They're still running
some chemical tests."

"What about the other thing?" I glanced at Mac, who had
put his shirt back on but hadn't rebuttoned it. He was sitting on
the floor with his back against an armchair, listening attentively.

"Garner flew back to Arizona this A.M.," Tark said. "I've
confirmed that he's there, now, at a ranch he owns near Nogales,
on the Mexican border. I've got someone on him."

"Has your person seen anything of Mom or Charlie there?"

"No—aren't they with you?"

I told him about their disappearance, and the blood. "I'm
inclined to believe the sheriff is right. There's no real proof of
foul play, and it's too small an island. If something serious had
happened, we'd know about it by now. Meanwhile, there's another thing—Lang. We were right about him. He warned Charlie, Mom, and Garner about our arrival last night. That's why
they were gone when we got there."

"I'll talk to him," Tark said heavily. "But Marcus isn't going to like this. He trusts Lang more than most. What about Devlin?"

"He . . . wasn't in on the meeting."

Tark was silent. Then he said, "You can't talk, can you?"

"No."

"Okay. So, answer questions. That's what he told you, that he wasn't in on the meet. Do you believe him?"

"I think so. I'm not sure. Listen, do you know why Charlie would have arranged that meeting with Sam Garner at a farmhouse Marcus owns?"

"Is that the way it happened?" Tark asked. "Browne chose the place?"

"That's what Mac says."

"Let me look into it. Right now, no. I haven't got a clue."

"Okay. Look, we're staying overnight in case Mom and Charlie show. I'm not sure yet about tomorrow. Will you call me if you hear from either of them? And see if you can find out what kind of business Marcus and Charlie might have together now?"

"Of course. But don't you want to talk to Marcus yourself?"

"No."

"He'll want to know what's going on with you—"

"No," I repeated firmly. "Just find out what's going on, okay?"

"Sure, but—"

I replaced the receiver gently on its cradle. Tark wouldn't mind. He was used to me hanging up when the subject came to Marcus. I'd been doing it, off and on, for two impossibly long years.

"Tell me about Mariana," I said, in that contrary way a woman will when she's slept with a man, and then suddenly, everyone he's ever known—every heart he's ever broken—takes on momentous import.

It drives most men nuts, that implied attack on their secrets, their freedom.

But Mac didn't seem to mind too much. We were sitting on a porch-type swing on the veranda of the inn, drinking hot coffee from deep, heavy mugs. We had spent the night together, and now it was morning. A time to face reality—except that with Mac, the surprising reality was that he was still here. He hadn't gone off in the night, hadn't woken up aloof and irritable, wishing he were anyplace but in bed with me. Instead, we had made love, and then we had laughed and tickled each other and goofed around, tracing scratches from the adventure in the thicket the night before.

Amazing.

Neither Mom nor Charlie had shown up. Tark hadn't called back with any news. But someone from Captain Ludden's office had phoned and said Ludden was on his way here. He wanted us to wait.

"It was a long time ago," Mac said, in response to my question about Mariana—the woman he said he had loved, the one whose death Sam Garner was responsible for.

"Do you mind talking about it?"

"I used to, but no . . . not anymore. What do you want to know?"

"Well . . . she died seven years ago?"

"Going on eight, now. Like I said, she had been working in Central America for ten years or so before that, with a relief agency. Helping people in the town where her family grew up."

"But she was born in Kansas?"

"Yes. Mariana was a year behind me in grade school, but we hung out together. Played marbles in the schoolyard, that sort of thing. Later, I helped her with her homework . . . actually, we helped each other. She was a whiz at English. Geometry was my thing."

His face was relaxed, almost happy in the reminiscence. But

when I asked him when he and Mariana fell in love, there was a flicker of pain.

"We went steady all through high school. Her parents, for many reasons, disapproved—but they finally allowed it. Grudgingly. I think they thought that if they were to forbid us to see each other, we'd run off."

"Would you have?"

He smiled. "I don't know. Maybe."

"How did Sam Garner fit into all this?"

"He and I were friends. But I was on the football team, while Sam rode motorcycles and dressed in leather. He was the one the girls were all a little bit afraid of—and attracted to."

"They must have been attracted to you, too."

He looked sort of wistful. "You think so?"

"I'm sure of it."

He shook his head and took a sip of coffee. "I don't think Mariana was attracted to Sam. Not then. She and I planned to marry. We were certain—in the way only young people blindly in love can be certain—that we could overcome her parents' objections."

"Why did they object?"

"The Samoranos were aristocracy in Central America. They wanted Mariana to marry her 'own kind.' "

"Ethnically—or financially?"

"Both. My father owned the town newspaper. A small weekly, respectable, but no real money in it. My prospects—if I took one of the football scholarships offered—were solid, but not exciting."

"And Mariana buckled under their objections?"

"Not at first. She stood up to them, had a terrible argument with them. The next they knew, she was in Central America, living with relatives. This was in 1968. I planned to go down there after her, but her father came and talked to me. It was the first time I'd ever seen him act like a human being. He was genuinely concerned for Mariana's future. We finally agreed that if she and I still felt the same way after four years of college, he'd be willing to consider our marriage."

"But you went into the Air Force, instead of college?"

"Yes. The draft was still in effect, and if I was going in, I wanted to fly."

"And Mariana?"

"She stayed in Central America. We wrote to each other nearly every day. Then Nam wound down, for the U.S., at least, and Sam and I stayed on to fly cargo—"

He broke off, his expression as bitter as the dark brew we were both drinking.

"After a few months," he began again, "Sam and I split. He took a job flying for a private airline in Central America. He and Mariana met again there."

"And they ended up together," I said softly.

"Funny you should think that. I was never sure. But her letters started to sound different. Withdrawn, somehow. And there weren't as many of them anymore. Finally—"

"You were back in the States, and you went down there. To see what was wrong."

"Something like that," Mac said. "It was '74 . . . '75. She was awkward with me at first, and when Sam was around, she couldn't look me in the eye. I guess I was burned out . . . didn't have much heart left for the chase. I finally got the message, and left. But then Mariana started writing to me again, and over the years . . . Hard to believe, but it was ten years . . . ten long years of getting back into civilian life. They just sort of slipped on by. Anyway . . . we got to be friends again, writing letters. Closer, maybe, than we'd ever been. I began to hope—" He shook his head, and made a short, angry sound. "About seven years ago Mariana wrote and asked me to come down there, said she needed my help. When I got there . . ."

"She was dead?"

"Yes."

I gave him a few minutes. We rocked in the swing, and looked off down the lawn and to the water. A boat was approaching, but it was too soon to see if Ludden was in it.

"I don't suppose I should blame Sam," Mac continued. "Mariana was helping a child in the village, a little girl, who was dying. She mediated an illegal sale of pharmaceuticals, to get the drug this kid needed. I talked to several people—people I felt I could trust—and they all said that she had gone to Sam to help put the deal together. But you know, I just can't help feeling that if she'd gotten the drugs some other way—and that if Sam Garner hadn't been involved—it wouldn't have all gone sour. It's that way with Sam. Things always go sour."

Mac's caustic tone matched his expression. Any pretense of devil-may-care was gone. Weary lines deepened along his mouth, and I knew he must be thinking, too, of the trouble Sam had gotten into in Vietnam, causing the partnership to break up. "What did Garner mean the other day, when he said you owed it to Mariana to make this delivery?"

"He said that the kid Mariana did the deal for—the one who was dying back then and needed the drugs—was in trouble again. She's nineteen now, but it's one of those diseases kids get in the third world countries, and never get over. It keeps coming back. And Sam says that she needs this medicine, and I owe it to Mariana—who gave her life so that this girl could live, all those years ago—to help her stay alive now."

"I don't see what the problem is. Why doesn't he just deliver it himself?"

"That's the part Sam hasn't seen fit to tell me yet."

"That's a pretty heavy guilt trip to lay on you," I reflected. "Do you believe that story?"

"I don't know. That's the thing . . . with Sam, you never know."

It was all we had time for. The motor launch was tying up at the dock, and Captain Ludden was on it. His arthritic limbs moved jerkily over the rail, and he landed on the dock with a wince that was visible from here. We walked down the path to meet him.

Ludden's face was pale; his eyes didn't quite meet mine. A chill swept through me, despite the sun glittering on the blue water, despite Mac's arm, which had suddenly gone around me.

"I'm sorry," Ludden said. "Your mother . . ." His morose brown eyes shifted to mine, and away.

"What? What about her?" I stood looking at him, waiting, while his old face worked miserably. *"What?"*

"She's dead," Ludden told me. "I am so very, very sorry. Her body was discovered on the main island . . ."

I screamed, then, I think. Mac grabbed hold of me, and everything went black, then red. I began to hit. I struck with my doubled-up fists, over and over, and didn't even realize I was hitting Mac, or that he was allowing me to do so, until I looked into his eyes and saw tears of sympathy there. Then I started to cry.

Chapter 22

▼ ▼ ▼

I don't remember the boat ride. I remember spray in my face, knowing the fact of it, yet not feeling it. The river, from island to island, might have been encased in a bubble. There was no longer any connection, for me, to anything solid; no sense-matter, no emotion, no joy, or even grief.

Captain Ludden talked, and now and then words came through: "Ravine . . . purse . . . hotel."

I heard Mac ask questions, heard the name "Browne." Ludden shook his head. "No sign of him." Mac never left my side, and vaguely, I knew that he was treating me with great fragility.

I used to wonder what it would be like when my mother died. Sometimes I'd rehearse it in my mind: getting the news, attending the funeral. I thought that in some way, that might alleviate the pain of the real thing when it happened. A psychological trick.

But nothing had prepared me for this.

She wasn't in a morgue; there wasn't one on the island. The coroner's office used the facilities of a local funeral home. Dimly, I was aware of dolorous music, of the too-sweet scent of flowers, of an unnatural hush that was worse than the silence of death. I was aware, too, of the way I was shaking.

They had put her in a small "preparation" room. Outside the room were a desk and a couple of file cabinets. Ludden pulled a large brown envelope out of a drawer. "Your mother's effects," he said awkwardly.

I sat at the desk and opened the envelope, delaying the moment when I'd have to go into that room. Reaching inside, I pulled out my mother's watch, the one Charlie had given her when they were married. It was gold, outlined with diamonds and emeralds. In its center, at the apex of the hands, was a green emerald *K*. The crystal had shattered. I passed a hand over my eyes. Mom's rings were in the envelope, and a beige scarf. Aunt Edna had taken me shopping one Christmas when I was eleven, and we'd bought it for Mom. It was old silk, thin and soft now. I couldn't believe she'd kept it all these years.

My hands shook, and I couldn't go on. I left the envelope on the table and stood. Ludden opened the door to the preparation room, and I paused on the threshold, looking in. At the center of the room was a table draped with sheets. On it, a still form. It, too, was covered. I don't remember anything else about that room.

Mac came with me. At the table, Ludden pulled the sheet off—from the feet up, as if preparing me for it gradually. I squeezed my eyes shut. Mac grabbed me. His chin moved against my hair. I turned and shoved my face against his shirt. "It's all right," he murmured, "it's all right."

At last I drew away, thinking I was ready. I was wrong. My eyes fixed on something peach: Mom's silky, peach skirt, and the tunic-length, unstructured jacket. My reluctant vision traveled down the slender legs to her low-heeled, white pumps. I recognized a scratch that she had tried to repair with shoe polish at my apartment, that morning before Toni came over. It had been too deep. She had laughed and said, "Oh, well! Who ever looks at anybody's feet, anyway?"

No one, maybe . . . unless they're the feet of someone who's dead: their flaws exposed for all the world to see. My hand went out to protect my mother, then fell. My throat hurt, and I tried to swallow and couldn't. Panic set in. My heart pounded. "I can't . . ." I reached for my neck, clawing with my fingers. ". . . can't breathe." Mac pulled me against his chest again, massaging the back of my neck and telling me that I *could* breathe, that I just had to do it slowly, that I was hyperventilating and everything would be all right. "Steady now," he said. "Steady. Nice and slow." I tried, but I thought I would strangle and die, I was sure of it. "I can't do this," I said, hearing my voice rise hysterically. "I can't—"

I felt Mac stiffen. "Jesus Christ!" he yelled, jerking away.

I stared up at his face in shock. "What? What is it?" Mac was focused on the table—at Mom.

I whirled and looked. At Mom's blond hair. Pale and uncovered now. Blond hair—

Blond hair—

"You goddamned fucking idiot!" I screamed, wheeling on Ludden and swinging with every ounce of strength I had. He fell back against something that clattered, slack-jawed, rubbing his cheek. "Whaaaat?" he croaked. "What's wrong?"

"You fucking idiot! This is not my mother!"

And goddamn fucking Charlie Browne—he'd done it to me again.

"It's not even the same color hair!" I stormed, pacing in the outer room before the worried sheriff. "Mom's is brown, with a little gray. It's even on her license that way."

"But women color their hair all the time. We thought, since

164

she'd recently been married . . . And it *is* her license." Ludden's expression was one of embarrassment and chagrin. Mac, who stood by the door, arms folded, looked angry for me—but greatly relieved.

The sheriff had a point. It *was* Mom's license. I'd checked it. And her clothes. In addition, the innkeeper had motored over in the early dawn hours and made a "positive" identification, before Ludden informed me. They had thought they were saving me pain.

But this only confirmed my cynicism about organized law, as opposed to organized crime. Organized crime at least knows what it's doing half the time. These bozos—

"The innkeeper said that this was the woman who'd been staying in Mom and Charlie's suite?"

"Absolutely."

"What do you know about this innkeeper? Jordan, is that his name?"

Ludden rubbed his chin. "He's been at Greenspire since the original owners sold it, thirty-two years ago. I'd swear to his honesty."

I thought a minute. "Hang on."

Using the phone on the desk, I found an empty line and called the inn. "Give me the innkeeper, please—Mr. Jordan. This is Jessica James."

I was put through to him right away. At first, he went on and on with condolences. Until I told him about the mistake. Then there was an ambivalent silence, during which I could hear him thinking: *Oh, shit.*

"I don't know what to say," Jordan began worriedly. "I am so sorry—"

I'd had enough apologies for one day. "What about the man who was staying with this woman? What did he look like?"

"Mr. Browne, you mean? Well, he was extremely tall, blue eyes, with silver hair—"

"Wait a minute. *Extremely* tall?"

"Quite, I'd say. I'm six-foot myself, and Mr. Browne was several inches taller than I—"

Charlie is five-eleven. The man with my poor dead "mum" in the room next door had been another ringer.

And when I caught up with Charlie Browne this time, I would fry his balls in hot Crisco.

I thanked Jordan, assured him that everything was all right, and hung up.

"Mac? I need to get home. Is the plane ready? Do you need to fuel up or anything first?"

"All done, taken care of when we first got here."

I turned to Ludden. "Do me a favor?"

"Anything." The captain looked relieved to have a chance to make up for my earlier grief.

"Don't tell anyone this isn't my mother, okay? Keep your report the way it is for now?"

"Well, now, Miss James, I don't know—"

"You said *anything.*"

He groaned as he stood, all stiff movements, rubbing the small of his back. "Give you forty-eight hours," he said reluctantly. "No more. Then I gotta report it to the state, all the appropriate people."

"Fine. Forty-eight hours."

I glanced around the funeral parlor office. On the wall were sales photos of caskets. The dreadful music sounded from another room, along with subdued voices. The file cabinets in here, presumably, held only records of people who were dead.

Not one of which—thank God, thank God—was my mom.

We were home by early afternoon. It was a crystal-clear day in Rochester; the smog that had been plaguing the city more often in the past couple of years had been washed away by a morning shower. The weather report on the car radio promised sunny skies and only warm, balmy days to come.

I had left Mac at the airport to take care of business. He'd be along in an hour or two, he said—and I'd promised not to do anything until then. Ordinarily, that was the kind of promise I'd never keep. But some of my sharp edges had gone. I was feeling, well . . . more amenable.

I saw everything in brighter colors now, too. The trees lining Genesee Park Boulevard were of the deepest, purest green. The blue sky was bluer, the puffy white clouds like magic carpets carrying passengers on their way to Nirvana. Sounds were more gentle. Honking horns were lullabies . . . birds sang with the bell-like pitch of flutes.

I hadn't realized how close the threat of death can bring one to a grateful heart. I remembered a prayer Sister Benedict had taught us at Mercy High: *Keep me, oh God, from pettiness . . . let me be large in thought, word, and deed.*

It's not often I "get religion." But for a moment there, I was almost ready to forgive Charlie Browne.

Until I heard the sound of MTV drifting from my open living room windows.

Mom! Only Mom watches MTV in my house. And she doesn't really watch it—but uses it to exercise by. If she was exercising, that meant she was all right—

My relief was instant and overwhelming. I nearly cried. But then I remembered that if Mom was here, Charlie couldn't be far behind. With that, I saw red.

I jerked the Dodge to a stop, yanked on the parking brake, jumped out, and slammed the door. Running up the porch and then the inside stairs, I rehearsed all the things I was going to say, and do, to Charlie Browne. I would insist Mom get an immediate divorce, for one thing. That she leave the country, if need be. I'd even go with her to see that it got done, and that Charlie didn't persuade her to change her mind. I'd see to it she lived out the remainder of her life in a convent—

Then I'd deal with Charlie Goddamned Browne.

I tore through my door, loins girded for battle—

To see a vision in purple. Purple socks, purple tunic, purple tights . . . and topping it all, a mop of orange, from which emanated clouds of smoke.

The vision stood before my television, snapping her fingers to the beat of some horrible rock song on MTV. When she saw me she sucked on her cigarette, then grinned.

"It's about time you got home. Don't you have any herb tea around here? And what about fresh veggies? I can't find a goddamned thing."

Aunt Edna.

Chapter 23

▼ ▼ ▼

I'm shorter than I'd like to be, at five-four. But Aunt Edna is shorter still. I ran across the living room, grabbed her up, and hugged her so tight I nearly broke her ribs. "I don't know what you're doing here, but I sure am glad to see you!" I yelled.

I had to yell, to be heard over the music.

"You were playing George Michael when you called," my mother's sister hollered back. She brushed at her frizzy orange hair. "Anytime you move up from classic jazz to soft rock, I know you're in trouble."

She turned MTV down and gestured with her cigarette at my tape collection. "Also, your taste in music is always behind the times. *One More Try* was popular years ago, for heaven's sake, and he's got a whole new album now. Maybe I should go through your tapes while I'm here and toss out all the out-of-date stuff. I'm sure I'll find John Denver—"

"You do, and I'll trash your Simon and Garfunkels next time I'm in California."

But I didn't mean it, and neither did she. I laughed and hugged her again, just glad to have Aunt Edna here, in my camp.

A while later, tucked into bedtime sweats and spooning down Häagen-Dazs, I said, "What are we going to do about Mom?"

Aunt Edna stopped her frenetic pacing around the bedroom and blew smoke my way. I inhaled, reaching for that old familiar buzz by osmosis. I'd never smoked, but presumably have enough tar in my lungs—from growing up around Aunt Edna— to pave any New York thruway. It's something I don't worry about for now, figuring that if life turns out to be short, with Aunt Edna around it will at least have been swell.

"First of all, I don't fully agree with you about Charlie," she said. "I've seen them together more than you have—and he cherishes that woman." She waved a negligent hand my way. "Oh, I know, it's an old-fashioned word, Jesse, but if it ever fit, it does now. Charlie may involve Kate in mysterious schemes, but only because she insists on it. She *yearns* for it."

"Yearns? Mom *yearns?*" It was a strange new concept.

"You thought she would just get old and die, without making a mark of some kind? An O'Donnell?"

"Well, she always—"

"Kate's life was never her own while your father was alive. She wasn't herself all those years. But I suppose you'd have to have known her before her marriage, to know that."

It was more or less what Mom had said last fall: that she'd been acting a lot while I was growing up. Getting through, the best way she knew how . . . pretending to a happiness that wasn't there. "It's what you do," she had said, "when you've got a child to raise and a husband who's determined to pickle himself to death. You laugh a little, you pretend a little, and you make the best of things."

That's not, of course, what they recommend these days. These days, Mom would be called a co-dependent, an enabler.

But she didn't know that then; didn't have the kind of information that's available to people now. And while we might all agree that it makes us smarter and more "together" to understand these things today, I suspect we owe a large debt of gratitude to the moms who raised us with guts, and cunning, and managed to throw in a little laughter on the side.

"So you think that wherever she and Charlie are, they're okay?"

"I didn't say that." Aunt Edna plopped down on the end of my bed and crossed her legs yogi style. "What I said is that Charlie's heart's in the right place. That doesn't mean he's beyond landing them both in deep trouble. That man has more secrets going on, at any given time, than Houdini."

"An interesting correlation," I mused. "Charlie is somewhat of a magician, isn't he? A master of illusion . . ."

It had occurred to me in the Thousand Islands that there was only one way the switch at the Greenspire Inn could have been pulled off: Charlie had set the whole thing up. Certainly his resources were endless, his scheming boundless.

Why he'd have done that—and why the woman posing as Mom had been killed—was another matter.

Before Mac and I left the funeral home, Captain Ludden had said that he'd check the dead woman's prints. "And we'll get people at the inn to help us with a sketch of the man she was with. We'll put it out over the wires, in case he's left the islands."

It seemed likely that Charlie's impostor knew his companion was dead, and had purposely disappeared. Unless, of course, something had happened to him too.

"There's just no getting around it, Aunt Edna. Whatever Charlie's involved in now, it's not good. That woman up there was murdered. Stabbed, it looks like, in the hotel room—and then most likely taken to that ravine in the hope she wouldn't be found."

"You don't think Charlie killed her!" Aunt Edna said.

I was startled to find that I didn't—that the thought hadn't even once occurred to me.

The phone rang. I picked up, hoping it was Tark returning my earlier message. It was.

"Things are heating up here," he said. "Lang's disappeared. And Jess . . . that pilot friend of yours?"

"Mac?"

"He's disappeared with him."

I laughed, but even so, my spine grew cold. "That's crazy. I left Mac a couple of hours ago. He should be on his way over here by now."

"Don't bet the rent on it."

I glanced at the clock radio by my bed. It had been close to three hours since I'd left Mac at the airport.

"Damato was making a pass at the airport again," Tark went on, "looking for some sign of Sam Garner or that Beech 18 of his. I'd told him I didn't want him telling Lang anything for a while. I've been isolating Lang, trying to figure out what he's up to. Anyway, who should Damato see at the airport an hour ago, than Lang himself? He went into CHARTER 10, and when he hadn't come out a half hour later, Damato went in. Some woman was there, working, but no sign of either Devlin or Lang. The woman said Devlin had gone out on a charter, but wouldn't tell him anything more."

"Holy shit. You think Mac was hired to fly Lang somewhere?"

"Damato asked around, talked to some maintenance people at the hangar. They described Devlin's passenger: three-piece suit, business type . . . blond hair."

My mind was racing. "Mac must have filed a flight plan," I said.

"I'm working on that. Thing is, Lang's supposed to be letting me know his every move. In fact, he was due in my office around the same time Damato saw him at the airport. And Marcus isn't talking."

"Is he upset? About Lang?"

"Strangely . . . no."

We were silent, both of us thinking, I knew, that that was strange indeed.

Another phone rang in Tark's office. "Hang on. That might be my connection at the airport." He put me on hold.

While I waited, I told Aunt Edna what was happening. "There's some weird connection between Marcus and Charlie. I'd have sworn Marcus didn't know him until last fall—"

Tark came back on. "Jess? I've got it. They're flying into Phoenix, Arizona. And the reason it took some doing to get the flight plan is that Devlin didn't take his own plane."

"Well, he does borrow from other companies some-times—"

Tark made a sound like a snort. "Other companies, hell. He's got Marcus's private jet."

I sat straight. My aunt narrowed her eyes in a question.

"I think it's time you had another talk with the boss, Jess. He never lies to you—not outright, anyway."

"No. He *avoids.*"

"Even so . . ."

"Unh-uh. He'd only tell me he was 'handling things,' and to 'stay out of it.' " That brought up another question. "Are you going to drop out of this now? Marcus won't want you helping me out, if he's this deep into it."

"I thought we discussed all that months ago," Tark replied softly. "I don't take those kinds of orders anymore."

It was what I'd hoped to hear.

"Jess? There's one more thing. A couple matching your mother's and Charlie's descriptions is registered at the Camel-back Inn, outside Phoenix. The name's different—Phillips—"

It rang a bell. "Phillips! That's Charlie's father's name—Justin Phillips Browne."

"I know that," Tark said in a tone of utmost patience. "Which is why—"

"Then it *is* Mom and Charlie. I've got to get down there!"

"Which is why," he continued patiently, "I've hired an executive jet to take us there."

"Us? You mean, you and me?" I grabbed Aunt Edna's knee, the way I used to in darkened movie theaters when things heated up.

"No—me and the Lone Ranger," Tark said. "Who do you think? Of course, you and me."

"But that's great!" For the first time in twenty-four hours, I had a feeling I was catching up with Mom.

"When do we leave?" I demanded.

"Within the hour. Pack your spurs."

"And my Colt 45's?"

"Round 'em up, head 'em out," Tark replied.

Chapter 24

▼ ▼ ▼

*T*ark didn't look much like a cowboy. He looked like what
he was: a man who'd been a mob bodyguard most of his
life, but who had recently expanded his horizons. His too-hard-
to-be-handsome face bore the scars of battle, but he looked
steady, capable, and sure in a business suit with running shoes,
no tie. The gray suit jacket was open, but pulled taut across
shoulders so broad, they nearly overwhelmed the rest of Tark's
six-foot-four-inch frame.

We had been in the air ten minutes. Aunt Edna, who had
insisted on coming along, was in the rest room, while Tark and I
sipped ginger ale from champagne glasses. A bucket of ice held
the Canada Dry bottle on a table nearby. We sat in facing swivel
chairs that were soft and cushy. There was a television with a
VCR, movies on tape, a phone . . . and freshly cut flowers.

I could get used to this, I thought. Sure beats the hell out
of coach.

But the charter had cost Tark a small fortune. I had watched
him pay the guy at the executive charter service; he hadn't
blinked an eye at the exorbitant price.

"Did you tell Marcus what we were doing?" I asked over the ginger ale.

"He wasn't in the office. I left word with Alfred that I'd be gone a couple of days."

"Not where, or why?"

"No."

I just looked at him.

"I've got vacation time coming," he said with a shrug.

"Uh-huh."

"And Marcus doesn't have to know everything. We sure don't."

I raised a brow. "You sound testy. Something new?"

"Not new."

"C'mon, it's a long trip. Spit it out."

He avoided my eyes, leaning back in the swivel chair and studying his glass. "He was out at that farmhouse."

"Oh." I tapped my own glass against my teeth. "Doing what?"

"You don't want to hear this."

"I can't *not* hear it, now. Tell me."

He shook his head, obviously not able to believe what he was about to say. "He's digging. *Plowing.*" Tark's laugh was scornful. "Whatever."

"Plowing?"

"Soil. For a vegetable garden."

"You mean, he's overseeing the work."

"No . . . I mean he's preparing the soil himself, according to Alfred, who doesn't believe it either. A 'labor of love,' he told Alfred—with a grin and a jaunty wave as he sailed out the penthouse door, leaving appointments to be broken and myriad apologies to be made."

Labor of love. That's what building the Tancook Whaler had been, for Marcus and me. For nearly two years, we'd worked on that boat . . . together.

I pictured Chris out there at the farm with Marcus, the two of them working happily side by side beneath a hot sun. And Chris's froufrou mother, trotting out to the fields in a pink and white frock, with tall, cold glasses of lemonade for the field hands.

"Shit," I said.

"Presumably, that's part of it." Tark attempted a smile. "The garden, I mean."

I drummed my fingers on the arm of the chair. "Christopher has really changed things, hasn't he?"

"I warned you that he would."

I just hadn't known how far Marcus would go to make his son happy. I *should* have known. But sometimes I close my eyes to things, look the other way, until reality smacks me in the face and yells, "Wake up, wake up! Life is passing you by!"

"Thanks for not wanting to tell me."

We were silent, listening to the low whine of the jet engines. The plane hit an air pocket and bounced. My nerves didn't even jump. I was numb.

So what was all that with Mac about, my nagging conscience said, *if this can hurt so much?*

I wasn't sure. I sometimes behave like that—with another man—and ask questions later. Samved says I'm covering all bases, so I won't be left out in the cold, alone, if the relationship I'm in goes sour. He says it's a common enough reaction when you've grown up in an alcoholic home and feel abandoned all the time.

He also says I've got to grow up someday, and put all that aside.

Many minutes later, Tark spoke again. "I've got no quarrel with Marc's feelings for Christopher. It's made him a better person, in a lot of ways. But she's not right for him, Jess. You are."

"Have you and Marcus talked about her? Has he told you for a fact that they're getting married?"

He shook his head. "You know Marcus. In all the time he's known you, he's never once talked to me about his relationship with you."

Nor had he talked to me—except once—about the bimbo. It was a code Marcus had, something his mother, a good, Italian-Catholic woman, had raised him with: You don't talk about a woman you're with; to do so is disrespectful.

So Marcus, who scammed all day to relieve business cronies of their goods and cash by almost any illegal means that worked —and who boasted of it freely—became an altar boy about his other life, the one that took place between the sheets at night.

A strange dichotomy—but one I understood. When you're raised Catholic, you're taught that women are the Virgin Mary here on earth. It's verboten for a woman to smoke, drink, or swear. It is okay to fuck, of course—so long as she propagates and populates.

Marcus had done his share to populate, with Christopher. The propagate part would by necessity include marriage—in the Church. Marcus and the bimbo would go to Mass together, they'd be a stunning couple there in the front, paid-for pew. He'd become like that mobster in New Jersey, or wherever it was . . . the one all his neighbors loved because he gave to the Church and to the poor (who shouldn't even be spoken of in the same breath, since the Church and the poor would never be one and the same).

I realized suddenly that my bitter thoughts were raising hell with my stomach lining.

"There's one other thing, Jess. . . ." Tark squirmed in his chair, looking more uneasy than ever.

I sighed. "Spill it."

"Alfred says that Marcus wants to see you. Specifically, at the office. He wants to talk."

My blood ran cold. And yes, it does happen that way, sometimes. Given enough trepidation, the blood becomes ice water. "He said that, precisely—*at the office?*"

Tark looked miserable.

We both knew what it meant. Marcus chose to meet with people at his office when he had something unpleasant to tell them. When he fired them, or dropped them from his life in some way.

So I'd lost him, then. It was definite now.

I fought back tears. It was happening even faster than I'd expected. I wasn't prepared.

"Do you think he knows I've been seeing Mac Devlin?" Marcus had overlooked my brief fling last year in California, but even he had his limits. Had I pushed him into an early decision about Chris's mom, with that night in the Thousand Islands with Mac? Had he somehow found out about it?

"I don't know, Jesse. I don't understand Marcus at all these days. I think sometimes that he doesn't tell me things because he knows I'll tell you."

"Would you?" My life had turned to quicksand beneath my feet. I suddenly wasn't even sure about Tark. "Would you tell me if you knew something?"

"Hey." Tark drew a handkerchief out of his pocket and leaned forward, dabbing with his big, sensible hand at my cheek. "What's this? Tears, from an outlaw?"

"Never mind!" I took the handkerchief and blew my nose. "I'm a big girl, I can take it. It's just hard to get used to."

Tark was angry, though—whether more with himself for breaking the news, or with Marcus, wasn't clear. "When we get back—" he said darkly.

"When we get back," I finished, "I'll march into that goddamned penthouse office of his, and knock Marcus Fucking Andrelli on his ass!"

Tark smiled, then, obviously relieved that I wasn't going to fall apart while we were trapped together in an airplane cabin the size of a millionaire's bathtub. "That's the spirit."

"Absolutely," came another voice from the area of the rest room. "Fuck 'em all roundly," my favorite aunt said.

———

Mom and Charlie led us a merry chase, but we caught up with our quarry—more or less—in the end.

A blast of heat struck as we stepped off the plane. "Dry heat," I'd heard people say about the Arizona desert. "You don't feel it that much."

It was a lie. The place was an oven. In the few minutes it took to walk from the plane to the waiting black Mercedes that Tark's man had brought, I longed with all my heart to be back by the Genesee River, the lakes, the green, green trees and fresh spring rain.

Bobby Dell—Tark's man in Phoenix—was dressed in jeans, boots, and a blue plaid cotton shirt. He met us with a drawl, a tall, booted swagger, and the news that Mom and Charlie had checked out of the Camelback Inn. "They're down at a ranch south of Tucson. Moved in, bag and baggage, 'bout an hour ago."

"Must have heard we were coming." I glanced at Tark. "But how?"

He shook his head. He and Bobby had worked together often, he'd told me, when Tark was Marcus's bodyguard. Bobby had been assigned to the Andrelli Enterprises Southwest office eight years ago, and kept a confidential eye on things for Marcus, from San Diego to Dallas.

"He's picked up a drawl here," Tark had told me, "and he thinks he's the Sundance Kid now. But Bobby's loyal. There's not a chance he'll talk."

Still, someone had talked, if Mom and Charlie were on the move.

"What about Devlin and Lang?"

"They landed a few hours ago," Bobby said. "Refueled and took off again, but I think I can track them down."

We climbed into the Mercedes; me up front, Tark and Aunt

Edna in the back. Bobby drove, hunkering over the wheel and riding the Mercedes' saddle at 80, 90 mph. After a while we branched off from Interstate 10, and our scout's sharp blue eyes scanned the two-lane highway constantly—for possible trouble, I supposed. But the road was smooth and empty; I hadn't seen this much open space in my entire life. Mountains rose on either side, changing color as we moved, in the manner of certain art. Grays became cocoa, then brilliant salmon, fading to slate blue as evening approached. The word "ranch" had scared up pictures of whirling dust and horses, of creaking leather, and sand in the teeth. I have to admit I've never much cared for all that—never longed to play "cowboy" as a kid, in spite of my hapless misnomer. As much as I wanted to see Mom, I wasn't looking forward to our destination.

But the Mercedes was large, comfortable, and air-conditioned. A digital readout on the dash showed the outside temperature to be hovering at 105 in Phoenix, then climbing as we neared Tucson and points south. On the tape deck played the Eagles' greatest hits. Don Henley sang my latest self-appointed theme song—one I'd been playing a lot lately at home. "Desperado." Bobby, his tan cowboy hat tilted over his forehead, was tapping on the wheel and humming along. As the melancholy prose continued, Bobby broke out in a deep bass voice with the lyrics. His drawl was richer than Henley's—the husky rumble of his voice making it too bittersweet, too trenchant.

When the tape was on its second turnaround, I asked Bobby if he'd mind if I played something else. I was weary of hearing how I'd better let somebody love me "before it's too late." Bobby glanced at me in surprise. "Sorry, Ms. James. I thought you'd like it. It's Mr. Andrelli's favorite song . . . plays it all the time when he's out here."

I sat there staring at him, my mouth working. Then I stared at the tape deck . . . and finally, at the road.

" 'Least, it used to be," Bobby said.

He popped the tape, and we were left in silence. We wound around a mountain and through a pass that was straight from an old movie. I imagined Apaches on either side, poised to descend upon their trapped victims—the greedy, pioneer land-grabbers. All the old clichés came back, and my scalp prickled. I wondered where I'd gotten those pictures from, since I hadn't seen many westerns. Then I remembered that Pop used to watch *Rawhide*. I'd sit on the floor by his knee and watch, too. It was the only way, sometimes, to be near Pop. I'd shared his attention with cowboys, Indians, and multiple six-packs of Genny beer.

By the time we reached our destination, the temperature had landed at an astonishing 112. I stepped out of the now-dusty car, nearly fainted from the furnace blast, and almost immediately began hallucinating. Like in the old Foreign Legion movies, I was seeing a bright green oasis with splashing fountains, acres of cacti, a swimming pool, a Jacuzzi. . . .

I pinched myself and found I wasn't imagining things, after all. We were at the "ranch" that Charlie and Mom had moved into, according to Bobby—and there wasn't a horse, nor a dust bowl, in sight.

The house was sprawling, contemporary, and gleaming—a white adobe and glass castle on a sloping, cactus-studded hill. Its floor-to-ceiling windows winked with bright pink and azure in a slowly setting sun. To the side of the house was the pool I'd seen, a long turquoise rectangle bordered by a natural rock formation. On a deck slightly above it, a Jacuzzi. Behind the house, a higher hill rose. The sky beyond it was a Hollywood backdrop, so blue it might have been splashed there by a child with a paint box and a new sable brush. Three-armed cacti studded the hill, their green in dramatic relief against the improbable sky. The air, as the sun dipped lower, had mercifully begun to cool. I looked at the sky, and drew in a breath.

Wasn't it Edna St. Vincent Millay who wrote: *Above the world is stretched the sky—no higher than the soul is high*? In "Renascence," I think. My heart expanded to meet that tented turquoise sky. It was streaked with colors I'd only dreamed of while drunk . . . old-gold, rose-arbor green . . . and changing, parrotlike tints that one only finds—I'd thought—in some exotic jungle, or perhaps beneath the sea. It was almost too much—an embarrassment of riches—when I realized that from horizon to horizon stars had appeared, so close and so brilliant, you could almost feel their beams pierce your heart.

I felt a nudge at my elbow. Tark was saying, "You all right?"

I nodded, embarrassed. I hadn't quoted anything aloud, had I? Christ! I was beginning to wish spring would get its visit the hell over with and head on home.

Bobby got our meager luggage, and I followed Tark up a path of finely crushed white stone, past scarlet flowers and irrigation water trickling happily between stone fountains and man-made brooks. Lights were on in the house, as well as throughout the grounds. I hoped at first we'd been seen arriving, and that Mom would come running down the path, throw her arms around me, and cry, "What on earth are you doing here, Jesse?"

But no one came running, and no one answered the bell when we rang. It tinkled like wind chimes, clear as the stars that were popping out now by the thousands while we waited.

Finally Tark said impatiently, "Isn't there some kind of Rule of the West—something about hospitality on the trail?" He turned the knob of the massive Spanish door and twisted it. It opened, and we stepped in.

Chapter 25

▼ ▼ ▼

"Anybody here?" Tark called.

Silence.

We stood in a blue-tiled foyer, with touches of white. White roses on a softly tinted blue and white table, watercolors of southwestern scenes in pastel tints of blue, white and peach . . .

"Lights are on a timer," Bobby said, behind us. "I'll check upstairs, and you down? See if anybody's here."

Tark nodded, and Bobby took the stairs two at a time, as if he knew precisely where he was going. Aunt Edna looked at me sharply, then followed him. Tark and I entered the living room. It was built on a grand scale, with glittering curtains of glass overlooking the desert and hills. The color scheme was blue. Blue was everywhere, from turquoise to slate . . . and again, in here, there were pinpoints of white.

Tark and I checked out the rest of the downstairs. There were two bedrooms, two baths. Each bedroom had a wall of glass looking out to a lush desert garden, and beyond that, the hills. The huge baths had windows over each marble tub. Decor throughout was southwestern, but not in that overdone way that's now a cliché. The blue and aqua color theme continued.

There was a movie once, *A Man Called Peter.* It was about Peter Marshall, who became known as "Minister to the Senate." Or maybe it was to the President; I tend not to remember details about religion these days. But in the movie, Peter Marshall surrounded himself with the color blue. Supposedly, he did this in real life too.

There was only one person I knew who did the same.

We wound up our search in the kitchen, and found no one else in the house. But in the bedrooms, we'd come across Mom's and Charlie's clothes. I had recognized a couple of Charlie's shirts—and Mom's yellow robe, the one I'd looked for and not found at the inn in the Thousand Islands. For the first time, I felt a certain sureness that Mom and Charlie were really here.

But why had they come here? And for that matter, where the hell were they?

Bobby appeared as we stood in the kitchen, wordlessly looking around. Tark leaned against a counter, arms folded: his thinking position. His cool gray eyes fixed on Bobby.

"Nobody up there," Bobby said. He looked questioningly at Tark—who shook his head.

Bobby turned to me. "Your aunt is making some phone calls. I put her in a guest room. Would you like some food?" He'd removed his cowboy hat. His thick blond hair was ruffled, and that, along with his shy smile, gave him a boyish, innocent look.

Which neither Tark nor I bought. We both gave a restrained nod. "Sure." We watched as Bobby took wrapped plates from the fridge, along with a couple of beers and a pitcher of juice. He moved easily from fridge to counter to sink, putting sandwiches together with bread that his hand had unhesitant reached into a cupboard for.

"This juice for me?" I crossed to a square, blue and white table and lifted the pitcher.

"Well, yeah, I thought—" Bobby shrugged. "There's more beer, if you want it."

"No . . . this is fine."

Tark's eyes met mine again. Bobby caught it and shrugged again. He had the grace to look awkward. "Marcus said to make everybody comfortable. And to get plenty of juice in for you. That's all I know."

"This is Andrelli's place?" Tark asked the question, but he'd already figured out the answer, same as I. "It seems there are a lot of things lately that I don't know about. How long's he owned it, Bobby?"

"A couple of years." Bobby took a knife from a wooden block and cut the sandwiches in half, putting them on thick turquoise plates. "I don't think anybody knew, until lately, except me. He told me not to talk about it."

As Tark had said earlier, Bobby was loyal. But—to Marcus. The only question now was: How did that apply to us? Were we pawns on this chess board, or bishops, or . . . no, certainly not kings. In Marcus's world, he was the only king.

"I need some air," I said.

I went out through double glass doors to a terrace—*patio*, I guessed it was called here. It had red clay tiles and spanned the length of the house, overlooking the same mountains, valley, and—from this angle—the narrow, private road we had just traveled. Marcus's southwestern castle was effectively isolated from the rest of the world, just as his cabin was in Irondequoit—and the farmhouse he'd bought for Christopher and his mom. It was a requirement of the kind of life Marcus had made for himself, this kind of protective isolation. One never knew when some jealous Family "cousin" from the Old Mob might lob a grenade into a bedroom, or spray AK-47 bullets along one's dining room table.

I thought about how far apart Marcus and I were now. It had begun last summer, actually, and despite the fact that we'd worked on the Whaler and spent weekends together since then, he still wasn't telling me things. I'd be going along, thinking everything was all right—that we had an "understanding" of sorts. And then whammo, I'd find out there were secrets. Things going on that affected me somehow, that he should have told me about but was silent on.

The sky was dark, now, the stars bright but cold. I felt alone, suddenly, stranded on a continent of my own making. *We create the kind of life we want,* Samved had told me, time and time again. *Often, we don't realize it until much later . . . but that doesn't change the fact that we've manifested precisely what we want.*

I heard boots on the tile, and turned slightly. Bobby stood beside me, hands in his jean pockets. "I guess you're upset. I didn't tell him you were coming . . . but he knew."

"Marcus?"

Bobby nodded. We looked out over the dark outline of mountains. "Anything I can do for you?" he asked finally.

I'd never met Bobby Dell before today. I wondered how far his apparent "friendliness" would extend. "You could tell me what's going on. Why are my mom and Charlie Browne here? And Mac Devlin, and Lang? Where are they?"

Bobby rested a booted foot on the low stone wall that surrounded the patio. He gazed off at the hills and said, "I don't really know. Not exactly, that is."

"C'mon, Bobby." I looked around us, at the sweeping spread, and made a gesture to include it. "Marcus obviously trusts you."

"To an extent. Much as he trusts anyone, I suppose. So—I know your mother and Browne are here, along with this pilot, Devlin, and Lang—and a guy named Sam Garner. But the only reason I know is because Marcus gave me descriptions and told me to keep an eye out for them—and on them. He said they were comin' here, and he told me you and Tark were comin'. My job is to let him know what goes down."

I looked at Bobby's wide-open face and candid blue eyes and wanted to believe his story. "Did he send all of them down here?"

"I can't tell you that. I just don't know."

I looked back into the kitchen. "Aunt Edna still upstairs?"

He nodded. "Taking a shower."

"Where's Tark?"

"In the living room, making phone calls." Bobby peered into the distance. "And that, if I don't miss my guess, will be company."

Headlights announced a vehicle winding along the road, perhaps ten miles away. Bobby went back inside, and I stood watching as the lights grew larger. The speeding vehicle bounced over ruts the Mercedes had taken smoothly, and when it finally jerked to a stop at the side of the house, below me, I saw it was a Jeep Cherokee—dusty black in the glow from ground-hugging landscape lights.

From it stepped Mac Devlin . . . and Charlie. They looked up and saw me standing there. Their clothes—jeans, work shirts, and boots—were as weary as their expressions.

I waited for one more figure to step from the jeep. When it didn't, I hugged myself against the chill that swept over my heart, and mouthed to Charlie: "Where's Mom?"

He shook his head, the lines deepening in his face. After a few murmured words to Mac, he came up the path toward the patio as if he were meeting his executioner.

Mac watched him, met my eyes again, then looked away. Holding an arm against his waist as if it hurt, he took the other path—away from both of us.

———

"Where is she?" I said.

Charlie stood a couple of feet from me, arms hanging limply at his sides. I'd never seen him look so defeated. I was prepared to hear him lie, but he didn't. "Garner has her," he said.

I wasn't even angry—there was too much fear in my heart. "Why?" My jaw was rigid; the word barely came out.

"Insurance. I'm certain he won't hurt her."

"Insurance against *what?*"

"Not against. For. He wants to be sure we'll do what he wants."

I tried to control my voice, but I was near the edge. *"Which is?"*

Charlie sighed. "He wants Mac to fly a delivery of medical supplies to a village in Colombia."

"That's all?"

"Supposedly."

"Why doesn't he fly them himself?"

"Apparently, there's a price on his head. Garner was nearly killed there last month. He got away, but all the landing strips in the area are being watched."

"The cargo is drugs? Illegal drugs?"

"According to Garner, no."

I gave a snort. "You believe him?"

"Ask Mac Devlin. He flew the supplies down here in Marcus Andrelli's jet."

"From Rochester? Him and Lang?"

Charlie nodded. "Devlin swears there's nothing but legal drugs—medicines—in the lot."

"Maybe they're stolen, then."

"Mac says he's got genuine bills of lading. Receipts."

"Where have you and Mac been? Where did all this happen?"

"Your mother and I met Devlin and Lang earlier today, when they landed at a strip about twenty miles from here. It's the one Andrelli uses when he comes here. I helped Mac and Lang transfer the cargo into Garner's plane."

"Is that where Mom is now?" I had to sit on the wall; my legs had gone weak.

"Yes."

"But why you? What did you and Mom come here for?"

"I owed Devlin a favor, from years ago. He asked me to connect him with some people, to find out what Garner was really up to."

"Did you?"

"Yes. But we never came up with anything to contradict Garner's story. He took a job to deliver relief medical supplies to this village—he claims—and he needs the money from it to pay somebody off. That *may* be drug-related; he seems desperate enough about it. But the rest of his story checks out with my source in that area. Garner was hired to do this job, and there's big money in flying cargo down there because of the danger—especially with this recent flare-up of trouble in Colombia."

I rubbed my face, and rested it for a moment in my hands. Then I looked tiredly at Charlie. "Did you check out this cargo yourself?"

"As much as possible, in the short time I had before Garner pulled a gun on us and grabbed Kate."

I pictured it—the lonely airstrip, nothing but coyotes as witnesses. My naive, sometimes featherbrained mom, with a gun at her head. "Why did he do it?"

"Devlin was still refusing to fly down there. He knows Garner best, and saw some kind of hidden trouble in it. I figured his instincts were right. I backed him up, and when I told Garner we weren't going any farther than we already had, he lost it."

"Where is Mom now?"

"There's a small communications shack at the airstrip. Not much there except a phone, and gas tanks for refueling. Garner's holding her in the shack. Mac is supposed to take off from there at dawn, and when he gets to this village, somebody'll call Garner and let him know the job's done. He'll release Kate to us then."

"Oh, right—just like that! A complainant to a kidnapping?"

"I—"

"Wait a minute, let me get this straight. Sam Garner is holding my mother—your wife—out in the desert, in some miserable shed in the middle of nowhere—and you and Mac together couldn't figure out a way to get her out?"

Charlie passed a hand over his eyes, then clenched a fist and stared at it miserably. "You think we didn't try? Devlin is inside now, cleaning up a gunshot wound."

I remembered the way Mac had favored his arm. "Must not be much of a wound. He's walking."

"Jess . . . please stop." Charlie lowered himself heavily on the stone wall, his handsome features tired and haggard. His crisp silver hair was dull with sand and dirt. "I could use your help on this, now that you're here."

"God damn you, Charlie! If you hadn't been so busy playing games from the first— What the hell was that business at the inn, up in the Thousand Islands? Do you know that woman is dead? The one who was pretending to be Mom?"

His shoulders sagged. "Yes. I know."

"Well, who the hell was she?"

"We were being followed, and I was worried about Kate getting hurt. I hired those people as decoys, to distract the person following—"

"Charlie, it was *Lang* following you—for *me!*"

"No. I knew about Lang, almost from the first. This was a whole other deal. Nothing to do with the trouble between Devlin and Garner."

"Oh, Christ. It's that old shit, isn't it?"

"What old shit?"

"The *shoes*, Charlie! The goddamned shoes."

"I don't know what you're talking about," he said flatly.

"The shoes . . . the codes . . . the lining. What does 4-0-2-2 mean?"

Surprise entered the cool blue eyes. And speculation.

"There was an alligator shoe on my living room floor," I told him. "After you left. I had it x-rayed."

One thing about my new stepfather, he recovers quickly. Charlie threw his head back and laughed. "You actually had one of my shoes *x-rayed?*"

"It's not just any old shoe, Charlie. It's one of those things you get in a package with a plain brown wrapper, no return address—"

Charlie put an arm around me, hugging me to his side. "Jesse, Jesse . . . you do have a grand imagination."

Someone else might have seen his gesture as impulsive. I saw it for what it was, and pushed against him, backing away. "That doesn't work anymore," I said softly.

"What—flattery?" He was still smiling.

"Distraction. You can't distract me with charm anymore, Charlie. Not with my mother in the hands of some killer, and not when it's because of you—"

Another voice entered the scene. "Killer! Some killer's got Kate?"

Aunt Edna had come from the kitchen and was standing behind Charlie. Her mouth was open; an unlit cigarette stuck to her bottom lip. She grabbed it and crushed it in her fist. "What are you talking about? What's happened to my sister?" Aunt Edna jammed her hands on her hips and stood there like a fiery avenger—her carroty hair sticking out in every direction.

Charlie looked between the two of us—accusing bookends —and sighed. He began his wretched tale again.

Chapter 26

▼ ▼ ▼

We had come inside, finally, and were having a powwow with Tark, Mac, and Bobby, in the living room. Aunt Edna had laid into Charlie about not taking care of Mom, and he'd had the grace to look humbled for another forty seconds. Now he was anxious and pacing, discarding ideas as fast as we'd come up with them. Tark stood by the fireplace, arms folded, listening. Mac sat in a chair, his long legs stretched out before him. The bandaged arm was held stiffly against his chest as he rubbed it, and from his gray eyes came that probing stare. We hadn't talked; my mother's life was in Mac Devlin's hands, and what did I really know about him—putting that night in the Thousand Islands aside? How far, to help someone I loved, might Devlin be expected to go?

"The shack is out in the open," Charlie said. "Nothing around it—no other buildings, no trees, nothing larger than tumbleweed and cholla for miles around. And Garner's in this dried-up water tower that hasn't been used since the old railroad days. He's got a two-way radio, the very latest in cellular phones, and a bolt-action Remington that's equipped with a scope for night vision. Given that, and how bright it is out there tonight, he's in a perfect position to see anything that moves in the surrounding valley. There's absolutely no chance we can sneak up on him, not on a night like this."

The tall range of windows revealed a moon now, casting far too much brutal, shadow-free light everywhere.

"The man must have an excellent income," Charlie continued. "He's even outfitted that old Beech with up-to-date technology."

"Sam always was into gadgets," Mac said. "But maybe we can use that . . ." He lapsed into a thoughtful silence.

"Garner's plan," Charlie added, "is that when Mac makes the drop in Colombia, his man down there will call and confirm it. That's when he'll let Kate go." Charlie's ordinarily husky voice became thin and brittle. "I've thought about calling Garner. I could insist on coming back—staying with Kate until it's over. Then I could distract him, while you—"

"If he wouldn't let you stay in the area before," Tark countered, "why would that change now?"

"If I tell him Mac won't make the delivery otherwise . . ."

Bobby spoke. "Tark is right. Garner holds all the cards—and besides, he'd only suspect what you were up to."

"At least this way," Tark added, "he thinks he's got the upper hand."

"Well, dammit, as long as he's got Kate, he *has!* I've got to somehow turn that around."

"If we wait until Mac takes off at dawn," Tark said reasonably, "he'll be watching the plane, distracted—"

"On the contrary," Charlie interrupted. "He'll be expecting us then."

"I agree," Bobby said. "Anybody who's used to this desert, the way Garner is . . ." His background check on Garner had shown that he'd bought his ranch near the Mexico border several years before, on arriving in Arizona.

"By the way," I asked Mac, "where's Lang? I understand he flew down here with you."

"Lang's on a fact-finding mission," Charlie answered. "When we hear from him, we'll know better how to proceed. And Marcus wants to be in on it."

"Oh? How much of this does Marcus know?"

"I told him about your mother," Tark said, "over the phone, a little while ago."

"And?"

"And he said to do everything necessary to ensure her safety."

"Generous. And how like Marcus, to handle it all from his ivory tower."

My bitter tone reaped a scowl from Aunt Edna.

"Marcus is doing everything possible from his end," Tark said loyally. "He's got Lang in Phoenix, meeting with a source from this branch of Greater Pharmaceutical, the company Marcus just took over. When he's heard from Lang, he'll call us."

"Lang is finding out more about this cargo of Garner's," Charlie explained.

"Marcus sent Lang down here?" I turned to Mac again. "That's why you had the Andrelli jet?"

"Part of it."

"Marcus has some other reason to want to be in on this?"

Silence.

"Dammit, are you going to tell me, or do I have to drag it out of you?"

Tark's answer was calm as he glanced at his watch. "Hang in, Jess. Marcus should be calling any minute."

There didn't seem much else to say, so we all kind of sat around having private thoughts. An unlikely bunch—the two mob men, Mac, Charlie, Aunt Edna, and me. Aunt Edna was still glowering, and I finally broke the silence after a similar scowl in Mac's direction. "How do we know you're not just in on this whole thing with Garner?"

Mac was clearly offended. The gray stare became cool and distant as he looked away. I remembered Samved telling me once that Scorpio Eagles, when insulted, will turn you off faster than a fireman at a leaking gas-cock. They may seem happy-go-lucky, all smiles, unshakably self-confident—but they're not, not always. It's a mask. Underneath, Scorpios have sensitive nerve endings, and you never know, when you open your mouth, if you're going to bring on that look of displeasure and be frozen into something resembling a smelly cod fillet.

I had to admit, this looked like a typical Eagle to me. Mac sat there rubbing his bandaged forearm, yet poised and cool, gazing at a distant wall. This fine-feathered friend didn't even bother to answer my question. Forget cod—I might have been one of any thousand worms in a boneyard.

When the phone rang, we all jumped.

Tark was the first to reach it. "Marcus?" He held the receiver to his ear. "Right." He punched a button on the phone, and my sometime lover's voice came in, clipped and solid over the speaker.

"I just heard from Lang. The cargo is medical supplies, just as Garner said. The twist is that they're generic drugs that were supposed to have been burned or dumped by Greater Pharmaceutical a couple of years ago. They're all outdated—expired—and some are simply useless, others bad. Both are downright dangerous, or could be. Once introduced into the black market in Central America, they could kill people who need the active drug to save their lives."

I interrupted, my voice laced with suspicion. "Marcus? How long have you known this was going on?"

A sigh. And a pencil tapping. "Hello to you, too, Jess. Cordial as always, I see. Well . . . I've suspected, since shortly after I acquired Greater Pharmaceutical, that someone in the company was pushing these drugs instead of destroying them. Selling them to the black market in third world countries, and paying big money to have them flown there. It was all in the paperwork, if you knew what to look for. I've had Lang working on it at this end, where the drugs originate—but this final piece with Sam Garner was what I'd needed all along. So when Charlie came to me for help, it seemed to our mutual benefit. Lang's now found someone in the branch office there in Phoenix, who—with some healthy monetary persuasion—was willing to talk facts and figures."

"Is there some way to stop these supplies from getting into the mainstream," Mac asked, "once I drop them?" He had begun to pace, flexing the wounded arm, making it work despite the pain that crossed his face.

"Negative," Marcus said. "According to Lang's source, Garner will have his people right there when you land. It's why he wants you going out at dawn, instead of now. By then he'll have everyone in place to move the drugs into the villages quickly, and they'll simply disappear. Into the melting pot, so to speak. The problem is that there's so little tracking of these things in the outer villages. There are paraprofessionals working down there—volunteers—and they're grateful for whatever they can get. No one asks questions when medicines come in that can save lives, even if they're from questionable sources."

"Who are the buyers of this particular cargo?" I asked. "Where's the money coming from?"

"Honest clinicians, for the most part. They're backed by private parties—well-to-do businessmen and philanthropists— who finance these things with all good intent and purpose."

"You can't just get word to them that this is happening, so they won't use these drugs?"

Marcus answered. "That's what your stepfather is doing."

I looked at Charlie. "I have some contacts down there," he explained. "The problem is that once the bad drugs are mixed in with the good, the only thing they can do is stop using *all* of them. People will die, either way."

"Can't we deliver other drugs—good ones, that are marked as such—and make sure they *only* use those?"

"I'm working on that," Charlie answered. "And with Marcus's help, we could get some down there pretty fast. But there's a relatively new viral strain in Colombia, in some of the villages, and the one drug that will work is in short supply. They've got some down there now—but again, if Mac makes this drop and the expired drugs are mixed in . . ."

"The virus attacks children, for the most part," Marcus added.

We were all silent. I studied my boots awhile, and when I looked up finally, I wasn't at all surprised to see that all eyes were on me.

"What you're telling me," I said slowly, "is that there's no way Mac can make this drop without putting children's lives in danger. And the only alternative is to let Mom die—"

Charlie said angrily, "That's not going to happen!"

"No?" I was on my feet. "Well, why don't you big-shot men tell me just what *will* happen? I'm sure you have a plan, all you Monday-morning quarterbacks. Now that my mother's wonderful new husband has gotten her into this mess, let's see you get her goddamned out!"

The strategy meeting was over, and I didn't much like the outcome. Tark and Charlie had insisted on giving me nothing but scut work to do. Marcus, they said, didn't want me involved in any real danger.

That was the thing that pissed me off these days about Marcus. When I first met him a couple of years ago, he had welcomed my help with things. Now he was trusting me less and less to protect myself. Come to think of it, it had been months since he'd repeated his offer to put me to work as his bodyguard.

Aunt Edna was pacing and smoking in a small garden area

next to the living room. Mac and I were sitting on the patio wall. The night air was cold and sharp, the stars like cutout openings into some fantasy world.

"I remember Mom sticking those glow-in-the-dark stars on my ceiling once when I was little," I said. "She had come home after a double shift at the greasy spoon where she cooked and waited on tables, and it was one of the few times I saw her on a tear—so angry, and so driven, she couldn't stop moving."

I picked absently at a flowering shrub, pulling a small red bloom off and holding it to my nose. The scent was overly sweet, like the cheap perfume I'd given Mom at Christmas as a kid. *Evening in Paris.* When I was twelve or so, I'd gone through her drawers once, looking for a scarf, and found four or five of those blue glass bottles, unopened. "I'm saving them," Mom had explained later, soothingly, "for something special."

"That night with the stars?" I went on. "Mom got home sometime around two, three in the morning. She yanked a kitchen chair into my room, banging it against the hallway walls. We were in a kind of 'railroad' apartment then, all the rooms in a row from front to back, with a long narrow hall connecting to each. I could hear her coming a long way off, and at first I thought it was Pop on one of his drunks, stumbling and bumping along.

"When Mom got to my room she threw the light switch, and the ceiling bulb came on. I sat up and opened my eyes, but couldn't see a thing until they adjusted to the light. I mumbled something like 'What's going on?' and rubbed my eyes.

" 'I've had it!' Mom said. I remember the phrase because it was 'in' at the time, and Mom had never been 'in' before. She'd been picking things up, though, at work, and the strangest phrases would tumble out of her mouth and into my ears. Things like 'Go with the flow, Jesse,' when I'd tell her some teacher was on my case at school."

She had stood in my room like one of the Furies—hands on

hips, her stained yellow waitress uniform rumpled and sallow, like her tired face. Mom's hair was a glossy dark brown, then, her eyes a fiery green.

" 'I am sick to death of this life!' Mom said. 'I am sick to death of never having a dream. If I die tomorrow, Jesse, I'm going to leave you with one last thought: Don't be stupid like me! Live life while you can!'

"It was winter—the desolate days in Rochester, and it was dark still, not even dawn. I listened to Mom and realized the gravity of her standing in my room, waking me up at this hour. My heart felt all funny and wobbly. I said, 'Mom . . . what's wrong? Are you sick?' What I wanted to say, but was afraid to, was, 'Are you *dying?*' "

I looked at Mac, and wondered if he was listening. I didn't know why I was even telling him all this. Words just kept tumbling from my mouth.

"Even then, I was expecting something awful to happen all the time. I remember looking at Mom, and seeing from the sides of my mind that room—and it was like my eyes had been opened for the first time. I saw the wallpaper by my bed, so old it had lost most of its original gray print and was stained and peeling. I'd tried to paint it one day, thinking I might surprise Mom. But the paint had soaked into the walls. They were too old and porous. It was ugly green paint, anyway—something I'd found along the street on trash day.

"So anyway, there's Mom—and she's got this thin package in her hand, like a plastic envelope. And she climbs up on that chair and starts pulling things out of this package and sticking them on the ceiling. I didn't know what the hell they were, and I thought she'd gone nuts. I tried to talk her down. She ignored me.

" 'We may not have much money for Christmas,' she said. 'But I can give you a dream! I can teach you how to *dream,* dammit, I can do *that!*'

"Then she told me she'd lost her job, that they were hiring someone younger—with Christmas only three weeks away."

I could still see Mom on that chair, her hair straggly and her lipstick bitten off. In that awful light from the ceiling she looked a hundred years old. Funny . . . she must have been only in her thirties then. And she looks younger, actually, today.

"So anyway, Mom had stopped at an all-night drugstore on the way home. And instead of the triple six-pack of beer Pop always bought when he was fired, she'd gotten these stars. I ended up standing on my headboard and helping her stick them on in the corners of the ceiling. When we finally finished and turned the lights off, the whole ceiling glowed . . . like this." I looked up at the black sky, studded with pinpoints of silver. And remembered the feeling of awe and wonder that had swept over me at the sight of those phosphorescent ceiling stars. "Once, when Pop lost a job," I said, "he tried to kill himself. Mom wasn't like that; she'd fight back from some level when things went bad—even if only in her head."

I got up from the wall and began to walk toward the jeep. Mac walked beside me, his good arm around my shoulders, and when I got there I turned to him and said, "I want the keys to this thing. And I want you to tell me how to get to that airstrip. I may not be able to get near the place, but I want to see it." My voice was unsteady. "I want to at least feel that I'm near Mom now. Before all the shit comes down."

Mac walked me around to the passenger seat, helped me in, then circled the jeep again. He slid behind the wheel, pulling out keys and sticking them in the ignition.

"We'll go together," he said.

The floor of a valley lay before us. Using a back road that Mac remembered from when he'd flown in earlier, we had coasted the Cherokee in most of the way. Leaving it far behind, we had then made a careful, nearly silent approach to the shack, and were now far above it. One window revealed an inside light, while spotlights—front and back—lit up a circle of perhaps 150 yards in diameter around the shack. Just within that circle of light was the old water tower where Sam Garner supposedly waited. We couldn't see him—but hadn't expected to. "He'll be out of sight," Mac had told me. "Sam always covers his back."

On a long, dusty airstrip stood Garner's Beech 18 cargo plane—side by side with Marcus's private jet. The moon glanced off their hulls, brilliant on the shiny finish of the jet with its blue *Andrelli Enterprises* logo—duller on the Beech. Mac had told me that the Beech was a guts-and-glory plane, all thunder and smoke . . . an old gal, but decked out inside with the latest finery, instrument-wise. Sam Garner's livelihood, apparently, depended on his getting in and out of tight places, and on being completely independent of any ground/air support.

We were sitting in a crevice between two boulders the size of my kitchen at home. Gentle slopes at our backs kept us from being silhouetted by the lighter sky. "I don't see how we can get any closer," Mac said. "With this moon, he'd spot us before we were off the hill."

My nails bit into my palms. The valley was unrelieved by shadows, except for the occasional tumbleweed and clumps of cholla.

"Be careful," Mac had said, leading me away from patches of the nasty stuff. "If there's a purpose for cholla, I can't for the life of me think what that is. It's the damndest, most painful cactus around."

I looked below, and wanted to shove whole fields of cholla down Sam Garner's throat. I wanted to run down there and break into that shack, and just grab Mom up and hustle her home. She was so close, and yet—with Sam Garner in that tower waiting to pick off any moving thing—impossibly far away.

Mac went on, then, with the quiet conversation we'd begun

to pass time, a few minutes before. "In Nam, Sam began moving drugs. He pulled a double cross on the wrong drug lord, whose son turned up dead. Sam ended up with a price on his head. Same as now. He ran off to Central America, leaving me holding the partnership alone. I heard that Sam started out down there flying weapons to South America. Then, on the back-haul, he'd load up on drugs—bring them into the States, either over the border here and in California, or from the Caribbean islands into Florida. If Sam's got a ranch down here now, it's almost certainly a base for that sort of thing—not a retirement home."

"Was he flying for the CIA, a kind of latter-day Air America company in Central America?"

"Not Sam. He was always in it for the bucks, and the private drug lords paid more than the CIA. Air America was pretty wild, but it was tame stuff in Nam, compared to what Sam was involved in there."

"What about you?"

He laughed softly. "Believe it or not, I flew honest cargo. I liked the excitement, the physical risks of flyin' a chopper through the jungle or over enemy fire. But legal risks were something else—it just wasn't in me. Sometimes I think—"

He hesitated.

"What? What do you sometimes think?"

"Oh . . . Mariana. I've always wondered why she got involved with Sam Garner, down in Colombia. Couldn't she see through somebody like him?"

Good question. Why are women sometimes drawn to men outside the law—or even simply off-the-wall?

"What kind of person was she?"

"Mariana? She was good. I don't know any other way to describe it. When she was growing up, she did everything her parents told her to do. She was in by whatever curfew they set, and in school, she never caused trouble, got straight *A*'s. Her teachers loved her, friends adored her . . ."

"Maybe she was too good," I said. "Maybe she needed to

be bad once in a while." I didn't know where that came from. Probably from thinking about myself at the age of twelve to fourteen—running with boys, heisting cars, landing in juvie. "Maybe Mariana was going nuts, trying to tiptoe around her parents' imminent disfavor every day."

Hear that, Samved? I have learned a few things since sobering up. Mom always used to tell me, when Pop was drinking: "Don't make him angry. It'll just be worse for both of us." All that walking on eggshells. "Maybe it finally occurred to her," I said to Mac, "that she wasn't doing her parents any favors, either, letting them control her life."

"I thought of that. I'm almost sure it's why Mariana went to Colombia in the first place—to get away from them awhile. The Samoranos meant well, but they were too sure, always, that they knew what was right for Mariana."

"Why did they let her go to Colombia? Wasn't it dangerous down there, even back then?"

"Absolutely. But they had no choice. Mariana wrote to me; she said that one day, she simply got on a plane and left. The next her parents knew, she was down there in the old village with her aunts and uncles. They couldn't force her to come back."

"Did she tell you why she left like that? It seems strange, if she'd always given in to their wishes before."

"She said they had been getting letters all that summer from an uncle, about the conditions down there in the village. She'd been looking for something worthwhile to do with her life, something to offset all the craziness going on in the world. She was horrified by Vietnam, but in a spiritual way—Mariana was never an activist. She felt that by simply doing good, herself, she could somehow make up for what was going on elsewhere."

"What did she look like?"

Mac smiled. "Beautiful . . . but not in a classic way. Her nose, she thought, was too big." His tone was gently amused. "And she thought she was way too short."

"How short?"

"About five-one, full-grown. She barely came up to my chest. When we were kids in Kansas, she'd come running across the fields and barrel into me—all eighty pounds or so, then—and I'd scoop her up like a football and run with her to some imaginary goalpost. She'd laugh, and we'd fall on the ground and wrestle—"

He broke off. Then he said simply, "Life was pretty good back then."

There was movement below, from above the water tower. I gripped Mac's arm. "Did you see that?"

He leaned forward, peering into the bright circle of light. "A bird . . . probably an eagle."

It was perched at the very top of the tower—a few feet above where Sam Garner must be. I'd seen the dark shape earlier, but thought it was part of the structure. Something had startled it, apparently, because it had flapped its wings and was now repositioning itself. "I didn't know eagles came down this close to people. I've always imagined them hanging out in the hills, alone."

"Golden eagles are different. They'll nest on trees, sometimes power poles . . . it's a wonder, though, that they survive these days. If they're not getting shot, they're trapped. Or poisoned."

"You'd think they'd learn to stay away from people."

"Maybe they like the risk. Goldens are agile fliers, good at getting out of dangerous situations."

"What about you?" I was thinking of Mac's mission at dawn—the one we'd all talked about and planned in the living room earlier. "Are you good at getting out of dangerous situations?"

He shrugged. "I did all right in Nam."

"It's been a long time since Nam."

I didn't see, but could hear the arrogant grin. "I've seen a few Indiana Jones movies."

"Mac—"

"Hell, darlin'—takin' risks is like ridin' a bike. It'll come back." He drew his knees up and rested his one good arm against them. The leather jacket creaked, and the silver wings on his lapels glinted in the light of the moon. He looked like a little boy playing the part of pilot—or a *Top Gun* hero, displaying the wings he'd earned in some fight-to-the-finish sky battle.

Pilots who'd come back from Vietnam, I knew, had declared it the toughest war ever to fly in. With the jungles and swamps, enemy fire from almost any direction, and the difficulty of maneuvering a chopper through those complicated skies, it had taken a skill even greater, it was said, than that of the seat-of-the-pants World War II fliers.

So I shouldn't fault Mac for wearing his wings; he'd earned the right to be proud of them. But could he cut it still? Or had he been away from the front too long—had he softened up too much in civilian life?

Whatever Mac Devlin was, being around him these past few days had been like soaring with the eagles . . . one minute adventure, the next a kind of focus that was reassuring. A kind of *let's-just-get-the-job-done* effect, and *this, by golly, is the way we'll do it.*

If Mariana had indeed ended up "with" Sam Garner, she was a stupid, stupid woman. Garner might have had more flash —more *derring-do*—but Devlin was solid. He was here beside me, helping me out, when he didn't need to be. He could have gone off—left me and Charlie to free Mom without his help.

I almost wished he had.

"I wish you weren't doing this," I said, surprised at feeling protective, suddenly.

"We talked about it back there. It's the only way."

"It's *not* the only way. There have got to be six hundred other ways. We just haven't thought of them yet."

"This is the fastest, the simplest—"

"Simplest! You could be killed—"

"—and the most direct. It's the safest for your mother."
His hand gave a gentle tug at my hair. "C'mere, Outlaw."

I leaned back into the curve of his arm. "Sometimes we just
have to do things, Jesse. Put ourselves on the *line* . . . make
some sort of commitment, some sort of statement to the world.
It may be that one heroic gesture is all we've got to leave behind."

There was a strange intensity in the way he said "heroic
gesture." But I didn't have time to think about it then. There
was another movement from the tower. This time, a figure appeared and stepped to the top of the wooden ladder. Mac stiffened, dropping his arm from around me. He leaned forward in a
crouch. "What the hell is he doing?"

It was Garner. He had slung the Remington over his shoulder and was coming down the rest of the way, hand over hand,
his boots slipping once when a rung gave way on the rickety
ladder. But he was nimble. He grabbed the rung above his head
again and hung on, righting himself within seconds.

"We should have brought a gun," I said.

"We'd never get close enough to use it. Besides—you really
think you could shoot, if it came to that?"

He had a point. He'd seen my ignoble moment at the Davies School of Defense.

"Well, what about you?"

He laughed softly. "I hate guns . . . I have ever since I
came back from Nam, in fact. I'll tell you something, pretty
thing, if you promise not to tell anyone. I'd have flubbed that
test worse than you. Why do you think I do my best to stay out
of trouble now?"

It was a rare gem, a gift—Mac Devlin admitting to a "weak-
ness."

"Well, you're in a heap of trouble here," I said.

At the bottom of the ladder, Garner now stood looking

around. He raised his shaggy blond head as if sniffing the air. I wondered if he sensed we were here. My breathing slowed, as if that would make the difference between exposure or cover. But then he moved on. Toward the shack.

"He's going in to Mom," I whispered anxiously. My shoulders were tight, and my stomach felt like tiny little bungee jumpers were diving into it, off my ribs. I didn't realize until Mac stood up that I'd grabbed his arm again. I stood with him. "What's he doing?" The question wasn't meant to be answered; what I'd really meant was, *Is Garner so stressed out, or so evil, that he'll do something to Mom now? Without waiting until dawn?*

"He won't hurt her," Mac said.

"But if he's as bad as you say—"

"He's not self-destructive. And he really wants the money from this job. He knows he'll have to produce your mother, and that she'll have to be well, before I'll take off with that cargo."

But Mac didn't sound as sure as I'd have liked. We watched Garner take keys from his leather vest pocket and unlock the door to the shack.

He stepped in, and the door closed.

There were no sounds, no movements discernible from up here. I stood it as long as I could, then burst out, "What's he *doing* in there? We've got to go down!"

Then a loud, foreign sound emanated from the cabin. A *whooosh* . . . a strangled, gushing, coppery noise like old bones rattling through the whole damned valley—

I let out a long, relieved sigh, and Mac grinned. It had taken only a moment to get over the shock and to realize the sound was that of a toilet flushing. An old toilet, its rusted pipes knocking through the silent ground.

"Mother Nature," Mac said. "Gets even the black hats now and then."

But after that it was silent again. One, two minutes, passed, and I was going nuts. "I've got to go down there," I said, tasting blood from having ground down, with my teeth, on my lip. "What if he *is* hurting her in some way? Mac, this is our chance—"

"No. He could come out any time. Wait here." Mac pressed my arm and stepped down from the crevice onto solid ground. About fifteen yards down the hill, he stopped on a small outcropping of rocks. With legs spread, he bellowed, "Garner! Sam Garner!" The words ricocheted over the valley, seeming to bounce off the black, flattop mountains and return—a vocal boomerang.

The door to the shack flew open. Garner stood outlined against the inside light momentarily, before the cabin light was cut, the interior left in darkness.

"Mac? Mac, that you? What the hell you doing here, buddy?" The voice was like hot oil running over cement—a hard base, but pure slick on top. There was another sound, a click, then a glint that the spotlights caught—the barrel of the rifle, possibly. That was all.

"Just want to see the lady," Mac called out easily. "Make sure she's still healthy and happy."

"You'll see her when you're in that cockpit at five A.M.," Garner countered.

Mac stepped forward. "Bring her out here," he yelled, "or I'm not showing up at dawn. I'm calling this thing off, right now."

"This some kind of trick? You got a gang of people out there, ready to pick me off?"

"You know better than that. You've had a three-sixty-degree view out here—you know there's nobody within range. Besides, since when didn't I play it straight? I told you I'd do the job, and I will. But the lady's daughter is worried, and I don't like her worried." Mac's voice became hard. *"Do* it, Sam."

A long silence before Garner answered.

"Stay where you are," he finally said. "I see anything suspicious out there, the lady is dead."

The door closed, and a light appeared again at the one window we could see. While we waited, even the eagle atop the water tower grew restless. It was moving about as if sensing danger and preparing for flight.

Garner pulled Mom out into the circle of light.

She was dressed in jeans and a pink shirt. The soft tinges of gray in her brown hair weren't really visible from here; my imagination—my need to touch her—only made it seem that way. Garner's rifle was at her throat.

I didn't think about it—I just stumbled forward over rocks, my boot heels catching and twisting as I ran down the mountain toward her. I'd have passed Mac right by, if he hadn't jumped down from the rocks and grabbed my arm, yanking me back so hard I nearly fell. "Easy does it, Jesse! Don't scare him off!"

I tugged at his restraining hand, then stopped. I knew he was right. I wet my lips, then nodded. After a moment, Mac let go. I called out: "Mom, are you all right?"

"Jesse?"

"Are you okay?"

Even from here, I could see her chin go up. "Of course I'm all right, dear. You think I'd let myself be intimidated by a no-good fool like this—"

Sam Garner yanked her back, pulling her closer to the cabin door. "That the daughter, Mac? Who else is up there with you? You're playing it close to the line, comin' back here like this. What kind of trouble you bringin' me, pal?"

"No trouble," Mac assured him easily. "Just wanted to see that the lady's safe and sound. Figure Jesse and me'll just sit out here and wait until dawn, make sure."

"You can sit till the cow-tits burst and the roosters crow, you ain't seein' nothin' more, pal. Might as well go home."

"Jesse?" Mom called out. "Honey, I'm fine. You just go on back to the house, now. *Please.*"

It was her best mothering voice. I was surprised not to hear her add, "And drive carefully, dear."

"No way, Mom. I'm here until this is over."

"Sam," Mac called, "tell you what. Let the lady go, and I'll stay here in her place. I'll take this drop and anything else you want me to do—from now on, for as long as you want. Just let her go."

"And have that husband of hers swoop down on me, the minute I do?"

Or that eagle, I thought. In the moonlight, the great golden bird was raising its wings, then slowly lowering them, as if gearing up for flight. Or dinner.

"It never should have come to this," Mac said heavily. "Back in Kansas—"

Garner interrupted. "You were a naive, small-town kid back in Kansas. You didn't know squat about life, about the way some of us had to live to survive."

"My dad tried to help you out," Mac countered. "You thumbed your nose at him."

They were talking in natural voices now. Yelling wasn't necessary; their words floated over the hard-edged valley and reverberated in every direction, like drops of lead striking a steel pan. "You were the other side of me," Mac said. "We were best friends—"

Another harsh laugh from Sam. "I hated you from the first. And you've hated me—since Mariana."

I felt Mac jerk in surprise beside me.

"If you're here, pal," Garner went on shrewdly, "it's not for any grand purpose, like saving this lady's life. It's to get back at me for killing Mariana."

With that, Garner shoved Mom inside the shack. He raised the Remington to firing position, and began scanning with the night scope, moving it side to side.

Mac lurched forward. His boot must have kicked a stone; it clattered down the hill, louder than a bowling ball. He was clearly outlined by the light of the moon now, and there was an explosion of sound. Bits of sand and rock rained down from somewhere just above us.

"I don't want to hit you, Devlin! Just stay back!"

In the next two or three seconds, Mac disappeared. He was there one moment, then he was gone.

I looked frantically around. "Mac?"

"Jess, get down!"

There was movement several yards ahead, farther down the hill. Mac was flat on the ground, crawling quickly from rock to rock. They were small rocks, giving almost no cover.

I slid down the hill after him. Bullets struck below us, tearing up sand and stone. I heard Mom scream from within the cabin, "Jesse! Dear God, *Jesse!*"

I landed a foot or two behind Mac, and plastered myself to the ground. "What the hell are you doing?" I breathed. But I knew. Garner was right about Mac; he might have come here for me, but now that he was here, he was set on revenge. *If you ever hurt a Scorpion, get out of the way of its lethal tail.* I hear you, Samved.

"What did he mean, that he killed Mariana? What the hell is going on?"

But Mac wasn't listening. "What happened, Sam? What really happened seven years ago?"

A heaviness, like a depression, floated through the air from Sam Garner's direction. "She was coming home to you," he said. "Did she tell you that?"

Mac's eyes closed briefly. A long sigh escaped his throat. "No. She said she needed to talk to me. She never said—"

"She always loved you, Mac. You were the knight in shining armor—the one who could do no wrong."

"But you and she—you told me—"

"You really believed that? I didn't think you bought that story. Shit, Mac—Mariana used me. She *used* me to get supplies for the kids in that village. She used my connections, and the way

I could get in and out of tough places. But she hated my guts. It was always you."

"What happened, Sam?" Mac's tone was deadly now. He rose and began to move with deliberate anger downhill, toward Garner and the shack. I grabbed his arm, but he shook me off as if I were weightless.

"Don't come any closer," Garner warned. He fired a single shot that echoed and bounded off mountain walls. Mac halted.

"She crossed me up," Garner said after a moment. "She was supposed to set up a meeting in the village, so I could score a back-haul of drugs into Florida—the biggest I'd ever had. I needed the money bad, Mac—real bad. There were people after me—"

"There are always people after you! You fuck-up, you goddamned fuck-up! Why did you involve her?"

"I wouldn't have fucked that one up!" Garner yelled. "It was Mariana—she screwed it for me, on purpose. Fixed it so the contact wasn't there when I got there. I had to get out fast, and I lost the deal—"

"And you killed her for *that*? You goddamned *killed* her? Jesus Christ, Sam!"

"I didn't mean to. Shit, I was mad, that's all—I was mad, and I left her in some hut out in the boonies, tied up—" There was a sound from Garner . . . a high-pitched, nervous laugh. "I had to get out of the country, Mac. I just forgot. I forgot to tell somebody to go after Mariana . . . and it was so goddamned fucking hot that day—"

Mac stumbled forward again, and although I tried to hold him back, his rage gave him too much strength.

"Get back! Get back, or I swear I'll kill the lady here!" Garner screamed. The cabin door opened, and his figure moved across the lighted doorway. He raised the rifle.

I screamed at Mac, grabbing and tearing at the neck of his

jacket when I couldn't hang onto his arm. *"Stop!* He means it, he'll kill my mother!"

But he kept on, dragging me with him down the hill. Bullets smacked into the rocks around us and I was sobbing and gulping for air, hanging on to Mac in a panic, pounding on his back, trying to bring him down. I kept yelling "No!" and "Stop!" and cursing, over and over, "Stop, goddammit, stop!" but it wasn't having any effect. Then, all of a sudden, there was a blast of sound so close my eardrums hurt. The relentless force of Mac's downward plunge ended abruptly. He came to a halt— and the force of my weight, behind him, brought us both down. I let go of his jacket and raised up to see what had finally stopped Mac Devlin in his tracks.

Standing before us was a massive form, and in its hand was a shotgun. It was sawed-off and Sicilian—a *lumpara,* Tark had told me once. Light, short, and potent . . . a favorite of the mob.

As usual, Tark didn't raise his voice. "You are not going down there. You are not going to blow this thing for Kate and Jess."

Mac was on his feet instantly. "Get out of—"

"Not a chance," Tark interrupted. "My sole purpose in being here is to protect Jess and her mother. You get in the way of that, you're dead. That's a promise."

"She's going to die anyway! He's not going to let her live! Christ, let me go down there and get him now—I'll get her out of there—"

"You'd never make it down." When Tark said it, I knew it was true. "He'd kill you—or before you got there, he'd kill her."

"I want him! I want his ass!" There was incredible pain in Mac's voice.

"You know the plan," Tark answered implacably. The shots from below had stopped. Presumably, Sam Garner was trying to figure out what was going on—and how he could turn it to his advantage. "We've got to hold out until it's light," Tark said softly. "When you take off, when you do what we talked about, he'll be watching you. I'll move in on him, and Bobby will get Kate. That's the way it's going to be."

"It's a stupid plan," Mac protested. "You'll never have time, don't you realize that? He's not going to be distracted enough, no matter how many problems I tell him I'm having in the air. Not anymore. He'll be watching for a trap every step of the way."

"Yeah, well, he's going to have a harder time than you think." The *lumpara* didn't waver.

"What are you talking about?" Mac demanded.

"Charlie wants you back at the house. He's come up with something special for us . . . something that'll really take Garner's mind off things in the morning."

"I'm telling you," Mac said stubbornly, "I've known Sam Garner all my life. I've worked with him, I've seen him in combat. Whatever it is, he's not going to fall for it."

"He's going to have to," Tark said implacably, "because this is the way it's going to be." He turned to me. "Jess?" He tossed me a set of keys. "The Mercedes is up there. Take it back to the house . . . And take Devlin with you."

"No! I can't leave my mother. What if he hurts her? I need to be here."

"I'll stay. You let Garner know you're taking Devlin back to the house, so he won't be nervous about trouble from him anymore. He'll play it cool after that. He doesn't want this blown any more than we do."

I studied Mac. There wasn't a chance in hell I'd be able to strong-arm him to the car and all the way back to the house. "What do you think?" I said reasonably. "Hell, Mac . . . if Charlie's got something else, some other idea . . . let's give it a try. You can always settle the score with Garner later, when this is over. . . ."

Some of the fight had gone out of Mac. His fists still

worked, and his gray eyes looked haunted. But the rage had been tempered. There were a few tough moments while emotions warred in his face. Finally, he nodded.

I turned back to Tark. "We'll go. But I've got to send Mom a message first." I scrambled up on a cluster of rocks and cupped my hands to my mouth, calling out. "Mom? Mom, can you hear me?"

"I hear you, Jesse." There was only a small quaver in her voice.

"I'm taking Mac back to the house—it'll be safer for you that way. But listen, this'll all be over soon. And I've brought you a book. Booth Tarkington—you know, the one you like. We can curl up together and read for days."

"I can't wait," my mother called back bravely. "And I'm glad you're going back to the house, dear. Don't worry about me. I'll be fine."

Her voice was more sure, and more clear, now. She sounded greatly relieved.

Chapter 27

▼ ▼ ▼

The first thing we noted on approaching Marcus's Mirage was that there was a plane in the yard.

It wasn't a big plane—white, with green stripes, long, slender wings, and a single propeller at the nose—but it looked odd, standing there.

At least as odd as the four huge, white container drums beside it, with the numbers 4-0-2-2 emblazoned in red on each. Next to them was some sort of contraption that looked like it might have a pumping action.

Charlie met us at the door. He looked tired, but there was a light in the blue eyes that indicated hope. "Marcus called a neighboring rancher," he said. "A friend. The guy flew it down here for me, and Bobby drove him home."

"What're the drums? The ones with those interesting numbers on them?"

"Come with me," Charlie said. "I'll tell you about it."

So we stood by the plane and had a long talk—and Charlie

did tell us what the 55-gallon drums were for, and what our new plan would be.

He just never answered my question about the numbers.

"Later," he said. "It's not important now."

Mac and I sat in the southwestern kitchen, over thick black coffee. A gloom of depression had settled around him, but he seemed to want to talk. I listened, the way he had earlier when I'd gone on and on about Mom.

"I always suspected," he said wearily, "about Sam—that he'd done something to Mariana. But I wasn't sure. You know how you close your eyes to things? I guess I didn't want to believe that he'd do anything that evil." He sighed. "But Sam always was unpredictable—over the edge.

"The thing is, she was down there for ten or more years. We were writing back and forth, getting close again, and I hoped—

"She was getting tired, burning out. She seemed afraid of something. I thought it was just the political climate down there. Things were getting more and more crazy, with all the drug traffic. . . ."

He sipped at the coffee, but it had to be cold by then. Mac's hands, around the cup, shook. Anger replaced depression. I could see it in his eyes. And it should have been a warning.

When Mac went upstairs to rest for a couple of hours, Aunt Edna seized the opportunity to drag me out to the side garden and state her case.

"How is she holding up?"

"I think she'll be okay. She knows Tark is there."

"I'm coming with you in the morning," my aunt said, hands on hips.

"Please," I argued, sounding like Mom. "I want you here, where it's safe."

"She's my sister, Jesse. You can't treat me like some extra piece of baggage you brought along on the trip! I have to help."

"You *are* helping. You always have, just by being there."

Aunt Edna was there for me when Mom and Pop weren't, when I was growing up. The times when he was drunk—and when Mom was working day and night to keep the wolf from the door. It wasn't like Aunt Edna *did* that much. She kept me company—and sometimes that's all a neglected child needs. Somebody to put bright red polish on eight-year-old nails. To fuss with temperamental hair.

In that same way, she was here now—and it was all I needed.

"I know how much you want to do something. So I'm asking you, as a special favor to me, to do this. To wait here. Aunt Edna, if anything happens to Mom— And then if you—" I turned away. "I wouldn't have anyone left."

I think it was the tears that did it. And they were only a little bit of a con.

"You'll be okay?" I asked in that hour before dawn, as Mac, Bobby, and I were climbing into the jeep. I gave her a hug.

"Sure." Aunt Edna grinned. "I found some more Don Henley tapes, while you were off last night." She snapped her fingers, then fluffed her orange hair. "Forgive-*ness*," she sang off-key, rotating her pelvis. "Forgive-*ness.*"

She looked like a tiny little Lucy, performing against orders on Ricky's show.

That was Aunt Edna: adding a note of humor to a desperate situation. The quaver in my voice was real this time. "I'm sorry about dragging you down here and then leaving you like this. I just don't want you hurt."

Aunt Edna stuck a cigarette in her mouth. "They also serve," she deadpanned, "who only stand and wait."

Chapter 28

▼ ▼ ▼

*B*road bands of rose brushed the eastern sky. The desert was blue-gray in the dawn, with here and there a splash of ghostly pale white. I was in the Cherokee—on the hill above the shack, and far from danger—performing my scut work.

"We really need you monitoring that equipment," Tark and Charlie had said, before going about their masculine chores.

Yassuh, yassuh. Far be it from me to go against orders, suh.

First, there was the radio that served as ground/air control between Sam Garner and Mac Devlin. In addition, a cordless phone connected Garner to a set in the shack. It was the phone he expected to receive word on, once Mac had landed in Colombia. Charlie had rigged a receiver for me, so I could hear anything that was said, anyone Garner contacted at all.

The third piece of equipment was something special Charlie had put together: a radio with a private, unauthorized frequency that hooked up only Charlie and me.

Tark stood in jeans and a sweatshirt, several yards to the left and below the jeep, watching the scene around the shack. Bobby was off as many yards to the right. The three of us formed a kind of squat, spread-out triangle.

The Beech 18, a lumbering gray whale, was readying for takeoff. It was Marcus's field, built for his private jet, and he'd taken over the entire valley to expand the old runway. Through the earphones of the radio, I could hear Sam Garner giving Mac last-minute instructions about some of the newer equipment on the Beech.

"I can't believe you need all this shit," Mac was complaining. "The way you used to fly in Nam—"

"It keeps me out of trouble," Garner said.

"Handles a little heavy, though." Static crackled.

"She's a dream, what're you talkin' about?" was Garner's retort.

"I don't know, I just think she's holdin' back."

Garner laughed. "You ain't never seen no plane as sweet as this old girl. But then, you never did recognize a good woman when you had her."

I felt a jolt. Surely Garner wouldn't take the chance of angering Mac again at a moment like this! Still, there was silence at Mac's end, and it got me worried. *Please, oh please, don't let him blow it now.*

But Mac started talking again, asking calm questions and responding. "Yeah?" he would say. "Okay, but—" and "Oh, I get it," followed by "Wait a minute, what about—"

It went on like that—with Sam giving impatient lessons, and Mac playing dumb. But finally, he couldn't put it off any longer. The prearranged time arrived, the moment when he would have to take off, or risk being late for the drop outside the Colombian village. "No more," I heard Sam say. "You've got to get going."

"Check."

The Beech began to taxi. It lumbered down the runway,

and for a long, awful moment, it seemed like its heavy belly dragged the ground. But then it lifted, rising slowly into the clear azure sky. I felt the force of gravity as if I were in the cockpit too. That, and fear. I was afraid for Mac, wanting to somehow pull him back—get him out of that thing. He had looked too damned determined, too grim, when we'd parted at the jeep—despite the cocky thumbs-up gesture.

The Beech gained its altitude, and one wing dipped as it began to circle back for its southward run.

The radio crackled again. "Mac? Mac, what the hell is that?"

From a distance came the drone of another plane. Sam Garner had heard it first. I looked toward the east and saw nothing but a dot against the horizon—could have been a bird unless you were used to looking and listening for these things, the way pilots are.

"How the hell should I know?" Mac answered lazily. "Probably some weekend air-jock. Listen, Sam, I'm gonna make one more circle while you help me figure out the rest of these instruments."

"Forget the goddamned instruments, Devlin! You can fly that thing without—"

"I don't know the area! For Christ's sake, you want the cargo delivered in one piece, or what?"

I heard Garner mutter, "Fuckin' civilian, been out of it too long—"

Mac was making a wide, slow circle, and the other plane was drawing near. Garner began yelling instructions to Mac, and Mac responded, sounding confused. Garner's temper flared. "Goddammit, Mac!" The plane was still maybe a couple of miles off, but heading straight for us, for the shack and the water tower. "What if that's the law? We haven't even filed— Get the hell out of here now . . . just *go*, goddammit, *go!* We'll talk when you get the fuck away from here!"

"All right, all right! Sheee-it!" Mac ended his circle and began heading south, over the first jagged mountain. It was pink in the glow of the now-risen sun, like a piece of quartz on a coffee table of sand.

The other plane seemed to hang back—a glittering speck to my naked eye. I watched as the Beech skimmed the rough peaks, and heard Garner yell into the radio, "Too low, too low! Devlin, what the fuck are you doing? You're too goddamned low—!"

"Can't get altitude!" Mac shouted. "What's wrong with this fucking plane? What did you *do* to it?" Static shrieked through the radio. The engine of the Beech coughed and sputtered. The plane began to fall . . . slowly . . . dropping like a floating tin leaf. I felt my heart lurch. Mac hollered again, "I'm going down, Sam . . . down!" and Garner followed with, "God damn you, Devlin . . . pull out, pull out! What the shit!"

Mac's radio went dead . . . and with a dreadful finality, the Beech tumbled out of sight behind the mountain. A few more sputters—the frightening nonsound of a stalled engine—and then, silence.

Near-silence. Only the drone of the other plane remained, like a bee in a garden; you know it's there and you might get stung, so you can't relax. Meanwhile, Garner was going nuts. There had been no crash on the other side of the mountain, no explosion—and he wasn't buying any of it. "Fuck you, Devlin!" Garner bellowed into the radio. "I know what you're doing—"

Meanwhile, Tark, under cover of Mac's diversion, had been making a cautious descent down the hill. He carried the *lumpara*, not long-range but more lethal and thorough, and he needed only to get close enough to spray the rotting water tower with ammunition—to pin Garner down while Bobby went in after Mom.

But Sam spotted Tark, and he had the long-range Remington. He fired. Bullets struck rock, and Tark flattened himself behind the meager cover of a pile of rocks as Garner appeared at the top of the tower. "I warned you," Garner roared. "Man, you have blown it! The lady's a dead woman!" He began to scramble down the ladder, covering himself with a wild spray of gunfire.

"*Charlie!*" I screamed into the radio, dialing frantically for the channel. In my panic, I couldn't remember the special frequency, or even how to find it. I just kept hearing Garner's last words, and I shouted into whatever airspace might be there: "Charlie, *now,* goddammit, *now!*"

I threw the radio aside. The sound of my boots clattered over the dry ground and over my heart as I tore down the mountain. One side of my mind saw that Charlie, in the green and white crop duster, was closing in—while the other saw the tower, and Sam Garner heading down that rickety ladder with his rifle.

Garner saw the crop duster, too. Maybe he knew what was coming. He was poised a short way down, yelling, his longish blond hair like a dusty halo on a fallen angel. "Devlin!" he screamed. "You son of a bitch! God damn you, Devlin!" He shook the rifle at the sky.

The crop duster zeroed in, heading straight for us at frantic speed. Then suddenly it was directly overhead. And even though Tark and Bobby knew what was happening, and knew it was their moment to move, they stood transfixed as tons of orange powder billowed from beneath the crop duster's wings, raining down puffs of intense bright orange, clouds of tangerine-coral mist, a sea of bitter, chemical dust.

But Garner, the old soldier of fortune, was no stranger to diversion tactics. He recovered too quickly, and we lost some of the time we had hoped the stunt would buy. Shots sounded again from the ladder. Through the stinging cloud I saw Bobby Dell, halfway to Mom and the shack, go down. "*Tark!*" I screamed. But he had seen it. He flew across the sand in a frenzied race for the water tower, firing in Garner's direction. I veered toward Bobby, who had dropped his rifle in the fray and was skittering toward the underpinnings of the tower for shelter. Metal glinted on the ground, several yards before me. I stumbled toward it and grabbed Bobby's rifle up mid-run, heading straight for the shack.

Another blast, and I felt something hot on my arm. A prick —and my khaki sleeve bloomed with red. I kept running. My throat seared from the chemical fog. Mom screamed, and it sounded like she was pounding on the thin walls of the tin shack. "I'm coming!" I yelled. "Stay down!" Another smack of bullets —pinging off tin. My heart pounded so hard I thought it might blow up, and the air all around was thick with that acrid powder.

I saw Tark—nearly at the tower—go down.

Fear turned my mind to mush. I stood paralyzed, torn between covering Tark and getting to Mom. But Garner was too close, on that tower ladder, to Mom. All he had to do was finish his mad descent to the ground.

That settled it. I started running, running toward Sam Garner and fumbling with the heavy rifle.

And it all happened within seconds—like the awful moment at the Davies School, when I'd panicked and shot the woman and child. *I might end up dead,* I thought crazily as I ran, *but I will not—as long as I'm still on my feet—screw this up.* Flickers of knowledge came back from a class at Davies. *It's a Ruger,* I heard an instructor say, *a Ruger Mini 14, not a cobra. Touch it. Smell it. Remember how it works.*

Miraculously, my fingers made all the right moves. The Ruger bucked, stinging my hands, but I tightened my grip and kept squeezing away. The noise was terrifying. It bloomed through the desert air like a mushroom cloud, hot and searing. It filled my ears, my brain, my pores.

I must have hit Sam. He halted near the bottom of the flimsy ladder, his face a pale blob of rage. He had an arm looped around a rung, and the hand of that arm was pressed to his shoulder. He was shouting curses at me. I kept right on running, closing in, and was almost near enough to make out the gist of the curses when Garner twisted abruptly, raising his face to the sky. Consummate fear replaced rage, and he dropped his rifle, grabbing onto the ladder with that hand. I followed his eyes—

And froze. The Beech, with Mac, was no more than forty yards away. It closed in through the orange crud, heading straight for the tower. Garner hung there, immobile—perhaps stunned by the sight. The Beech's engine roared, gearing for speed, not for landing—its nose pointed straight at the tower and Garner—

"NO!" I screamed. *"NOOO!"* I felt something grip my arm, holding me back. "Mac!" I screamed helplessly, my mind all tangled and crazy as the Beech completed its mission of revenge and plowed with a deafening, sickening *BOOOOM* through the matchstick tower. Metal screeched into wood. A tornado-whirl of lumber rose into the rusty sky, then fell for hundreds of feet around, as if some terrible angry God were playing Pick Up Sticks.

There followed a long, ghastly vacuum of silence. Apricot grit settled on the pile of rubble, on the twisted, half-buried body of Sam Garner, and on one wing of the Beech—which had torn from the fuselage and was lying broken and ugly on the desert floor.

It's not on fire! I thought—half insane with fear and mingled hope. *We can still get him out—*

I yanked away from Aunt Edna, who—to complete the horrifying moment—was somehow beside me and had grabbed my arm. Her eyes were wide with terror, her hair a frizz of orange that nearly disappeared in the caustic haze that kept falling in billows from Charlie's plane.

"Get Mom!" I yelled, and Aunt Edna spun on her heel and raced for the shack. I began to run toward the Beech. Bobby had struggled to his feet and was limping toward the downed plane from the right. I didn't see Tark anywhere. I think I was hollering something. My lungs burned from the chalky chemical, and pieces of the tower had struck my shoulder, my legs. It was like they wouldn't move—like one of those awful nightmares where you keep running and running, and never make headway because the thing you're running toward keeps drifting away.

I was almost there when the Beech exploded.

The flames shot up to the desert roof . . . the tented sky . . . *No higher than the soul is high.* . . .

Above all the wreckage, an eagle rose, its great wings spread wide. It flew and flew, so high, so soaring, you could almost hear the beat of its brave, strong heart.

Chapter 29

▼ ▼ ▼

"It was a time of indecision, time to sit and think it through,

Was a time of inquisition, baby—

Don't know what you're going to do."

—"COMING HOME," BY D. R. LUNSFORD

Alfred was in a snit because I had a personal call coming in over "his" line. He sat behind his ornate desk, surrounded by tons of file folders and correspondence—all of it neatly piled and stacked—and glared at me. Sticking the receiver in my face.

"He's been calling every fifteen minutes," Alfred said, his thin brown hair as slicked-back as his voice. "I offered to take a message, but he wouldn't leave one."

I wasn't in a mood for Alfred's games. "Maybe he knows you wouldn't have given it to me." He hadn't even bothered to ask about my bandaged arm. The twit has no heart.

I grabbed the gold and white phone from his quivering, offended hand. "Hello!" I shouted irritably.

"Well, finally! Dammit, girl, Charlie said you were due there an hour ago!"

"I was on the phone with my Aunt Edna. So far as I can see, she's about the only sane person left in this goddamned story."

"Jesus H.! *Now* what are you being so ornery about?"

"That was a harebrained, asshole stunt—that's what I'm ornery about!"

"Nothing like what we did in Nam. Hell, gal, I've flown through fire, hail, thunderstorms, and rain—"

"Like your average postman, I suppose. I am not impressed. What if Tark hadn't gotten you out of that Beech in time? It was blown to smithereens!"

"But he did get me out."

"What if he *hadn't*? With Bobby disabled—"

"Jesse, Jesse . . . sheee-it, gal . . . we haven't got time for this. I got a question for you. How'd you like to just settle down awhile, now, and marry me?"

I held the receiver away and stared at it. *"Marry* you? Marry *you,* Mac Devlin? Why on earth would I want to do that? Why would *you* want to do it, for that matter?"

"Hell, girl," the receiver squawked, "where am I gonna find another woman as feisty as you?"

I put the phone to my ear again. "And don't call me feisty, I hate that word. It sounds like some little old lady with an umbrella."

"Will you just simmer down, and listen for a change? I asked you to marry me. Don't you ever take anything serious-like?"

Certainly not *this* anything.

But I had to admit my spirits had taken flight at the words —like an eagle, one might say. Maybe this day, once the dreaded talk with Marcus was over, could be salvaged in some way.

"Where are you?" I said.

"Out at the airport. Charlie and I just got in with the Andrelli jet. We had some business to clear up with the authorities in Phoenix. Can you meet me, say, in an hour, at your place?"

I glanced at the door to Marcus's part of the penthouse, which was closed. An hour should be about right, I thought with a sigh, for getting things over with here. *Really* over with. As in end of my life . . . kaput . . . finis. "Sure," I muttered. "An hour, maybe a little more."

"Okay. But hurry. I'm not feeling real patient today, gal."

The cocky act was in full gear, and it was good, for once, to hear it. I'd had a few bad moments when that Beech sheared the water tower. We'd talked beforehand about the chemical that Marcus had sent down from Greater Pharmaceutical, the inert filler used in a new, experimental sulfa drug. So the stalling plane, followed by the orange cloud as diversion, had been planned. But I'd clearly underestimated Mac's desire for revenge, his need to settle the score with Sam Garner.

When it was over, there was one sick instant when I'd wished he had let Garner live. But then I remembered what Garner had done to Mariana, and that he would have killed Mom just as easily—and I have to admit, I didn't much care that Sam Garner was dead, buried beneath the ashes of a flaming water tower. There are times when revenge feels right . . . and yes, I hear you, Samved: *Revenge is Mine, saith the Lord* would be his latest admonition. Back in the old guru days, he'd have said, *What goes around comes around, and you get back exactly what you give.*

So maybe I'll pay someday for being glad that Sam Garner is dead, and maybe Mac will pay for being the instrument of that death. I don't know about Mac—but I'll accept that, for my part. *Sufficient unto the day, Samved, is the evil thereof.*

Marcus stood with his back to me, looking out the wall of blue-curtained windows at Rochester—surveying at least some of his kingdom. He wore a light gray business suit. His back was rigid, his hands clasped behind it. I knew the pose: It was the one he assumed before all heavy-duty meetings, when he was running his energy, getting ready for some major strike on some unsuspecting soul.

Well, one thing: I wasn't unsuspecting. Marcus had summoned me here to the principal's office, and now he was figuring out how to tell the student that she'd flunked her grade.

"Hullo," I said.

For a man who usually moves with athletic grace, his turn was stiff and uneasy. No smile. "You were injured," he said.

"A couple of burns. A flesh wound." I shrugged. "Like they say in the movies."

He motioned to the open sliding doors, which went out to a terrace.

"After you."

So it was going to be like that: a kind of curt courtesy. No emotion, at least none that could be seen behind that careful mask.

Marcus poured a glass of something cold from a blue pitcher and held it out to me, along with a napkin. I took both, careful not to touch his hand, and drank—not tasting it, not wanting it, but not knowing, either, what else to do with my hands. I tried to brace myself, but my bones kept going in all the wrong directions. I knew what he was going to say, and I didn't want to hear it—not any of it, not now that it was here. If anything, I heard mixed emotions as they played a lament through my head.

I cleared my throat. "I was just on the phone with Mac Devlin. He did a great job down there."

Marcus looked at me. His black hair was still damp from a shower. A few tight curls grazed his forehead. He might have looked like a small, careless boy—except that his smile was so strained. "I know."

Of course he knew; Tark would have reported in.

"He's a brave man," Marcus said.

"Yes."

"A good man."

I nodded.

"He'd be good for you, Jess. And to you."

I couldn't speak. It was coming now. I sat heavily on one of the terrace chairs, with its nautical-blue cushions that had always seemed somehow jaunty, matching the pots of blue and white flowers that Marcus planted out here every summer. He leaned against the terrace wall and folded his arms. An employer, now, giving a troublesome employee the axe. I thought about just getting up and walking out. I didn't have to do this, after all. I didn't have to sit through the actual words of rejection.

But I couldn't move; there wasn't much fight left. And all the while I kept thinking: *You've known it would end with Marcus one day. You've never deluded yourself on that score, never dreamed any of the usual girl/boy dreams. If anything, you've deliberately avoided doing just that.*

"I've been doing a lot of thinking lately," Marcus said. "I've been thinking about life, and how insecure everything is these days. The world—and the absolutely terrible shape it's in. If we want a stable life, anything meaningful or lasting, we've got to make it for ourselves. We've got to construct our own microcosms, our own worlds separate from the fray. It's the only way to survive."

My head ached. I couldn't quite focus—or breathe.

"Marriage and family are more important now, I think, than at any other time in recent history. Or at the very least, lasting partnerships—with people who will stand with us against the craziness out there, people who are steady, reliable, who care about us day after day."

"Marriage . . ." That was the word I kept hearing. It escaped my mouth, dry as dust. It sounded like "death."

Marcus said stiffly, "I know that's always been a distasteful word to you."

I couldn't make my head work. It was the moment I'd always known would come, the moment he'd walk out of my life without a backward glance—just like Pop did when he drank that last bottle and drove off and killed himself without caring who he was leaving behind or how many years they might live with the pain.

Marcus was still talking, but I barely heard. My ears were ringing, and that was the frightening part; I didn't know until that moment, how much I cared. I'd thought that if I found someone else—that if I turned my emotional energies in some other direction—it wouldn't hurt so much when this moment came.

"Jess?" Marcus had stopped talking. His hand was on my shoulder. He must have thought it would be comforting, but it felt like seared metal, burning a hole through my flesh. I tried to pull away.

"Don't do that!" he said irritably. "Can't you give me an answer? Even now?"

I reached into my subconscious to see if I'd heard anything of his announcement, if anything had gotten through—

"I asked you to marry me, Jess."

My ears stopped ringing. My jaw dropped.

I stared.

"Huh?"

"I said . . . will you marry me?"

I saw then that Marcus's nearly black eyes were lit from inside, the way they get when he's on to a new idea—something he knows is going to save the world. He hunkered down beside me, taking my icy hands in his. "I've bought a house for us. It's in the country, the kind of house you've always wanted to live in, with lilacs—your favorite flower—all over the place. And trees. You'll love it. I've fixed up the kitchen and bathrooms, but the rest of the house is just waiting for you to furnish it—Jess?"

Tears were rolling down my cheeks like boulders.

"Don't cry."

I wiped at my face. "I thought . . . I thought . . . What about Christopher, and his mom?"

He looked bewildered. "What about them?"

"You aren't going to marry them? Her, I mean?"

"Marry Christopher's mother? Why on earth would you think that?"

My chin jutted out as I snuffled. *"Why? Why would I think that?* Because you've just been all over the goddamned world with them, that's why! And because you see them all the time, and because Christopher is your son, and because he loves the country, and vegetables, and it'd be just like you to want to make a home for him and his bimbo mother—and okay, okay, I know she isn't really a bimbo, I just like to think she is because I know I'm not as good as her—"

He gripped my good arm. "Will you, for God's sake, stop that? Why do you think like that? Why, when you think at all, do you always come out with less than the rest?" He loosened his grip and said softly, "Why is it you've never believed that I love you, Jess?"

"Well, dammit . . . you certainly haven't said it lately."

He sighed. "I say it to you in all kinds of ways, every time I see you. Every time I hold you, every time we speak."

I snuffled some more while he took the napkin from my hand and dabbed at my nose. "You do?"

He laughed gently. "I do. I always have. The burning question is: When will you hear it?"

"But you were so cold, last time I was here. You wouldn't even look me in the eye."

"I know. And I'm sorry. I was afraid."

My eyes widened in shock. "You? Afraid?"

His slightly nervous smile was rueful. "Pretty amazing, isn't it? But when you start acting tough and independent, it strikes terror in my heart. It's taken months to screw up the courage to even tell you about that house. I've been afraid you'd run."

"But Tark says you've been trying to get out of the Family and clean up your life. You wouldn't do that, except for Chris."

"Correction. I wouldn't be doing it except for *you.* You're the one who's been pushing on me now, for almost a year, to go legit. You're the one who keeps nagging at me to see Chris, to make him a part of my life—and to make a life that's safer for him."

"And you said you couldn't, that there was no way you could take a different path after all these years—"

"Jess . . . did it ever occur to you that maybe you convinced me I might be wrong?"

"I didn't think I could convince you of anything!"

"So, maybe *you* were wrong." He poked the napkin at my nose again and smiled. "You often are."

I was silent a long moment. "Well, for cryin' out loud, it was the goddamned *vegetables!*"

He rocked back on his heels. "Pardon me?"

"Tark said you were out there planting a garden, and I know Chris loves vegetable gardens . . ."

Marcus laughed. "Well, so do you."

"But you didn't know that."

"Sure I did. Chris told me."

"Chris?" I blinked.

"You told him, Jess." He frowned. "Are those gray cells so addled by old age today that you don't even remember that?"

I was ready to take offense about the age business. Then I remembered.

"Happy Birthday," Marcus said, kissing the tip of my reddened nose.

"Gosh . . . it *is* my birthday today."

"It is, indeed. And I've got a special dinner planned—out at the new house. It's part of my plot to win your stubborn heart."

"Me? I'm not stubborn."

Marcus laughed. "I guess that was some other Jesse James I just proposed to. Well . . . how about an answer?" The black eyes bored into mine, no longer distant or nervous, but steady. "I'd do everything possible from my end to make it work."

I couldn't answer. There was that ringing in my ears again. But this time, it sounded vaguely different.

Just possibly—in fact—like church bells.

Epilogue

▼ ▼ ▼

"And it feels like you're never comin' home . . ."

—"COMING HOME," BY D. R. LUNSFORD

"*H*e loves me," I said, my voice a little giddy. "He loves me and he wants to marry me."

"Then congratulations are in order!" Samved's seventy-something blue eyes were beaming.

I shifted in the director's chair that had HENRY DREEB painted on its canvas back. We were in the small television studio that Samved—Henry Dreeb in this latest incarnation—had rented for his Praise the Day! telethon. "But Samved," I said, "get this: Mac wants me to marry him too."

My guru/minister/shrink was clearly delighted. Only a Jewish matchmaking mom—or an Irish matchmaking mom—could have been more so. "Two proposals in one week?"

"Two in one *day*," I said, my tone conveying the fact that I was still in a state of stun.

"Praise be! You will, of course, accept Marcus? I will be happy to perform the ceremony!" He looked ready for it, in fact, in his stolid black suit, the one he'd traded in the flowing white robes for.

"Fat chance," I said. "Marcus is Catholic. He wants to be married in the Church."

"A Catholic wedding? Oh dear. With bodyguards and hired guns in attendance? Sounds a bit militant . . . but appropriate to the Faith, somehow."

In the two years or so that I'd known Samved, we'd taken on nearly every religion, both of us with a jaded eye toward the dogmatic organizational aspect of each. There was nothing personal in it—no real feeling of disrespect for anyone's beliefs. We just liked to yak.

"Maybe you could pose as a priest," I said. "Then you could perform the ceremony for us." Samved had been a New Age guru when I'd met him. This year, he was Fundamentalist.

He shook his head. "All that bowing and scraping and kissing of floors? Hardly. But then"—he clasped his hands to his chest—"this means you *have* decided to say yes to Marcus."

"I didn't say that. I mean, it's all so much to take in. He's bought this wonderful house out in the country for us, with a vegetable garden and everything—the house I thought was for Christopher and his mom, only it turns out that she wants Christopher to go to a boarding school in Switzerland, to get him out of this crime element here—and that's why they flew over there, to check it out. . . . And you know, he even put in a banister just like one I'd told him about a long time ago . . . the nice, wide, curving kind that a kid can slide down. I always wanted a banister like that. . . . And that house in Arizona? It's to go there winters, because I hate the cold and snow here so much. . . ."

I was rambling, I knew. "Hell, I haven't even been to confession in fifteen years, let alone Mass. How can I get married in the Church?"

"That wasn't actually my question. Are you going to marry Marcus Andrelli—or Mac Devlin? I don't see a ring on your finger."

I looked at the digit in question. It was decidedly bare. "I . . . I told them both I'd have to think about it."

"The master of indecision," Samved said with a sigh. "Were you ever to make up your mind about anything, I'd retire and hoe beans myself."

"One doesn't hoe beans, I don't think. One picks them. It's potatoes you hoe."

"Potatoes, shomatoes," Samved said. "If you blow it this time, you may not get another chance."

I frowned. "I'm not blowing it. I just want to be sure. After all—everybody gets a little nuts in the spring. Maybe they'll be sorry they asked."

"That's not the only reason, is it?"

"Meaning?"

"What are you leaving unsaid?"

"Just . . . well, you know. I've been hurt before."

"And?"

"And what if I say yes, and then get hurt again?"

"Count on it," Samved said confidently. "Anyone as prickly as you will be hurt consistently throughout life. You set yourself up for it. You're convinced that without pain, you wouldn't know you were alive. It's the adult-child-of-an-alcoholic syndrome."

"So, what's the alternative?"

"Joy!"

He said it jubilantly—the way Christians do when they've got The Answer and can't wait to share it with the world. "Joy is the answer! Embrace it! Joy is life—and life is joy!"

"Oh yeah? I thought life was a fountain."

He nodded, beaming even wider now. "And the fountain is brimming with joy!"

Mom and Aunt Edna were in the kitchen of the farmhouse that Marcus had bought, the one he wanted us to live in together.

Marcus hadn't arrived yet, but he'd invited them to have dinner with us. The move had surprised me, but only briefly. Marcus really was nervous. I hadn't said "yes"—and he wasn't sure I ever would. He'd called in the troops.

But then, so had I. In trying to imagine the years stretching before me in marriage to Marcus, I'd failed. I needed another perspective, one not coming from Mom anyway—who thought I was crazy for hesitating at all. So while she and Aunt Edna were oohing and aahing inside—over a house I might never live in, at least not as Sadie, Sadie, Married Lady—I'd dragged Charlie outside, to one of the gardens.

Charlie was in jeans and running shoes. We looked like a couple of twins in a Miller's Outpost ad. It was kind of comforting, sometimes, the way Charlie Browne dressed like me: a matching body language of fashion.

"Sometimes I look at you and Mom," I said as we walked, "and I think it just might work."

"Really?" He grinned. "I thought you didn't approve."

"I don't. Not of you, Charlie, or most of what you do. But all that aside, I like the way it works with you and Mom. I like the way you look after her, and think about her all the time, and protect her . . . Christ, when you came storming in with that crop duster, dumping orange smoke everywhere, it reminded me of every romantic flying movie I'd ever seen. You are one hell of a guy, Charlie Browne. You look after your own."

"Your mother looks after me, too. It's mutual."

"Yes. I guess that's what I mean. And Marcus is right—people need that more than ever today. Somebody in their lives who provides that."

I broke a purple lilac from a bush, and held it to my nose. "I . . . I guess I can't remember a single time that it was mutual between me and Marcus. I mean, he looks after me, he always has. Too much sometimes. But what have I ever done for him? I'm just this . . . this *problem* that's always around."

Charlie put an arm around me as we walked toward the wide front porch. He shook his head. "You still don't see it, do you?"

"See what?"

"The person you are. The one Marcus sees and wants to spend a lifetime with. You can't get past all the insecurities of your childhood, even now. Let it go, Jess . . . let the past, and the terrible things that were done to you, go."

The terrible things. Charlie was right. I remembered Pop saying once: "Jesse, girl, you . . . your mother . . . you're too much a burden on the heart." This was one night when he was stewed to the gills. Pop was a peace-loving guy at heart, but when the drink was on him, he tended toward morose. Anyway, he was sitting there in his overstuffed chair, still in the tired coveralls he always wore to climb down into those hot, gassy vats at Kodak, although he'd been fired the night before. He was horribly drunk and holding a gun to his temple. I was ten at the time, and I remember throwing up right there on the living room rug, and then crying until he stopped and put it down.

The world exacts a high price from men who would be poets, who dream of tossing words like silver birds into the sky, and wind up shoveling food into the mouths of dependents instead.

Later, he said, "Jesse, girl, you couldn't even let me die in peace." He said it heavily, with none of the usual twinkle in his eye, and I've always understood, no matter what anyone since has said—counselors, gurus, or well-meaning friends—that I'd screwed up yet again.

Someday, when the prisons are too full to put any more people in them, the courts will assign all miscreants an Irish Catholic father to instill perpetual remorse for their sins. Meanwhile, I'd had Pop. And later, all those Genesee Screws.

Charlie took my hand, and we walked up onto the porch. Marcus had installed one of those porch swings, the kind you see

in old reruns of Doris Day movies. Doris and Gordon MacRae—
swinging away and necking, by the light of a silvery moon.

It was something I might have expected from Grady North
. . . never Marcus Andrelli.

"I loved Pop," I said, resting on the swing with my knees
drawn up to my chest. Charlie sat beside me. He still held my
hand. "But he wasn't a father. A father should nurture, I think,
above all else. It's a tough, cruel world, and a good father should
blaze a path. He should lead the way."

My stepfather was silent. And I thought: Good old Charlie
Browne. Not much of a father figure. Years younger than my
mother, at forty-eight or so—and a man with a mysterious past.
In some ways a con, a prevaricator, a man with a dark side that
diminished the light. But hell, he was kind of fun. Whether he
was playing Peter Pan or just plain Pan, he took a nicely casual
approach to the world and all its foibles.

And he looked like Paul Newman. For now, at least, maybe
he'd have to do.

I leaned back in the swing, shoulder to shoulder with Charlie. Relaxing. Around us, dusk was moving in. Crickets chirped,
bees buzzed—

It wasn't bees. It was Mom and Aunt Edna, deep in excited
plans for my future.

"What do you think she'll say?" Mom's words came
through an open window.

"Well, you know Jesse, Kate. She's so damned stubborn.
But then, it *is* spring. And she was playing George Michael earlier. I'd say she's gaga in love."

"But with which one? It's time she committed to one
man," Mom said wisely. "She's thirty-two, for heaven's sake!"

"And what better man for her than Marcus?"

"I don't know . . ." Mom said. "Mac Devlin is one of the
good ones. And strong. She was quite taken with him, I
think . . ."

I looked at Charlie, and he looked at me—with a grin and a shrug. "You should have been in California when Kate and I met at the matchmaker's. I didn't stand a chance."

"I've always wondered why you went there in the first place, Charlie. I can see Mom doing that . . . but you?"

"Maybe you don't really know me," he said.

I gave a snort. "An understatement if there ever was one. And speaking of which—about those shoes, Charlie. Those *codes*. And that 4-0-2-2 on all those pharmaceutical drums . . ."

He chuckled. In the near-dark, his blue eyes were mischievous, but alert. "Don't you ever let up?"

"Can it, Charlie. That decoy for Mom—the one that was killed in the Thousand Islands? That's serious shit, pal."

"You're right," Charlie agreed, "very serious. But both those people knew the risk they were taking, and opted to do it."

"Do *what*? *For* what? Jesus, Charlie, what's it about?" I realized I had asked the question before. And up to now, I'd never gotten an answer.

"You may remember," Charlie said slowly, "a luxury yacht anchored at the Greenspire Inn while you were there?"

"Yeah?" I felt a prick of excitement, and dropped Charlie's hand to turn toward him—stunned that I was about to hear an honest-to-God explanation from my stepfather's lips.

"Well," said Charlie, folding his arms and kicking back with the swing, "that's it. It had to do with that."

"Yeah? Yeah, well . . . go on."

"I can't tell you any more now, Jesse. Maybe in a couple of months, when it's over—"

I leapt to my feet. "Damn you, Charlie Browne! Don't you do this to me again!"

"Do what?"

"Leave me hanging when there's all kinds of shit coming down every time you're around." I remembered something else.

"And what about that so-called burglary at Mac's office, when I found him tied up in the back room right after you'd been there—"

"A common burglary," Charlie said smoothly. "Ask Mac. The police caught the kid who did it. He'd been hitting all the offices along that stretch for weeks."

"Hmmmm. Well, okay . . . let's say that's true. Not that I'm saying I think it's true, mind you, but let's just *say* I do. I still never believed it was coincidence, you showing up at my door the first day I got together with Mac Devlin. You and Marcus *knew* about his involvement with Sam Garner long before he turned to you for help. You must have wanted to connect with him for your own reasons. So you were having him followed, and you knew he'd be at my place that night—"

Charlie shook his head, smiling. "Jesse, Jesse . . . the scenes you do cook up in that overly suspicious mind . . ."

I opened my mouth to argue. But Mom and Aunt Edna were coming through the door, and they looked determined.

"It's time, Jessica." Mom stood before me with folded arms and a firm chin. "Your aunt and I have talked, and we think Marcus could make you happy. We don't intend to let you cop out on this proposal."

"Cop out? What an archaic phrase," I said, smiling. "A little like 'I've had it'—or 'Go with the flow.' "

"Now what on earth brought that up?" Mom asked, bewildered.

"Stars, Mom. Don't you remember? A night long ago . . . when you taught me to dream?"

Marcus's limo had pulled into the drive and was nearing the house. I stood, twisting the lilac bloom between my fingers and thinking of all the things I had to talk to Marcus about.

Aunt Edna was looking at me shrewdly. There was an unlit cigarette stuck behind her ear. "Dream, huh? Does this mean you've decided on Mac Devlin? Are you going to marry him? He *is* dashing, and handsome, and he's crazy about you. Besides, he's a doer *and* a dreamer—"

Charlie and I laughed in unison. They were impossible.

But then, so was I.

"Decisions, decisions," I reflected. "Who can know?"

And I stuck the lilac in my hair, and left them standing there.